"I did...
softly.

"Neither did I," Melissa replied, her voice not quite steady.

"But I enjoyed it." He turned his head to capture her lips again.

Lightning isn't supposed to strike twice, Melissa thought as the touch of his mouth sent arousal sweeping through her veins. His kiss made her weak. She felt as if she could cling to him all night long.

A little alarm bell went off in her head. Melissa didn't want to *cling* to anyone, anytime. Hadn't she decided Hunt was exactly the sort of man she needed to avoid?

She broke away. His arms held her too close to let her move very far, but she tilted her head back to look at him. "This is a mistake."

Dear Reader,

Sophisticated but sensitive, savvy yet unabashedly sentimental—that's today's woman, today's romance reader—you! And Silhouette Special Editions are written expressly to reward your quest for substantial, emotionally involving love stories.

So take a leisurely stroll under the cover's lavender arch into a garden of romantic delights. Pick and choose among titles if you must—we hope you'll soon equate all six Special Editions each month with consistently gratifying romantic reading.

Watch for sparkling new stories from your Silhouette favorites—Nora Roberts, Tracy Sinclair, Ginna Gray, Lindsay McKenna, Curtiss Ann Matlock, among others—along with some exciting newcomers to Silhouette, such as Karen Keast and Patricia Coughlin. Be on the lookout, too, for the new Silhouette Classics, a distinctive collection of bestselling Special Editions and Silhouette Intimate Moments now brought back to the stands—two each month—by popular demand.

On behalf of all the authors and editors of Special Editions,
Warmest wishes,

Leslie Kazanjian
Senior Editor

CELESTE HAMILTON
Silent
Partner

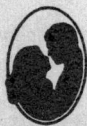

Silhouette Special Edition

Published by Silhouette Books New York

America's Publisher of Contemporary Romance

For Robert,
who loves me no matter what.
And for my parents, my brothers and sister,
who always believed I could do it.

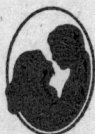

SILHOUETTE BOOKS
300 East 42nd St., New York, N.Y. 10017

ISBN: 0-373-09447-7

First Silhouette Books printing April 1988

America's Publisher of Contemporary Romance

Printed in the U.S.A.

Books by Celeste Hamilton

Silhouette Special Edition

Torn Asunder #418
Silent Partner #447

CELESTE HAMILTON

began writing when she was ten years old, with the encouragement of parents who told her she could do anything she set out to do and teachers who helped her refine her talents. The broadcast media captured her interest in high school, and she graduated from the University of Tennessee with a B.S. in Communications. From there, she began writing and producing commercials at a Chattanooga, Tennessee, radio station. Aside from a brief stint at an advertising agency, she stayed with radio and now works for Chattanooga's top country music station.

Celeste began writing romances in 1985 and says she "never intends to stop." Married to a policeman, she likes nothing better than spending time at home with him and their two much-loved cats, although they also enjoy traveling when their busy schedules permit. Wherever they go, however, "It's always nice to come home to East Tennessee—one of the most beautiful corners of the world."

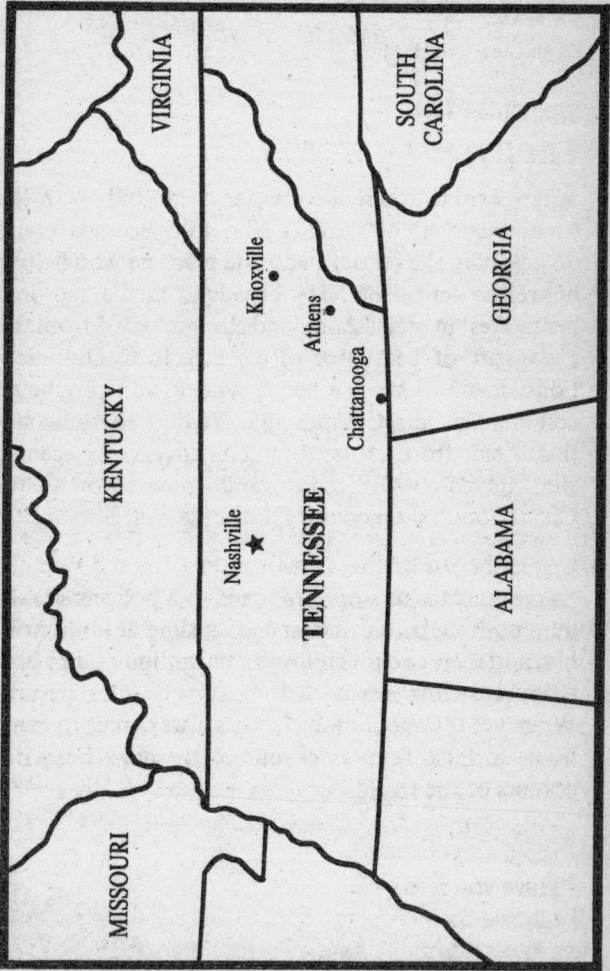

Prologue

The vultures descended as soon as the taxi drew to a halt. With flashcubes popping and microphones in position, they waited eagerly for their victim to emerge from her protective carriage into the cold December night.

"They're like scavengers, fighting over a juicy piece of Washington scandal," Melissa Chambers murmured, watching the press close in around her car. Gripping her small suitcase in one hand and the door handle in the other, she took a deep breath and plunged into the fray.

Their questions clawed at her like razor-sharp talons.

"Miss Chambers, has your father made a decision?"

"Will he announce his resignation tonight?"

"Do you know—"

"Have you seen—"

Ignoring their strident calls, Melissa followed a resolute path to her parents' house. A calm "No comment" was the only morsel she threw their way before the door opened, offering the sanctuary of the elegant foyer, away from the hungry horde.

"Melissa, thank God you're here."

"Mother." The word was a sigh. Melissa dropped her suitcase and stepped into welcoming arms. For a moment, just a moment, she allowed herself to seek some comfort. Then she pulled away and looked deep into shadowed blue eyes. "How is he?"

"Frightened."

The word startled Melissa. Her father frightened? It couldn't be; he slew dragons.

In a voice full of anger, she cried, "What gives them the right to ruin people's lives, Mother? How did this awful lie get started?"

Her mother answered her with silence.

The hideous fear that had been slumbering in Melissa's chest awoke and nearly choked her with its power. She gripped her mother's fragile shoulders fiercely. "Tell me it isn't true, Mother. Tell me."

Jenna Lewis Chambers's beautiful face crumpled, and there was no need for words. Melissa spun away and put a tightly clenched fist to her mouth, fighting hard to hold back a sob.

"Where's Michael?" her mother said at last.

Michael. Melissa couldn't stop the cry that tore from her now. Michael had been right.

"Melissa?"

The tears poured down her cheeks as she turned. "It's over. That's why I took so long getting here. I called him, asked him to catch the plane with me. He said no. He said he'd been rethinking our engagement. I couldn't believe it.... I went to his office. He said..." Melissa faltered, shivering as she recalled the cold impersonal look on the face of the man she loved, the face of her lover. "He said he'd never loved me."

"I'm not surprised."

"What?"

Again, Jenna's arms closed comfortingly around her daughter. "Michael Billings is an opportunist, honey. In that respect he's much like your father."

"Mother!" Aghast, Melissa jerked away.

The woman's laugh was low and bitter. "Why do you think your father considered Michael his heir apparent? He recognized a kindred spirit. Michael won't let himself be attached to any scandal. It could hurt his career. He'll tell the press your engagement was off well before this storm broke. Politics is merely opportunities found—" she paused and glanced at the door to her right "—and lost."

Melissa followed her mother's gaze to that door. Behind it, in his study, would be her father. "Is he alone?" she asked in a choked voice.

"Of course not. His advisors have to have one last chance to tell him what to do." Jenna sighed. "I'm going to bed, Melissa. Today has been hell, and tomorrow won't be any better." She stepped forward, and with a gentle hand, wiped the tears from Melissa's cheeks. "I'm sorry about Michael."

Melissa merely nodded.

"Your father will want to see you."

"I know."

"Good night, honey." After a final hug, Melissa was alone in the foyer, with only a trace of her mother's jasmine perfume left to comfort her.

Shrugging out of her coat, she went across the hall and into the family room. Brass lamps bathed the room in a golden glow, and a fire burned cheerfully. Its coziness seemed out of place on this night of pain. Suddenly cold,

Melissa went toward the blaze. Standing there, her attention was caught by the family photographs that lined the mantel.

There were her mother and father, looking young and tanned and blond, on the beach in Florida. There was her father, brilliant smile flashing, holding a small girl aloft at a victorious election-night party. There was Melissa's younger brother, Edward, looking solemn as he shook hands with the President of the United States. There was Michael, his arms around Melissa....

A violent oath ripped past her lips, and she seized the photo of Michael, jerked back the fire screen and tossed it into the fire. The protective glass shattered on the iron grate, and the picture erupted into flames.

God, it's all been so pointless, Melissa thought with resentment. So futile. All these years she'd done everything her father had asked of her. She'd smiled for the cameras. She'd made speeches. She'd gone to the school he'd chosen, fallen in love with the man he'd pushed at her. Her entire life she'd been a politician's daughter preparing to be a politician's wife. And now? Now what was she supposed to do?

"Hello, Melissa."

She turned at the sound of her father's voice and resisted the urge to fly into his arms. He'd hate that, hate any sign of weakness. She was Malcolm Chambers's daughter; she was a trooper.

"Father, I..." She faltered. He looked so old, his hair more silver than gold, the lines beside his handsome blue eyes carved with the brutal knife of fatigue. But still, there was no sign of the fear her mother had mentioned.

"I'm glad you're here," he said.

"I wouldn't be anywhere else."

"And Michael?"

She took a deep breath. "He won't be going anyplace with me. Ever."

"I see." There was no surprise on the congressman's face. "I'm sorry."

"I am, too. But what about you? Are you okay?"

He advanced into the room. "I'm resigning."

Melissa swallowed a cry of sympathy. "What do we do now?"

He took her hand. "We hold our heads high. I made a mistake, but life goes on."

"Oh, Father." Melissa gave in to the urge to hug him. Rather awkwardly, his arms closed about her.

"It's going to be all right, Missy," he said, using her half-forgotten childhood nickname.

"But how? It's so awful, so—"

"Don't." Grasping her shoulders, he stepped back. "Remember who you are. You have nothing to be ashamed of. Tomorrow, when I make the announcement, I want you looking beautiful. Smiling. We're going out looking like winners."

Her vague resentment turned to anger as Melissa watched her father. He was already preparing for the following day, psyching himself up to meet the press. Even here at the end, everything centered on appearances. But after tomorrow, when it was over, what would happen to her? He'd insisted that his career be the focus of all their lives. What was he offering to take its place?

"It's going to get worse, Melissa," he said now. "Much worse."

Shocked, she gazed at him in silence. What other revelations did he have in store for them?

"Whatever happens, I want you to promise me you'll hang on, that you'll set an example for your mother and Edward. I've always depended on you, Missy."

She merely frowned at him.

"Promise?" He smiled that glittering, winning politician's smile.

As always, Melissa responded. "I promise," she whispered.

He patted her shoulder and was gone.

Trembling, she sank down on the raised brick hearth. So, he was asking for one more performance. A curtain call for the perfect congressman's daughter. She couldn't help the rebellion that rose within her.

"I'll do it, Father," Melissa told the empty room. "I'll do one last turn. Then never, ever again. You won't own me anymore."

It was curious how saying those words made her feel—as free as a bird, as shaky as a newborn colt.

A log fell in the fire, and Melissa turned to watch the shower of sparks, each one as bright, as fragile, as the resolve burning in her heart.

Chapter One

One hand skimming over the dusty oak rail, Melissa rounded the curve in the staircase and raced down the remaining steps to the foyer below. "I'm coming, I'm coming!" she called as the pounding on the front door increased. Glimpsing a familiar carrot-topped head through the etched glass panel, she ran forward and jerked open the door.

"Beau Collins, where have you been?" she demanded of her favorite cousin.

"I've been banging on this door for half an hour." He leaned casually against the door frame and grinned, apparently unconcerned by her irritation.

Melissa sighed and forced herself to remain calm. Beau never got upset or in a hurry about anything. There was no reason to expect him to change now. "I mean," she said carefully, "where have you been for the past week? I've called your office over and over."

Momentarily she thought a flicker of worry darkened Beau's normally happy expression before he answered, "I've been out of town on business."

"I was afraid you had deserted me and my restaurant," Melissa said, stepping back to allow him to come inside. The door clicked shut, closing out the warm autumn sunshine and leaving them in the chilly gloom of the dusty-smelling foyer. For a moment, both of them were silent.

"It still seems strange to come here and know that Myra won't be coming down those stairs." Beau stood at the bottom of the broad steps, gazing upward.

"Yes," Melissa agreed in the same hushed tone. Being here without Myra Lewis, her grandmother, seemed more than strange. It was eerie. Even a year after her death, the big red brick home was indelibly stamped with Myra's personality—the Victorian furnishings she had loved, the mementos from her travels, the many photographs of family and friends.

Melissa had spent the past week sorting through her grandmother's clothes and personal things. Each time she had opened a hatbox or a drawer and caught a whiff of English lavender, she had looked up, expecting to see Myra, waiting to hear her throaty, uninhibited laughter. But she was never there, and for a moment the loss would be as sharp as when Melissa had first been told her eccentric, beloved grandmother was dead.

"You miss her still." Beau's sympathetic voice pulled Melissa back to the present.

"I'll always miss her. Won't you?"

"Yes," he agreed, favoring her with a slight smile. "But you've got an important part of her. She left you River Rest."

"You're right. I guess I'm the only one who loved this house as much as Grandmother. Goodness knows Mother didn't want it." Melissa leaned back against the satiny wood of the front door and gazed about the wide foyer with pride.

"You know, I was always jealous that Myra was your grandmother and not mine," Beau said.

"Well, she was crazy about you. In fact, she thought you were the best member of Father's entire family—including Father. You know exactly how she felt about him." Melissa smiled, remembering the many battles fought between her grandmother and Congressman Chambers.

"I think Myra just had a thing for redheads." Beau followed Melissa through a doorway and into the library.

"Especially *handsome* redheads," Melissa teased. She raised a small cloud of dust as she sprawled on an ancient blue velvet settee and surveyed her cousin.

He really shouldn't have been handsome. With his red hair and green eyes, Beauregard Perris Collins IV should have looked like the stereotypical television clown. Instead, he had inherited a handsome set of features, a tall, athletic build and skin that deepened to dark honey in the summer with just the faintest dusting of freckles. He was also a witty charmer who never met a stranger. Women had always loved Beau. Melissa often wondered how he had escaped matrimony thus far. However, at thirty-two, he was still a bachelor and claimed his advertising agency kept him too busy for domesticity.

"You really should get married and pass that handsome face down to a passel of young Collinses," Melissa teased.

Beau pretended to shudder as he wiped a coating of dust from the square desk and perched on the edge. "Mother would die if she heard you say that. We Collinses don't have passels. We create dynasties."

"Forgive me," Melissa murmured. "I momentarily forgot Aunt Martha's family pride. I guess I should just be grateful that she still speaks to me after the way Father disgraced us all.''

"Mother's only regret is that she can no longer talk about 'her brother, the statesman.'" Beau's voice was a perfect mimicry of his mother's affected Southern drawl. "Anyway, that was all over four years ago—"

"Yes it was.'' Restlessly, Melissa got to her feet again. She didn't want to dwell on the past. Four years ago she'd had no identity apart from her father and fiancé. Now she was on her own, not tied to anyone else's successes and failures. She wanted only to look ahead, to make her own mark in this world.

She turned back to Beau, ready to ask him again why he'd been gone for a week, but he was already asking her a question. "Have you heard from Edward lately?''

"Oh, yes.'' Melissa couldn't disguise the worry in her voice. Her twenty-year-old brother had called just last night. "He hates the new school.''

"How many colleges does this make?''

"Three.''

"Good Lord! Why do your parents put up with it?'' Beau asked.

"Edward's been through an awful lot,'' Melissa said, jumping to her brother's defense. "The scandal and Father's resignation, and then the divorce—''

"Those things didn't destroy you.''

"I'm eight years older than Edward.''

"Yeah, but that boy was born an adult,'' Beau said. "You know what I think—''

"Yes, I do,'' Melissa interrupted. "You think we should ship Edward to South America.''

"A little hand-to-hand combat and a few weeks trying to survive in a jungle would probably make him grateful to come back here and buckle down at school.''

Although Melissa had heard this suggestion of Beau's many times, she still laughed at the mental picture of her brother in his designer clothes in the wilds of South America. But Edward was not what Melissa wanted to talk about. "Enough about the family. What kind of business kept you away for a whole week? I was beginning to think you had changed your mind about my restaurant idea. I've been clearing out the top floors—"

Beau stood abruptly, interrupting her with a hastily cleared throat. "I can see you haven't made it down here to clean yet." He tapped a nearby lamp shade, unleashing a shower of dust that made Melissa sneeze.

"No, I've got a crew coming in tomorrow to help." Melissa clasped her hands together in excitement. "Beau, I know exactly how I want everything arranged. River Rest is going to be *the* restaurant here in Chattanooga. You're not going to regret helping me."

Again Beau cleared his throat and avoided Melissa's eyes. "I have to admit this is close enough to downtown to be the perfect location, and despite the dirt—" he paused to run a hand over the desk, wiping away the dust to reveal the gleaming beauty of the wood "—this house is really something."

"I know," Melissa said proudly. She glanced around at the room's generous dimensions. Floor-to-ceiling shelves, filled with books, covered most of three walls. On the fourth, a trio of arched windows overlooked the sweeping front lawn and the overgrown bushes that lined the circular drive. Outside, the shutters and columns could use a coat of paint, and inside, minor repairs needed to be done. But Melissa was confident that if she could make her restaurant idea work, the Colonial-style home would be restored to its former glory.

No "ifs" Melissa reminded herself. This had to work. With confidence she said, "I've made a lot of plans this week, Beau."

He turned away and stood gazing at the bookshelves. "More plans?"

Ignoring his less than enthusiastic tone, Melissa said, "Well, you know Grandmother converted part of the third floor into an apartment for her housekeeper. It's the perfect place for me to live. There are a few repairs that'll need to be done up there first. After all, the place has been vacant since Grandmother first got sick two years ago. But I don't think it'll be too expensive."

"That's good. You've got to save money any way you can."

"Believe me, I know about economizing. It seems like that's all I've done for the past four years."

"Your own choice," Beau reminded her.

"I know, I know. But I don't want to take money from my parents. I have to do something . . . make something of my own." Melissa watched for Beau's reaction. She knew he understood. After all, hadn't he built a thriving advertising agency without a penny's help from his own parents? They'd disapproved of his career choice, thinking he should follow family tradition into law school and politics. Despite their dire predictions of failure, he was doing well.

Pulling a book from a shelf, Beau blew off the dust and flipped idly through the pages. "I know what this restaurant means to you, Melissa. I just wish your grandmother had left you a little more money along with the house."

"Well, she didn't." Melissa stepped around the desk, took the book from Beau and put it back on the shelf. "I got a little money, but Grandmother left most of it to Mother and in a trust fund for Edward to use for his education. He can't touch it for any other purpose until he's twenty-five."

"Pity. We could hit him up for a loan," Beau said dryly.

Ignoring him, Melissa plunged ahead with her plans, pacing across the room and ticking off items on her fingers. "I've gotten bids for remodeling and adding on to the kitchen, for redoing the floors here on the main floor, for new wallpaper and carpet in the rooms I want to use upstairs. I've also gotten prices on tables and chairs which will blend in with the antiques. As soon as you write me a check we can get down to business."

When there was no response from Beau, Melissa turned around, her excitement changing to concern. Was he having second thoughts? For over three months, they'd been talking about turning River Rest into a restaurant. He'd said that Melissa's two years of experience with a Nashville restaurant were enough to get the place up and running. The last time they'd talked, a week ago, Beau had agreed with all of Melissa's plans. He'd promised her the money she needed. But that was a week ago. He'd been out of the office ever since. Suspicions growing, Melissa returned to the question she'd first asked him at the door.

"Beau, why have you been out of town? Where did you go?"

His expression changed from worried to guilty, and he managed a feeble smile. "Melissa, honey, I don't have the money."

For a moment she simply stared at him, waiting for the meaning of his words to sink in. Finally, she managed to say, "What did you do with it?" Visions of a wild Vegas gambling spree danced through her brain.

Beau shoved both hands deep into the pockets of his gray flannel slacks. "Everything's just gone to hell in a hand basket this week, Melissa. I've lost my two biggest accounts. And with them went half of my cash flow."

"Beau, that's terrible!" Concern for her own problems disappeared as Melissa considered Beau's situation. "What are you going to do?"

"The only thing I can do is take the money I was going to invest with you and use it to operate until I can find enough business to replace those accounts." Beau took a deep breath. "But everything's going to be okay, Melissa, I've found you another investor."

"Another investor?" Melissa echoed. The implications of that statement hit her gradually. Another investor wouldn't give her free rein with the restaurant. Another investor might not want her to live on the premises. Another investor would tell her what to do. So much for independence. "Beau, how could you?"

"Now, Melissa, don't go getting angry before you hear me out—"

"I don't have to hear you out!" Melissa paced the room. "We've already been through this. I don't want any other investor. I want this to be my restaurant, run my way. You agreed with all of my plans. You said you'd stay in the background and allow me to buy you out as soon as I could. Now who else is going to agree to terms like that?"

"Well, probably no one—"

"Exactly!" Melissa said triumphantly. "Anyone else would want a fancy agreement. They'd want to tell me what to put on the menu, how to redecorate and what the waitresses should wear—"

"And on the other hand, an experienced partner could help you make this place a success." Beau crossed his arms and gave Melissa a glare which matched her own in fury and stubbornness.

Angry color flamed in her cheeks. "Oh, so now you don't think I can do it on my own?"

"That's not what I said!" Now Beau was shouting.

"Then what do you mean?" Melissa asked, matching him octave for octave.

"I'm saying you should come down off your high horse and compromise, or go to your parents for the money."

"Never!"

"Then let me tell you about Hunt Kirkland."

"Who's he?"

"A man with money and experience. You've been to his restaurant before. You know...Kirkland's, in Knoxville, Atlanta and Birmingham—"

"Kirkland's!" Melissa repeated with obvious distaste. Vaguely she recalled bright, contemporary restaurants filled with people, plants and a casual atmosphere. That wasn't all what she had in mind for River Rest. "Good Lord, Beau, are you proposing I make my restaurant into a second-class beanery like Kirkland's?"

From the doorway came the sound of a throat clearing, and Melissa turned to meet a mocking brown-eyed gaze. Startled into silence by the sight of a stranger lounging so comfortably in her house, she simply stared at him for several moments.

Then, with elaborate politeness, he said, "I don't recall beans being on the menu of any of my restaurants. Perhaps you're thinking of someplace else?"

Melissa looked accusingly at Beau, who managed a feeble grin. "Melissa Chambers, meet an old college buddy of mine—Hunt Kirkland."

It was difficult for Hunt not to be amused by the flush which suffused Melissa Chambers's cheeks. Given the fact that she'd grown up in the public eye, she probably didn't find herself caught off guard too often. He continued to lean against the door frame, enjoying the spectacle. Actually there was something downright appealing about her flashing, angry blue eyes and the heated glow of her skin.

With her ash-blond hair and delicate features, Hunt could imagine that Melissa usually exuded cool composure. I prefer seeing her warmed by anger, he thought, watching her initial flushed confusion change to icy reserve.

Melissa inhaled slowly, allowing her politician's daughter poise to take over. It had gotten her through many awkward situations in the past, and she didn't believe it would desert her now. Summoning a tight little smile, she came across the room with hand outstretched. "So nice to meet you, Mr. Kirkland."

She moves like a lady to the manor born, even wearing jeans and a T-shirt, Hunt thought as he shook her hand. "Forgive me for barging in like this. I knocked but no one answered, and when I heard voices, I came on in. Beau was expecting me, so I thought it would be okay."

"Really?" The glance Melissa sent Beau's way could have fried an egg.

"Hunt and I used to play football together," Beau supplied, a little too brightly.

"Another Tennessee Volunteer?" Melissa asked Hunt.

"Halfback," he answered.

That explained his look of solid strength, Melissa thought. It was a quality she'd found that many ex-football players shared—a square-jawed, dependable aura. In Hunt Kirkland's case, his strong build was emphasized rather than diminished by the conservative blue pin-striped suit he wore. He had a pleasant, clean-shaven face. The nose was crooked, as if it had once been broken. His ruddy complexion went with the trace of auburn in his brown hair. He was handsome in a quiet, confident way. But it was the determination Melissa could read in his brown eyes and the set of his mouth that caught her attention. He looked like the sort of man who could take a situation, any situation, into his capable hands and mold it to suit his bidding.

This was definitely not what she was looking for in a business associate. If first impressions were right, and Melissa's usually were, Hunt Kirkland would never, ever be content as just a silent partner.

She straightened her shoulders and prepared to dismiss him. "Well, Mr. Kirkland, I'm really happy to meet any friend of Beau's, but I'm afraid you've come here under false pretenses—"

"Melissa," Beau warned, coming forward to stand at her side.

She cut him off with a look. "Beau, please you shouldn't have—"

"Excuse me," Hunt interrupted. "But I was told you were looking for a partner in a restaurant."

Melissa nodded. "Yes, that's true. But I have certain stipulations about the kind of partner I want, and since Beau is no longer able to assume that role, I'm just going to have to go the bank or something."

"The bank?" Beau and Hunt said in unison.

Their amused expressions attacked Melissa's pride. She raised her chin. "Yes, the bank. I haven't tried that route because I really didn't want to use the house as collateral." Melissa didn't want a huge mortgage. Even though she was convinced this venture couldn't fail, she wasn't willing to take even the slightest chance on losing her grandmother's beloved home. "That's why I wanted a partner, someone who was willing to take the risk with me."

"Well, you're right about one thing, the bank would definitely want some collateral. And even then they'd probably have doubts about the loan." Hunt strolled about the room, taking in the faded velvet curtains and the elegant lines of the furniture. Beau had been right about one thing; the house was a treasure.

"Don't you think this is a prime location for a restaurant, Mr. Kirkland?" Melissa asked with barely concealed challenge.

"Oh, definitely." He turned back around to face her. "A beautiful older home is very appealing to the public. The perfect setting. But banks don't deal much in romantic surroundings, Miss Chambers. And restaurants are particularly risky businesses, depending as they do on the whims of the public." Hunt shook his head. "And since you don't have much experience, I doubt—"

"Now, wait a minute. I spent two years running one of the Trent's Folly restaurants in Nashville. I have experience," Melissa declared defensively.

"Those are really great restaurants," Hunt agreed in a soothing voice. "Tell me, why aren't the Trents interested in going in with you on this venture?"

"Judy and Miles Trent don't want to expand out of the Nashville area right now."

"Why don't you wait until they do?"

"Because..." Melissa paused, trying to find the words to explain her position. How could she make anyone understand why she had to do this on her own? Judy and Miles had helped her take her first baby steps in the business. Now she had to break free. And as for not waiting? Well, that was simply a matter of timing. That much she could explain. "I think Chattanooga has room for the kind of restaurant I want to have here at River Rest. But six months from now it might be a different story. I want to make my move now and be ready for the holiday season. People will be going out a lot. They'll like having a new place to try."

"Good thinking," Hunt commented.

Melissa was surprised at how pleased she was by his praise.

"But the bank's still not going to give you the money," he added, canceling her pleasure.

Beau tried to explain. "Melissa, I have faith in your abilities and your instincts. But the bank doesn't know you. Two or three years of restaurant experience won't seem like much to them. That's just the way it is." He stopped and rubbed his jaw thoughtfully. "Of course, you could try one other thing."

"What's that?" Melissa prompted.

"You could get your father to cosign a loan—"

"Absolutely not!"

The vehemence of Melissa's response effectively eliminated that possibility, and Hunt intercepted a triumphant glance from Beau. Hunt had been wondering why Melissa didn't just go to her father for the money she needed. Malcolm Chambers might not be the political force he had once been in this state, but he was still a wealthy man. Obviously, father and daughter weren't on the best of terms. So Melissa's options for financing were few.

"Miss Chambers," he began.

"Oh for heaven's sake, call me Melissa!" she said shortly.

"Okay, Melissa. From what Beau has told me and what you've said, this restaurant isn't going to get off the ground unless you have a partner." Hunt didn't miss the venomous glance Melissa sent her cousin. "So why can't we sit down and discuss the possibility of me being that partner?"

"I don't think so," she answered firmly. She could kill Beau for telling this man so much.

"Melissa," Beau implored. "You don't even know what Hunt is willing to offer."

Struggling to ignore the reason in Beau's words, Melissa took a deep breath. She felt as if all her dreams were closing in around her. "Okay," she agreed at last, looking at Hunt. "Why are you so interested?"

"Because you're sitting on a gold mine," he said simply.

"I know that."

"I'm a businessman. I see a great opportunity. We each have something the other wants. You have the perfect house. I have money and the necessary experience—"

"I gather you would want to actively participate in the business?"

Hunt looked puzzled. "Of course. Who would be willing to become your partner and then leave it all in your hands?"

Melissa nodded in Beau's direction.

"You're kidding?" Hunt looked at Beau in amazement. "You were going to put this kind of money into the place without having any say-so about its operation?"

"I know Melissa will do a great job." Melissa was gratified by Beau's loyal tone.

"But she's a novice," Hunt stated, still incredulous.

"Now, hold on!" Melissa put her hands on her hips. Who gave this guy the right to make pronouncements about her? "You don't know that much about me or my abilities, Mr. Kirkland. In fact, I probably know more about running a *first-rate* restaurant than you do."

Hunt couldn't stop the slow burn of anger that stirred in his gut. Just who did this woman think she was? He knew her family background, as did just about everyone else in the state. Clearly she was a spoiled little rich kid whose daddy had handed her everything she wanted. And now, in her first feeble run at independence, she expected everyone to just go along with her plans like Daddy would. She didn't know anything about work and struggle, and he wasn't going to sit still while she insulted the business he'd spent the past nine years building.

"Are you saying, yet again, that my restaurants are second-rate?"

"Of course she's not saying that," Beau said, trying to keep the peace.

"And what if I am?" Melissa stepped closer to Hunt, all five-feet-four of her slender figure held ramrod straight.

"Then your ignorance is really showing," Hunt said tersely. "What would make your restaurant so much better?"

"Because I won't be trying to appeal to the lowest common denominator."

Hunt laughed mirthlessly. "This isn't Washington or even Nashville. There's no room for snobbery in this town when it comes to a restaurant."

"I'm not being a snob," Melissa protested. "I simply plan to cater to those who know quality and style—"

"You remind me of Marie Antoinette when she said 'let them eat cake'—just before they chopped off her head! You might keep your head, but you'll lose this business."

At the disdain in his voice, Melissa took a step back. She could feel her face color with anger. "I think you can go, Mr. Kirkland."

"I think you're right."

"No, you can't!" Beau stepped in between Hunt and Melissa. "You are both blowing a perfect opportunity."

Melissa exploded again. "Beau, you should have known better than to even try this. You know what kind of partner I was looking for—"

"The kind you'll never find!" Hunt interjected.

"I just know we can work this out," Beau insisted. "Be sensible, Melissa. You need him. And Hunt . . ." He turned to his friend. "You'll never find a better location."

Hunt and Melissa glared at each other, brown eyes locking with blue. But it was Melissa who looked away first.

The trouble was that everything Beau and Hunt had said was true. Getting money from the bank was going to be nearly impossible. Certainly, if she traded on the family name and connections, she might eventually find someone else willing to put up the money she needed.

But she didn't want to do it that way. If only Beau was still able to invest. Somehow borrowing money from him seemed different from going to any other member of the family. Beau had always been her confidante and friend. He understood how she felt. But Beau didn't have the money, and it looked as if Melissa was trapped. She had to at least consider Hunt's offer.

"Okay," she conceded with a frown. "I'm willing to think about it."

Hunt was surprised at the relief he felt. Somehow this deal didn't seem quite as smooth as it had when Beau had outlined it on the weekend. Working with Melissa Chambers might be a bigger aggravation than the restaurant was worth. But then, Hunt loved a challenge. And of course there was the house. He looked about him again in appreciation. It was exactly what he was looking for.

With confidence, he told Melissa, "You think about it the rest of this week and then give me a call." He handed her a business card. "I'm willing to put up the amount you and Beau had agreed upon." He named a figure somewhat larger than what Beau had promised.

Keeping her face perfectly blank, Melissa ignored the sly look Beau gave her and agreed with Hunt. Her cousin hadn't totally let her down after all. That extra money would do a lot of renovations.

Before they could talk further, Beau suggested that he show Hunt around the downstairs and the grounds. "Didn't you want to call that cleaning crew before four?" he asked Melissa, glancing at his watch.

She realized Beau wanted to get Hunt alone, perhaps to try and convince him she could indeed run the restaurant on her own. Taking his cue, she said, "I'll call you Friday afternoon or Monday morning, Mr. Kirkland."

"Oh for heaven's sake, call me Hunt," he said in faultless imitation of the tone she had used earlier with him.

He smiled then, and for the first time Melissa noticed the dimple that creased his cheek to the right of his mouth. It was an unexpected feature, one that made him seem younger and somewhat less self-possessed.

Forgetting herself, she smiled back. She walked to the doorway and paused, looking back over her shoulder. "Goodbye...Hunt." She left the two men alone in the dusty library.

"Beau—" Hunt began, but stopped when his companion motioned for him to keep quiet.

When Melissa's footsteps could be heard on the stairs, Beau said, "Isn't this place everything I said it was?"

"The house is terrific," Hunt agreed. "I don't know about your cousin."

"Oh, come on—"

"Why in heaven's name did you give her the harebrained idea that anyone would hand her the money she needs and expect nothing in return?"

Beau looked a little uncomfortable. "I was willing to do it, Hunt. She told me what she had in mind for this place. I thought her plans sounded good. I mean, Melissa is more like my sister than just a cousin. I said I'd finance it." He gestured for Hunt to follow him out into the foyer. "And I'd still give her the money if I could."

Pausing to glance in each of the rooms opening off the central foyer, Hunt said, "Getting the money from your family is one thing. But she didn't really expect to swing that kind of deal with anyone else, did she?"

"She was counting on me. And I had just broken the bad news to her when you walked in. If you'd been just twenty minutes later, I'd have had her convinced that you were the perfect partner. You always did have terrible timing, Kirkland." Beau opened the set of double doors at the end of the hall, and Hunt followed him out onto a wide back porch.

The scent of newly mown grass drifted to them on the breeze, and through the trees Hunt could see the green water of the Tennessee River glinting in the September sunshine. "This is really something," he said in appreciation.

"Can't you just see the ladies and gentlemen playing croquet on the grass?" Beau leaned against the porch railing.

"Yeah, I can," Hunt agreed, easily visualizing the lazy Sunday afternoon scene. What a gracious, beautiful home this must have been. "Why doesn't Melissa want to just live here? The house seems in good shape."

"The problem is money."

Hunt frowned, puzzled. "I was going to ask you about that. What about her father? From what I've read in the papers, Malcolm Chambers is still a rich man."

"She hasn't accepted a dime from him since he left office."

"They have a disagreement?"

"Nope. Melissa just declared her independence. She went to work for the Trents in Nashville. Then her grandmother died, and she inherited this place." As if anticipating Hunt's next question, Beau added, "Her mother and brother got what money there was."

"How did her grandmother expect Melissa to keep this place up?"

"I think she was issuing a challenge."

Hunt glanced at Beau sharply.

"You'd have to have known the old lady," the redhead explained. "She was completely independent, and that's the way she encouraged Melissa to live her life, too. It always bothered Myra that Melissa let her parents make so many of her decisions for her, that she was so concerned about what other people thought of her, of what the public perceived her to be. She was actually glad when Melissa's father had to resign."

"I'm sure Congressman Chambers just loved that attitude."

Beau laughed. "There was no love lost between the two of them. Myra thought he dominated Jenna, Melissa's mother. She was determined that Melissa wouldn't turn out weak and pampered." He nodded his head. "Yep. Myra knew how much Melissa loved this house. By leaving it to her without the money to maintain it, she was asking her to make something of herself, to find a way to make it work."

"I think this is a very complex family," Hunt commented.

Slapping him on the shoulder, Beau agreed. "You don't know the half of it, my friend."

"Don't tell me." Hunt strolled down the length of the porch, admiring the view. It was easy to picture a line of tables set out here, each one filled with appreciative diners. "Do you think Melissa will take my offer?"

"Let's just say I'm hoping her good sense wins out over her stubbornness." Beau fell in step beside him, and they walked down a shallow flight of stairs to the backyard. "To be honest, I'd feel a lot better if you were here to advise her. I still think she could have done it on her own, but together, I think you two can make this place a sensation."

As they completed the brief tour, Hunt couldn't help but agree with Beau's hopeful attitude. The large, airy rooms seemed made for dining areas. The kitchen would require extensive remodeling, of course, but there was plenty of room for expansion. Parking would be no problem since the grounds surrounding the house were large. Evidently, Melissa's grandmother had resisted the impulse to sell much of the land.

All in all, this house had everything Hunt wanted. He'd decided several years ago that a restaurant in an old mansion could work. He'd seen similar setups catch on well in Knoxville and Atlanta. If he combined the casual, fun-filled mood of his restaurants with this romantic setting, he just knew he'd have a winner. Yes, he loved the house and the idea. But he wasn't so sure about the owner.

How in the world did Melissa Chambers think she'd be able to pull this off without help? Hunt mused. She might have managed a restaurant for two years, but that restaurant had been well established. What did she know about building from the bottom up, about setting a menu or hiring a staff from scratch? He'd bet money that she'd turn tail and run at the first sign of trouble....

Hunt stopped dead in his tracks. That was it! She'd quit. With half an ear, he listened to Beau explain about the new heating and air-conditioning system Melissa's grandmother had put in just three years previously. But all he could think about was what should have been obvious from the beginning: Melissa didn't have the kind of backbone it took to build a business like this. She was used to an easy life and instant gratification. No matter that Beau said she was trying to break free of Daddy's demands. He'd still give her only six months before she was ready to sell out.

And he'd be standing by, ready to make her an offer she couldn't refuse.

Grinning like a puppy with a new bone, Hunt thanked Beau for the tour and headed for the dark blue Mercedes he had parked in the circular drive. He stood for a minute looking up at the graceful red brick home. "*My* restaurant is gonna be grand!" he said before getting in the car.

Chapter Two

Melissa turned her car into River Rest's driveway, following the pavement to the back of the house. She drew to a stop in front of the garage, and cut the engine, listening glumly as it sputtered several times. Great, she thought. All she needed was for her faithful Mazda to die on her. Where would she get money for a new car?

The five-year-old red RX-7 had been the last truly extravagant gift Melissa had accepted from her father. It had been her twenty-third birthday present, and Melissa could well remember the pride with which her parents had handed her the keys. That night seemed to belong to another lifetime. By her next birthday, her father was embroiled in a congressional scandal, her parents' marriage was over and the seemingly perfect fabric of their family life had ripped apart.

If none of those things had happened, Melissa surely wouldn't be sitting here worrying about money for car repairs. Money probably wouldn't be of any concern at all—especially funds for a restaurant.

With a dispirited sigh, she got out of the car and started up the brick path to the back porch. It was only Friday, and already three banks had turned down her application for a loan. The speed with which her query had been rejected was the unsettling part of the whole process.

After Beau and Hunt had left Monday afternoon, Melissa had gotten right on the phone. She'd filled out the necessary papers on Tuesday morning, taking her plans to all three institutions at once in order to save time. It was just as Beau and Hunt Kirkland had predicted. No one was interested. Not unless she mortgaged the house or found someone to cosign the loan. Two of the banks had told her a cosigner would make the deal very attractive. She knew without a doubt the cosigner they had in mind—her father.

Their attitude was only natural, she supposed, unlocking the door and walking into the sunny yellow and white kitchen. Malcolm Chambers had been born and raised here in Chattanooga. He and his younger sister, Martha, were the third generation of a socially and politically prominent family. Malcolm had gone to law school, joined his family law firm and run for the state legislature. He'd married Jenna Lewis, daughter of another well-known family.

His ambitions had carried him to Washington, where for nineteen years he'd served in the Congress. Though that career had ended abruptly four years ago and Malcolm had chosen to remain in Washington, there were those here in Chattanooga who still respected him. They'd certainly be willing to grant Malcolm's daughter a loan if he'd vouch for her.

Melissa laid her purse down on the kitchen counter and opened the refrigerator door. She poured herself a glass of orange juice and sat down at the rectangular table in the center of the room. "What do I do now?" she wondered aloud, not even taking a sip from the glass.

She knew without a doubt that her father would cosign a loan. He'd made it clear on more than one occasion in the past four years that he'd do a lot to reestablish the close relationship they'd once enjoyed. He had called last night, after having talked with her brother, wanting to know what she was doing in Chattanooga. Melissa hadn't told him about the restaurant, explaining instead that now that her grandmother's estate was settled, it was time to clear out the house and make a decision about the property. He hadn't offered any advice, but his daughter had known he wanted to. If Melissa just said the word, her father would swoop into town and take up all her problems. He had always fought her battles, made all her decisions, guided her life. Always, that was, until four years ago.

Malcolm Chambers knew that the fragile relationship he now had with his daughter depended upon the amount of space he gave her. So, in the distant, rather too-polite way they now dealt with each other, last night's phone conversation had ended with him simply asking her to keep in touch.

Melissa drew a hand through her hair, lifting it off her neck as she stretched her arms upward. The heavy, gilt-blond tendrils slipped slowly through her fingers as she sat contemplating the choices now left to her.

Maybe Beau could at least cosign the loan. The idea was discarded quickly. Her favorite cousin had enough business problems right now. Melissa just couldn't ask anything further of him.

So, what else?

Melissa thought momentarily of her mother. But that idea, too, was rejected almost instantly. Jenna Chambers now lived in Nashville and ran her own decorating firm. She was just beginning to sort out the pieces of her life again. And Edward gave her more than enough worry. Anyway, Melissa was determined not to run to either of her parents for anything. Doing that would put her back in the same old pattern of dependence. She just couldn't.

Having exhausted all other options, Melissa turned to what appeared to be her only immediate alternative—Hunt Kirkland.

She glanced at the telephone. The man's business card was lying on the counter next to it. Melissa got up, walked across the kitchen and picked up the handsome gray and maroon card. The number listed was in Knoxville, Tennessee, which was roughly a two-hour drive north of Chattanooga. A vision of Hunt Kirkland sitting at a big, important-looking desk rose to Melissa's mind, and she put the card down. I bet he's just waiting for me to call, she thought with momentary resentment.

She walked back across the kitchen and stood at the big window that overlooked the backyard. Hunt Kirkland was a smug one, she decided, remembering the sardonic twist to his mouth when he'd stood in the doorway after eavesdropping on her conversation with Beau. With a trickle of shame, Melissa also recalled the snobbish way she'd called his business second-rate. She hadn't meant that. She wasn't a snob. There was too much of her grandmother's teachings in her to allow her to feel superior to anyone.

Myra Lewis had accepted all her fellow human beings as equals. The fact that she'd been born to wealth and privilege hadn't prevented her from having close friends from all walks of life. Her only daughter, Melissa's mother, had rebelled against that liberal attitude, deliberately choosing a luxurious life-style. Not Myra's granddaughter. Melissa preferred to judge people by their characters, not their bankbooks.

So why in the world had she come on like a smug little princess to Hunt?

"He threatens me," Melissa explained to the empty room. She was truly afraid that if she went into business with a person like Hunt her own ideas would be pushed aside. Of course, she didn't know for a fact that Hunt's ideas for this restaurant weren't similar to hers. But she had a suspicion that he'd want to turn River Rest into something much like his other holdings. She didn't want that.

It wasn't that Kirkland's were bad restaurants. She just wanted River Rest to be different. Her plan was to recapture the charm and elegance her grandmother had displayed when she'd entertained. Myra's style hadn't been ostentatious; she'd simply served delicious food in comfortably refined surroundings. That sort of ambience was one Melissa thought anyone could appreciate. She wanted evenings in her restaurant to be an event. Not terribly expensive, just special.

But how am I going to get it off the ground? she asked herself, returning to the main problem. She glanced back at Hunt's business card, which seemed to beckon to her from beside the phone. Resolutely she let her gaze return to the chrysanthemums blooming just outside the window. Melissa could almost see Myra, wearing a pair of faded corduroy overalls and a bright yellow hat, energetically pulling weeds from the flower beds. "I wonder what Grandmother would tell me to do?" she asked, sighing.

The answer was simple. Myra Lewis always had one particular piece of advice for her sometimes timid, often overwhelmed, granddaughter. In fact, Melissa could practically hear her grandmother's clear voice saying, "Make the most of your opportunities, assert your own ideas and don't let anyone sway you from your convictions."

Was Hunt Kirkland's offer one of those opportunities? It did seem as if his was the only lifeline in sight for Melissa's restaurant. With strengthening resolve, she went to the phone and picked up the receiver. "I'm following your advice, Grandmother," she whispered before dialing Hunt's number.

After clearing a receptionist and secretary, Melissa soon heard Hunt's deep voice. "Melissa," he said, "I was hoping you'd call today."

His voice was strong and direct. It suits him, Melissa thought, before answering, "I knew you'd feel that way."

Hunt paused briefly. He detected a note of resentment in her tone. "Did you go to the bank?"

Melissa bit her lip. She didn't want to admit any failures to this man. "You and Beau are right," she hedged. "A bank loan isn't practical. I was wondering if you could come down here again so we could talk."

"When?"

"Would tonight be too soon?"

Melissa heard some papers rustling before he answered. "My calendar is clear. How about seven-thirty?"

"Fine." An idea sprang to Melissa's mind, and on impulse she added, "Come for dinner."

"That's not necessary."

"We both have to eat. Why not here?"

After only a slight pause, he agreed.

As Melissa hung up the phone she groaned. "Why did I ask him to dinner?" she demanded of herself. Then she grinned, glancing about the familiar kitchen. This room had been the scene of some of her greatest culinary accomplishments. I'll show him what an evening at River Rest can be, she thought, picking up her purse and heading out the door. It was getting late, and she had groceries to buy.

In his office, Hunt leaned back in his chair. So, Melissa Chambers was going to need him after all. Funny, but he didn't feel the surge of triumph that usually accompanied a successful business deal. Had he secretly thought she'd find a way to get her restaurant started on her own terms? Surely not.

Or maybe he was just getting blasé about success. "And there's danger in complacency," he added aloud.

The leather chair creaked as Hunt leaned forward to study his office. The cool colors of navy and gray and the stark, modern simplicity of the furnishings pleased him. From this plush suite on the second floor of his Knoxville location, he oversaw the operation of three restaurants. He'd come a long way from busing tables in a diner in his hometown. The desire to provide a service had attracted him to this business; the day-to-day challenges had kept him interested.

He'd always been intrigued by the details—the fluctuating cost of beef, the response to a new menu item, what the waiters and waitresses wore. He had built a thriving operation by watching the little things. He had trained his staff to do the same. Now, the whole business ran like a well-oiled top.

And he was bored.

Oh, he had plenty of time to pursue private pleasures. He was a regular on the raquetball court at his health club. There were several women with whom he could spend a night on the town or at the small but comfortable house he'd recently purchased. But for months now, Hunt had felt trapped in an uninteresting routine. His work no longer held his entire interest.

I need something new, he thought, not for the first time. And that desire for a challenge had made Hunt listen to Beau, had caused him to drive to Chattanooga, had propelled him into proposing a partnership with an inexperienced and stubborn woman.

A grin tugged at the corner of his mouth as Hunt considered the possibilities of this new enterprise. It was always much more fun getting a restaurant started. The tingle of victory Melissa's phone call should have prompted came to Hunt at last. Soon he'd have her eating out of his hand.

A little before seven-thirty, Hunt pulled his car to a stop in front of Melissa's house. In the fading September light the residence looked serene, its lighted windows gazing peacefully across the front lawn. Obviously, someone had been clearing the grounds. The boxwoods that lined the front porch had been thinned to a symmetrical row, and the fallen limbs and leaves had been raked away. Aside from the peeling paint of the four front columns and the shutters, Hunt supposed the house looked much the same as it had in its prime.

He got out of his car, smiling at the thought of how romantically inviting this place would be to future customers. He started up the shallow front steps, pausing when Melissa opened the door.

She made a pretty picture, standing there in the gracefully arched doorway, her slender figure silhouetted in the golden light that streamed from the foyer. The last time Hunt had seen her she'd worn jeans and a T-shirt. A blue silk dress and pearls at her ears and throat made a definite difference. There was even a friendly, apparently genuine, smile on her lips.

"The doorbell's broken, so I was watching for you," she explained, stepping back to allow Hunt to come inside.

He looked around in appreciation. The attention paid to the outside had also been given the inside of the house. The dust and cobwebs he'd seen on Monday were gone, leaving gleaming woodwork and furniture behind. Even the Oriental rug which ran the length of the foyer appeared to have been given a thorough cleaning.

"You've been working on the house," he observed as Melissa closed the door.

"I hired a crew to come in and help me. The place was spotless when Grandmother left it to enter the hospital two years ago. It was just dusty and had been closed up. It really didn't take too long to put it back in shape."

"It's beautiful." Hunt followed Melissa into a sitting room to the left of the foyer. It looked like a room that had been well used. Two comfortable looking chintz-covered chairs and a love seat were arranged in front of a marble fireplace. In the big bay window a table had been set with sparkling silver and china, candles and a centerpiece of live chrysanthemums. It had been an unusually cool day, and the windows were open. Through the screens came the pleasant buzz of early evening insects.

"My grandmother usually had her meals in here. The dining room is so big, it seemed silly to use it all the time. We ate there when the whole family was visiting or at Christmas." Melissa gestured for Hunt to take a seat.

He did so, noting that the low coffee table held an appealing spread of appetizers. A hollowed-out round of rye bread was filled with dip, and bread pieces and crackers were arranged beside it. Red cherry tomatoes, green celery and yellow squash formed a colorful circle around another dish of dip.

"You've gone to a lot of trouble," Hunt observed, sending Melissa a somewhat puzzled look. Why had she gone all out for a business dinner?

"Nonsense. I love to cook and I like good food, otherwise I wouldn't be in the restaurant business." Fighting an unreasonable stab of nervousness, Melissa crossed to where a bar was set up in the corner. "Can I offer you a drink?"

"Bourbon and water?"

"Certainly." She mixed his drink and poured herself some soda water. Handing him the glass, she nodded at the food. "Please, help yourself." She took the chair across from where he sat and leaned forward to select some of the fresh vegetables.

With a chunk of bread, Hunt scooped up some of the dip. It was delicious, a pleasing blend of cream cheese, spinach and mild seasonings. "This has to be homemade," he observed.

"Of course. My grandmother always served it at her open house during the holidays."

"Her recipe?"

"No. Grandmother didn't cook, but she had a wonderful housekeeper. This was one of her special-company concoctions. I used to spend almost every summer here, and Mrs. Barton taught me how to cook."

"Really?" Hunt took a sip of his drink and regarded the composed young woman who sat across from him. In her silk dress, it was difficult to imagine her as a youngster making cookies and a mess in the kitchen.

"Grandmother said it was a skill which was always in demand." Melissa laughed. "She said if I ever found myself in a jam, I could always get a job in a diner. I make a mean BLT."

Hunt had to laugh. The thought of Melissa Chambers working in a diner was even more preposterous than that of her baking cookies. "Is that why you got into the restaurant business?" he asked, helping himself to another dip-covered piece of bread.

"No." Melissa looked thoughtful for a moment. "After college—"

"Where?" Hunt interrupted.

"Vanderbilt, in Nashville."

"Good school."

She wrinkled her nose. "To tell you the truth, I wanted to go to the University of Tennessee, like Beau. He told me about all the parties."

"Beau liked to have fun."

"Didn't you?"

Hunt leaned back in his chair and stared at his drink. How did you explain to someone who'd always had money what it was like to barely get by? "I was on a football scholarship and considered myself extremely lucky to be in college at all. I studied. My parents expected me to make good grades."

"No fun?"

A slow grin slid across his face, deepening his dimple and bringing a teasing light to his brown eyes. "I guess I had my share."

He's very attractive when he smiles, Melissa decided, responding to his grin with one of her own. Her gaze slid to where his left hand rested on his knee. He wore no wedding band. It was unusual for a man as attractive and successful as he to be unmarried. She had to remember to ask Beau about it.

"Melissa?"

She jerked her gaze away from his ringless hand and her mind back to their conversation. "Yes?"

"You were telling me how you got interested in the restaurant business," Hunt prompted.

Forcing herself to relax again, Melissa said, "After college I went to work for a business my father had an interest in—a resort. The workings of the restaurant there fascinated me."

Hunt frowned. "So you really do have more experience than just with Trent's Folly in Nashville."

"Just a bit. I only worked at Moondance for six months."

Did Hunt imagine it, or had a shutter dropped on Melissa's expression? One moment she was relaxed and open, the next she seemed tense and strained. "Why did you leave?" he couldn't resist asking.

"My father's part in the business ended." Abruptly Melissa stood. "Can I freshen that drink for you?"

Hunt nodded automatically. It was suddenly clear to him why Melissa didn't want to talk about the job with her father's resort. Malcolm Chambers's interest in Moondance Resorts had started the chain of events that ended his career.

She returned with his drink, and he offered a quiet apology. "I'm sorry. I didn't mean to pry into something that must have been difficult for you."

With a quick wave of her hand she dismissed the subject. Her cool, businesslike poise was once more in place. Hunt couldn't help but admire her control.

She resumed her seat and said, "How about you? How did you come to start Kirkland's?"

He smiled. "I was practically born in a restaurant. My parents owned a little café in Athens, Tennessee. It seemed natural to go into the business."

His brief explanation didn't tell her how he had managed to build successful restaurants in three Southeastern cities, but a quick look at her watch reminded Melissa of her dinner. She excused herself and went to the kitchen.

The meal was superb, and Hunt wasn't shy about giving his compliments to the cook. He even accepted second helpings of the honey-basted ham, the baked sweet potatoes and the creamy asparagus casserole. He had two flaky, butter-drenched biscuits and considered a second slice of pecan pie topped with vanilla ice cream. And it wasn't until they were having coffee that the subject of business was brought up.

Melissa wasn't entirely sure what they discussed during dinner. Beau, food and movies were the only three things she ever recalled. All she knew was that she found Hunt to be an intelligent and altogether pleasant companion. In fact, she was surprised to find herself enjoying his company very much.

But he was a businessman, and when it came to business the easygoing manner disappeared.

"Okay," he said, after the dinner table had been cleared. He sat up straighter in his chair opposite the love seat. "I gather you've reached a decision about my offer, or I wouldn't be here."

"Yes." Melissa tried to think of her grandmother as she squared her shoulders. "I think it would be mutually beneficial for us to become partners—"

"I agree."

"—but I have a few stipulations."

Here it comes, Hunt thought. His coffee cup rattled on its saucer as he set it on the table. "Such as?"

She drew a deep breath. "I want to run the restaurant my way."

Hunt's eyes narrowed. "What does that mean?"

"It means that I want to be in charge of selecting the menu, planning the layout, hiring the staff—"

"Hold it." An enigmatic little smile played about Hunt's mouth, and if it weren't for the way his right hand flexed and unflexed, Melissa might have thought he was completely relaxed.

"Do you have a problem with these conditions?" she asked, managing to keep the challenge out of her voice.

"You know I do." Hunt's smile disappeared. "I told you Monday that no one, least of all me, will just hand you a check and then walk out, leaving you to run this place."

Melissa swallowed hard. "I understand that. I'm perfectly willing to discuss my plans with you. As long as the final decision rests with me."

"That's impossible."

Her chin lifted. "Why?"

Hunt sighed, and he began to speak in a soothing tone, as if he were explaining things to a child. "Melissa, I think you're probably a very sensible person who did a good job for the Trents in Nashville. In fact, they spoke very highly of you."

"You called them?"

"Of course. Before Monday I didn't know anything about you."

"Well, I'm glad you talked to Judy and Miles. I'm sure they said I was perfectly capable of running this restaurant."

"They said nothing of the sort."

A ripple of shock spread through Melissa. She'd always done a good job for the Trents. Why had they betrayed her?

The hurt on her face made Hunt feel ashamed, so he hastened to explain. "They said you were perfectly capable of running *their* restaurant. That's not the same as having your own."

Melissa's nails dug into her palms as she clenched her hands. "I'd like to know what the difference is?" Now she wasn't bothering to hide her belligerence.

"There's nobody to turn to if there's a problem at your own place. You have to make all the decisions, assume all the risks and take all the blame when things go wrong. And things will go wrong, Melissa. You can be assured of that."

"I had to do all those things in Nashville!" she declared hotly.

"Really?" Hunt stood up, put his hands in his trouser pockets, paced a few steps and then whirled back to face her. "How often did you have to worry if there was enough money in the payroll account?"

Melissa's proud posture faltered a bit. "I...uh...Miles handled the payroll."

"And the suppliers? Did you haggle with them?"

"Sometimes! Especially when..." Melissa bit her lip. "Especially when Miles and Judy were out of town."

"Did you set the menu and the prices?"

"I helped!"

"It's not the same." Hunt's voice was quiet, but he punctuated his words with the chopping motion of his hands. Impulsively, he sat down beside Melissa on the love seat. In the same low tone, he said, "I don't want to imply that I think you're not a capable person. The Trents said you had a lot of terrific ideas, that they trusted you implicitly. But, Melissa, it was their restaurant. You only worked there."

The puzzled, hurt look was back in Melissa's dark blue eyes, and without thinking, Hunt took her hands in his. For some inexplicable reason, he wanted to comfort her.

Melissa stared down at their joined hands and frowned. Hunt was treating her as if she were some kind of weak little fool who needed the rudiments of business explained to her in the simplest of terms. Never mind that there was something very pleasing about the feel of her hands in his warm grasp. That simply wasn't the point. Jerking her hands away, she got to her feet.

"If you don't think I'm a sufficiently knowledgeable partner, then what are you doing here?"

"Damn it, I didn't say that," Hunt barked out. He leaned forward, hands on knees, shaking his head. "I'm saying that I won't hand over the reins of this place to you without reserving the right to have a say in the running of it."

"By a *say*, you mean make all the decisions, and I just go along with them, right?"

"You keep putting words in my mouth!"

"They're the right words, aren't they?"

"No, Melissa." Hunt's shoulders slumped. "You know, I drove all the way down here thinking you had probably realized the sense of what I said to you Monday. We had this nice dinner. You seemed so pleasant. And now we're right back where we started. I'm sorry, but I don't have time to waste on someone who just won't face facts. You're not an idiot. In fact, you seem very intelligent. But you're not ready to undertake something like this on your own. If do you find someone who will put up the money for you, then all I can say is—I wish you good luck." He stood and started out of the room, pausing in the doorway to look over his shoulder. "Thanks again for dinner. I really enjoyed it."

Melissa stood alone in the center of the room and expelled a long breath. He was leaving, and with him any chance of having this restaurant anytime soon was walking out the door. Wasn't she giving up on one of the opportunities her grandmother had counseled her about? What would she do now, appeal to her father? That thought spurred her to action.

"Hunt!" she called, dashing out of the room and into the foyer. "Wait, Hunt!"

He had just opened the front door when he heard her call to him. Turning, he watched her hurry toward him, struck for not the first time by how lovely Melissa really was. Not beautiful. Lovely. Especially now, with her blond hair tumbled about her shoulders like errant moonbeams and her face aglow with angry color. She wasn't nearly as pretty when she had perfect control of herself, when her features were set in a mask of polite interest. Hunt couldn't help but wonder how her face would look alight with passion....

"Hunt, don't leave!" she said urgently, breaking his train of thought. "I'm really sorry. I know some of what you're saying is true. It's just that I've got in my mind how I want this restaurant to be, how my grandmother would want it be—"

"And are you so sure our ideas are completely at odds?"

"No," Melissa admitted. "I'm not. But I do know my ideas are going to come to nothing if I don't have a partner, some kind of partner."

Hunt scanned her flushed features. It seemed to cost her a lot to admit she needed help of any kind. "Maybe you should tell me what you've got in mind for this restaurant."

She gave him a smile that trembled a bit. "I want it to be like tonight."

"Tonight?"

"Simple but good food. Pleasant surroundings. I want everyone who comes here to feel like they're visiting my home, Grandmother's home."

Hunt shut the door and leaned against it, thinking back over the meal he had just shared with her. He thought of the gentle glow of candlelight, the fragrance of the fresh flowers, the mellow sheen of the china and silver. He remembered the generous helpings of traditional Southern food. There wasn't much about the evening that could be compared with the contemporary casualness of his own restaurants.

"I have to admit that's not what I had in mind for the place."

Melissa seemed to sag. Her vulnerability pulled at Hunt in a way he could easily understand. He knew what it was like to have a dream, to want something so terribly much that any setback was like a physical blow. He sensed that Melissa Chambers felt that way about this restaurant. And for some damned reason, some totally illogical reason, he didn't want to watch her dreams shatter.

"Maybe we could reach a compromise."

With his quiet words, Melissa's chin lifted and she looked into his eyes. "You think so?"

"Maybe." What that compromise was going to be Hunt had no idea, but right now it seemed worth saying anything just to see the hope light up her blue eyes. "The point is, I still think this is the perfect place for a restaurant—any type of restaurant. And I think as two reasonable people we should be able to agree upon the particulars."

"That sounds like a sensible plan." Melissa's voice was little more than a whisper.

"I might even be able to go a step further." Speaking slowly, Hunt found his attention caught by Melissa's pink, finely shaped mouth. "After we decide on all the major things, I might be willing to leave most of the decisions up to you, providing I at least get to hear about and okay your plans. I promise to be reasonable, but I couldn't let you do something I thought would hurt the business." He raised his eyes back to hers.

Melissa seemed to consider his words carefully. "I guess that's fair," she agreed finally.

"Then I think we're partners." Hunt put out his hand.

"This is crazy," Melissa said, putting her hand in his. "I don't even know what kind of plans you might have for River Rest."

"Well, I probably would want to make a few changes to your ideas," Hunt agreed.

"Changes?" Melissa's blue eyes narrowed in suspicion.

"We can work it out." Hunt looked down. He was still holding Melissa's hand. Damn, that seemed to come so naturally. Otherwise, why did he keep doing it? This was no way to be behaving with a business associate. But he still didn't drop her hand. He looked back up at her. "I'm going to stay at a hotel tonight. Why don't I come over tomorrow morning, and we'll hash the whole thing out? If there's absolutely no way we can agree, we'll call it quits. But we'll have given it our best shot."

"Yes, we will have." She continued to gaze directly into his eyes, and Hunt felt an unexpected warmth rush through him.

"Well, I guess..." he cleared his throat. He was strangely reluctant to leave. "I'd better be going."

He dropped her hand, opened the door and stepped out into the cool evening air. He glanced back once. Just as earlier, Melissa was silhouetted in the doorway, and even from this distance he could appreciate the rounded femininity of her figure. He hadn't noticed that before. His body tightened in response.

That's just great, he told himself as he got in his car. All he needed to complicate this situation even further was to be attracted to her.

During the short drive to his hotel in downtown Chattanooga, Hunt berated himself for his foolishness. He should have kept on walking out that door, away from Melissa's plans. Away from Melissa.

He checked into the Read House Hotel, sparing scarcely a glance for the historic structure's beautifully refurbished surroundings. He headed straight to his room, and once there, called room service and ordered some brandy. While he waited for it to arrive, he replayed the evening yet again.

It was clear that he had underestimated Melissa. She wanted this restaurant very badly. She probably wouldn't give up on it as easily as he'd thought. And for some reason he seemed hell-bent on helping her. What was it about the woman that brought out his every protective urge?

"And those aren't the only urges she arouses," he said morosely, just as room service tapped on his door.

A few minutes later, with a glass of good brandy in his hand, Hunt decided there was only one thing to do. He glanced at his watch; it was only eleven o'clock. He picked up the phone and punched in a number.

"Hello."

Hunt smiled at the familiar voice. "Hey, Dad. What're you and Mom up to?"

"Gettin' ready for bed. What about you?"

"I'm down in Chattanooga."

"Been talking about that new restaurant, huh?"

"That's right." Briefly, Hunt filled his father in on the details of his evening with Melissa.

"So she wants a different kind of restaurant, does she?" Hunt could almost see Bill Kirkland scratching his salt-and-pepper beard as he considered the possibilities of the situation. "You can change her mind, can't you?"

"Maybe. I have a feeling she's going to be kind of stubborn."

"I see. Well, Son, since the day you were born if you set your mind on something, you got it. I figure that if you want this restaurant bad enough, you'll either agree to her terms or change her mind."

"Yeah," Hunt agreed absently, swirling the brandy around in his glass. "Did I tell you she fixed me dinner tonight? I think she was trying to soften me up."

"Could be."

"Did I tell you she was really pretty?"

Bill let out a low whistle. "Stubborn and pretty, huh? Sounds like your problems are more than just the restaurant."

"Maybe." Hunt laughed. "Just talking to you about the whole thing brings my feet back down on the ground. I can work it out."

"Well, let me know."

"Okay. And, Dad, as long as I'm heading back to Knoxville tomorrow, I thought I'd stop in for a visit." Though Hunt tried to make time for his parents, his busy schedule didn't allow him to see them very often.

"Your mother will be glad. See you then, Son."

Hunt replaced the phone receiver in its cradle, a smile still lingering on his lips. People like my parents should have lots of children, he thought fondly.

However, there'd been only him. He'd been born late in life to Bill and Lois Kirkland, but they'd resisted the urge to spoil him. In fact, there'd been little opportunity. Running their restaurant took most of their time and provided them with a small return on their investment in labor. There was no money to indulge their only son with material things.

Hunt has spent a lot of time at the tiny café. From the time he was six he was waiting and busing tables, cooking, and washing dishes. He'd liked being there, liked seeing the pleasure people got from good food. He'd quickly decided that someday he'd have his own successful restaurant.

A standout high school athlete, Hunt accepted a scholarship to the University of Tennessee. The campus in Knoxville was only about an hour from his hometown, and his parents never missed a home game. After college, a supportive alumnus gave him a job as an assistant manager in his restaurant. Hunt worked his way up to manager. A few years later, when the man decided to sell, he offered it to Hunt first. Only Hunt's parents had made that dream possible.

With the warm support Hunt had always received from his family, it was hard for him to understand what it must be like for Melissa. Beau had said she wouldn't go to her parents for anything.

"Why?" he wondered aloud.

Surely this desire she had for complete independence wouldn't last forever. Oh, Beau had said she'd been on her own for the past four years, but during that time she'd had a pretty good job with the Trents, who, after all, were probably friends of her family.

No, Hunt decided yet again, it's just a matter of time before she tires of this whole restaurant scheme. Right now she's starry-eyed with plans, but that'll end soon. I've just been letting my reaction to her pretty face get in the way of my original plans, he thought.

He set down his empty brandy glass and began preparing for bed, his mind busily figuring what kind of return he could expect to see from his initial investment in this venture.

But when he turned out the lights and tried to go to sleep, Hunt's profit and loss statements gave way to the memory of Melissa's gentle smile.

"Damn it, Kirkland," he muttered in the darkness. "You're in a mess."

Chapter Three

Hunt was on Melissa's doorstep at ten the next morning, clutching a box of doughnuts and telling himself she wouldn't seem so appealing in the bright September sunshine.

He was wrong.

In tight, faded jeans and an oversize pink cotton sweater, Melissa was every bit as beguiling as she'd been in silk and pearls. Maybe even more so. Her face was scrubbed clean of makeup, and the blunt-cut ends of her shoulder length hair were damp, as if she'd just stepped out of the shower. She looked rumpled and a bit out of sorts; Hunt wondered what she'd do if he leaned down and kissed the sleepy look off her face.

That thought kept him standing on the porch moments after she'd opened the door.

"Well, are you coming in?"

The barest hint of impatience in her tone brought Hunt down to earth quickly. He had to keep his mind off her more obvious attractions and concentrate on the business at hand. "I'm in desperate need of a cup of coffee," he said, stepping inside.

"I'm making some right now." Melissa led the way through the house to the kitchen. She gestured Hunt to the table, poured steaming coffee into blue ceramic mugs and joined him. After several swallows, she looked up to find him watching her in some amusement.

"It's obvious that my new partner isn't a morning person." Hunt smiled and raised his own mug to his lips.

Melissa grinned sheepishly. "I need at least one cup of solid caffeine to get the old adrenaline pumping."

"Add some nice, healthy white sugar to that, too," he said, flipping back the lid on the box of doughnuts.

"Thanks. I'm starved." She jumped up to get a couple of paper towels from the dispenser underneath the cabinet.

Very casually, Hunt said, "I tell you, Melissa, I've been thinking..."

Melissa paused in midmotion, practically holding her breath. Had he changed his mind? And if so, how would she feel? She'd lain awake half the night, vacillating between hoping he'd back out of this deal and praying he wouldn't. Either way, she knew she was in trouble. Trying to muster a bright smile, she turned back around with a handful of paper towels. "You've been thinking about what?"

"Dinner last night."

She blinked. "What about it?"

"It was delicious."

She sat down, picked up a sugar-glazed pastry and sent him a puzzled look.

"I think we should include some meals like that on the menu," he continued.

"Of course we should. That sort of thing will *be* the menu." Melissa's tone was assured.

Hunt bit into his own doughnut and took his time washing it down with coffee. "Well, that's just not the sort of thing Kirkland's is known for, you know?"

"I know." Melissa was careful to keep any hint of disparagement from her tone. She didn't ever want to sound critical of his business again. "But then, this won't be a Kirkland's, so I don't see that it matters."

Mouth open and ready to take another bite of doughnut, Hunt stared at her. He put the pastry down. "What do you mean?"

Melissa cleared her throat. "I'm merely pointing out that since this is *River Rest* and not Kirkland's, it shouldn't matter if the menu is a little different from your other restaurants."

"That's what I thought you meant," he said dryly.

"Well, surely you didn't think I'd want to call the restaurant Kirkland's, did you?" Melissa avoided looking at Hunt's face by pouring herself another cup of coffee.

"I guess I did."

"Why?"

"Oh, little things like a nine-year-old solid reputation, recognition as one of the most enjoyable places to eat in Knoxville, Birmingham and Atlanta. Just inconsequential matters like that."

His voice was tight, and a peek at his face told Melissa he was getting just as irritated as he'd been the night before. That wouldn't accomplish anything. "Listen, Hunt," she said, putting her hand on his arm. "Why don't you give me a chance to explain what I want the restaurant to be? Then I'll listen to your ideas."

The feel of her hand against his skin was warm and soft, unreasonably pleasing. Hunt found his attention centered on the contrast of her delicate, pink-tipped fingers against the broad muscle of his forearm. He liked having her touch him. The thought must have shown in his eyes, because when he looked up at her, Melissa jerked her hand away as if stung.

And for a long, breathless moment they stared at each other across the table.

What is it with this man? Melissa thought, feeling a blush crawl up her neck to her cheeks. Last night he kept holding my hand. And this morning an impersonal touch becomes . . . becomes what? She wasn't sure. She dropped her gaze to the open collar of his yellow knit shirt, noting the furring of dark hair visible above the third button. Her eyes flicked back to his face, noticing for the first time how the morning sun highlighted the auburn in his brown hair. Displeased by the personal direction her thoughts were taking, she dropped her gaze to the honeyed sheen of the maple tabletop.

"I'm waiting," Hunt said quietly, and Melissa's attention snapped back to his face.

"What?"

"Tell me your plans." A slight smile turned up the corners of his mouth.

He's playing with me, Melissa thought. He doesn't think I have any ideas, and every time I act uncertain, he'll steamroll over me and do things his way. Her chin lifted. "I'd rather show you than tell you."

She left the room, returning just minutes later with an armload of blueprints, which she spread across the table.

At first, Hunt was captivated more by the excitement in Melissa's blue eyes than by the drawings she had to show him. When, in smoothing the plans out, she brushed close to him, it was her soap-and-water fresh scent which drew his attention, rather than the details of her plans for remodeling the kitchen. However, the quality of what she was presenting soon penetrated the web her attraction had spun. He was surprised by how much he liked what he saw.

"So you want to expand the kitchen out onto part of the back porch," he said, tapping the blueprint.

"We have to. There's got to be more room than this for food preparation."

"And in warm weather, while people are waiting for their tables, they can sit or stand on the rest of the back porch, enjoy the view of the river and have a drink."

"Exactly."

"And what about a beverage center and a place for supplies?" he asked quickly.

"The old butler's pantry and the big closet under the back stairs," Melissa supplied, showing him the neatly blocked-in squares.

"A place for the employees to keep their personal things?"

She pointed to what had been the housekeeper's office.

"Adequate rest rooms?"

"Here."

For every question Hunt fired at Melissa, she had a ready answer. He began to see that her plans for this restaurant were no overnight scheme. Hours of careful study had been put into the proposed renovations. She had even drawn up the table arrangements.

To illustrate her ideas, Melissa led Hunt from room to room. He trailed in the wake of her rustling papers and charts, utterly fascinated by the detail in which she had planned. She knew the color she wanted the walls, what paintings she wanted to hang where. She wanted a plant here, blinds instead of curtains there. An urn filled with ostrich plumes in this corner, an intimate table for two by that window. This room was to be a bold Chinese red and blue, that one would be a subtler blue and gray.

She swept from the front parlor into the wide central foyer, so carried away by her plans that she forgot she was trying to impress him. "And we'll bring the grand piano out of the music room and set it here." She stepped into the recessed nook underneath the curve of the stairs. "And we'll put chairs and couches up and down the hall for the people who are waiting to be seated. And at night the lamps will be on, and all the tables will have bouquets of fresh flowers."

Melissa fairly danced across the floor and halfway up the stairs, cheeks glowing as she warmed to her topic. "And when the ladies go up to the lounge, they'll sort of glide back down the stairs." She demonstrated the movement. "And below them, the men will stand like Rhett Butler watching Scarlett O'Hara before the picnic at Twelve Oaks." She pretended to lift a long, flowing shirt and simpered coquettishly down the stairs.

And though she bore no resemblance to the actress who'd played *Gone With The Wind*'s famous heroine, Hunt had no trouble at all imagining Melissa as a bewitching Southern belle, preying on the hearts of a dozen suitors. In fact, his own heart suffered an unexpected jolt when she reached the bottom stair and bounced to a halt in front of him.

"Every woman in this town will want to come to River Rest and walk down our stairs!" she enthused.

"But will they and their men want to eat at our tables?" Hunt asked, almost believing her prediction of success.

"Of course." Melissa whirled away, her blond hair lifting about her face like a fairy cloud. Still clutching her charts and plans in one hand, she punctuated her words with emphatic gestures. "We'll serve the tenderest prime rib, the spiciest barbecue chicken and rice, sirloin steaks that melt away from the bone, creamy honey-mustard salad dressing, chocolate pies with meringue this thick..." She paused to show him a two-inch spread of her fingers. "We'll have coconut cakes with pineapple in the middle and ice cream that's churned by hand. River Rest's food will be so good and the atmosphere will be so perfect that we'll have 'em lined up outside."

As if exhausted, Melissa dropped to a seat on the stairs. "Now that's my idea for a restaurant. What's yours?"

She looked like an earnest young student, just daring her professor to refute her hypotheses. Hunt found himself wanting to agree with her wholeheartedly, but he had his own ideas. He couldn't allow his common sense to be swayed by her appealing but whimsical plans.

"First," he began in a no-nonsense tone. "Where's the bar?"

"I told you, we'll have chairs and couches here in the hall—"

"Not good enough. You make money on liquor. It would be better to turn the sunroom and the smaller back sitting room into an actual bar—"

"But I planned for those to be eating areas!" Melissa got to her feet, blue eyes flashing, ready to do battle.

"You can put at least one more table in each of the other dining rooms, and that will be plenty," Hunt continued blithely. "And what about all these antiques?"

"What about them?"

"Do you want your grandmother's favorite settee ruined by a spilled piña colada?"

"But the furniture is part of the whole plan!" Melissa's voice was practically a wail.

"It's yours to ruin. Personally, I think we should look around for some affordable reproductions. Have you considered the insurance?" Hunt fixed her with his most sensible, brown-eyed gaze.

"You're reducing the whole concept to a consideration of costs!"

He pretended to be surprised. "Oh, are you planning to run the restaurant free of charge? If that's the case, we ought to just set up a soup kitchen in the back. You can give tours of the house to all comers."

Melissa almost stamped her foot. The man was so crass! "Of course I want to make money. But the next thing you'll be suggesting is that we cover up the original wood floors with carpeting!"

Hunt shot a quick glance downward and then looked back at her. "That's not a bad idea."

"Oh, for heaven's sake, don't be ridiculous." Melissa's clipboard full of figures and plans clattered to the floor, and she resumed her seat on the stairs, arms crossed defensively across her chest. "What else do you not like?"

Leaning with casual grace against the newel post at the end of the stair rail, Hunt systematically tore down many of Melissa's romantic schemes. Her traffic flow was all wrong. They wouldn't be able to afford all those fresh flowers and plants. Was new wallpaper really necessary in the hall? It looked fine to him. He didn't think every room should be full of antiques.

"I guess you were thinking about adding some chrome and glass and wicker," Melissa said in an acid tone.

"As a matter of fact, I was. I think the contrast of old and new will be good." He grinned.

"You're nuts."

"Nuts enough to know what people like in three successful restaurants," Hunt quipped with self-assured ease.

"I hate smug men."

His smile just grew larger. "I could take my checkbook and leave."

Melissa groaned. He was right. "I guess we'd better start compromising."

"Lead the way."

And so they argued. Throughout the rest of the morning, over another pot of coffee and three more doughnuts each, they haggled over details. Melissa hauled out her estimates on furniture, remodeling and decoration. They agreed on the kitchen expansion. Melissa swung a deal with him for new wallpaper in all the rooms. In turn, Hunt got a bar full of chrome and glass and wicker. They even compromised on the name Kirkland's at River Rest.

The discussions moved from the foyer to the kitchen and back to the foyer until at three o'clock, just as they were preparing to do battle over the menu, Hunt called a halt to the proceedings.

"I'm starving. How does a pizza sound?"

"Marvelous," Melissa said. "My stomach's growling." She found her purse and followed him to the front door, and Hunt caught himself wondering about a woman who didn't pause to fuss in front of mirrors.

Outside, the beautiful early autumn day had disintegrated underneath a canopy of threatening clouds. Thunder rolled in the distance, and on the quickening breeze there was the scent of rain. In Hunt's Mercedes they took the Veteran's Bridge across the Tennessee River and sped through the older residential section of North Chattanooga, stopping at the first pizza place they passed.

"You really must be hungry," Melissa said a few minutes later when Hunt ordered a large pizza with practically everything on it but anchovies.

"Pizza is one of my favorite foods."

"Do you serve it at Kirkland's?"

"No. People want pizza at pizza places. At Kirkland's they want a mile-long salad bar, chicken fingers, steak and

shrimp, baked potatoes smothered in cheese and all kinds of
other good stuff.''

"You have very definite opinions on what the customer
likes,'' Melissa commented.

Heavy rain had begun to pound the pavement outside,
and Hunt paused to watch it fall before answering. He supposed he did sound a little opinionated, but he knew what
seemed to work in his business. "I wasn't always so sure,''
he said finally.

"I can't imagine.'' The wryness of Melissa's tone was
softened by her grin.

While waiting for the waitress to return with the pizza,
Hunt told Melissa about the first year after he'd bought the
restaurant in Knoxville. "It was creative accounting of the
first degree,'' he said with a laugh. "Some weeks I had just
enough money to keep the staff. At the end of the month I
would rush out to pay the electric bill so they wouldn't cut
off the power. I didn't allow myself one dime for nine whole
months. I just barely managed to pay my father.''

"Your father was working for you?'' Melissa was finding it a little hard to believe the self-assured man seated
across from her had ever struggled. She'd imagined his restaurants had known instant success.

"Mom and Dad sold their own place in order to help me
get started. I had to make it work. If I sank, so did they.''

The raw determination on Hunt's face was something
Melissa could understand. How had he turned the dream
into a reality? She had to wait until after their pizza had arrived to ask him.

"I remember the very night that things turned around,''
he said quietly. "A group who worked in one of the downtown office complexes came into the bar. They were the
usual three-piece-suit crowd, not big partiers, just people
who liked good food and fun. My bartender had quit, so I

was manning the place myself, and I struck up a conversation with them."

"And they told you what they wanted in a restaurant?" Melissa prompted before biting into a thick slice of pizza.

"That's the crazy part. They liked everything the restaurant already had. They'd heard one of the radio commercials Beau had put together for me, and they just happened to be driving by and stopped. They must have spread the word, because from that moment the business started growing." Shaking his head, Hunt started on his own pizza.

"It was really just incredible luck, wasn't it?"

"At first. Then I really had to work," Hunt said. "The service had to stay friendly. The surroundings always had to be neat and clean. The food had to be of the best quality. Prices couldn't rise quickly, no matter what my suppliers were trying to charge me. There are a hundred and one headaches that go with keeping a successful place on top. Getting started is the fun part."

Melissa laughed, a full, happy sound that brought an answering chuckle from Hunt. "Do you mean to tell me that today was the most fun we're going to have with this partnership?" she asked, merriment dancing in her eyes.

"We're in trouble, aren't we?"

As quickly as it came, her laughter died. "You do think we'll make it, don't you, Hunt?"

There it was again, Hunt thought, gazing at her thoughtfully. That elusive vulnerability. There was something in Melissa's dark blue eyes, some softening of her delicate features that made a man want to gather her close, to murmur all the comforts and reassurances she might possibly want to hear. How was it this small, stubborn woman he'd known less than a week could twist his gut inside out with just a glance?

"We will be a success, won't we?" she prompted.

What had made this restaurant so all-important to her? Hunt asked himself. He summoned a smile. "I don't undertake losing causes."

"I guess that's all I'm going to get by way of a guarantee." Her voice had lost its strident edge.

"Take it or leave it."

"Just finish your pizza."

They both smiled and reached for another piece.

There was no more talk about the restaurant. Instead, they dawdled over the meal, watching the steady rhythm of the rain. And when it was time to go, they dashed through the downpour to Hunt's car and ended up dripping all over the expensive leather interior.

Melissa dried her face with a clean handkerchief, and without thinking, held it out for Hunt to use, too. Watching him wipe the moisture from his features, she was struck by the intimacy of it all—the close quarters of the car, the simple sharing of a piece of cotton cloth. She took the handkerchief back and crumpled it in her hand, imagining that if she held it to her face, it would smell of wind and rain and musky maleness. The thought made her shiver.

"Looks like it could rain all night," Hunt declared, peering through the streaming windshield.

"It'll be a good night to stay at home. Do you have to go back to Knoxville?" Resolutely, Melissa ignored the tiny voice inside her that wished he would stay.

"My parents expect me tonight."

"Oh." The disappointment showed in her voice, and Melissa felt rather than saw the questioning look Hunt sent her way. She hastened to explain herself. "I just thought we might get the menu hammered out."

"I think that can probably wait. I'm going to have the agreement papers drawn up according to the terms we've discussed, and we'll need to establish a business account. I think you can go ahead and get started on the renovations.''

"And you're sure I can't have the floors redone in the library and foyer?'' That was one point Melissa had been unable to get him to agree to during their discussions.

"I just don't think it's necessary. It's expensive, and we need to conserve as much cash as possible. The floors look fine, and a little later on, it will be more practical.''

"Okay, okay,'' Melissa agreed, her mind frantically digging for some other place to cut costs so that the gleaming, flawless look she wanted for the foyer could be achieved.

They talked very little the rest of the way back to River Rest, but as the car drew to a stop in front of the house, Hunt turned to Melissa. "You know, I hadn't even thought to ask. Where are you going to live now?''

She almost gulped. Hadn't she told him that part of her plans? "There's an apartment on the third floor. I was hoping to stay there.'' She held her breath, half expecting him to object. But, after all, it was her house.

"That's probably a good idea,'' he said slowly. "I'd like to look around upstairs. I know the ladies' lounge will be up there, and eventually, I think we'll want to put in some private party rooms—''

"And I thought we'd put the office up there, too.''

"Great. I want to take a look before I leave.''

The stormy afternoon made for deep shadows inside the old house. Melissa flipped on lights as she led the way up the curving staircase.

"Don't you ever get scared here by yourself?'' Hunt said. In the gloomy light, the house looked like the perfect setting for a murder mystery.

"Scared? At home?'' Melissa laughed. "I doubt there are any ghosts here who would harm me.''

Hunt wondered why this should seem like home to her. What about the houses she'd shared with her parents? He didn't ask. Any mention of her father seemed to send Melissa into a deep freeze.

The upstairs was as carefully preserved as the rest of the house, full of family antiques and with pleasantly worn Oriental rugs on the floor. Melissa showed Hunt the two rooms she thought would make good private banquet facilities. "They're close to the back staircase, which leads to the kitchen," she pointed out.

She opened another door to show him the bedroom she was going to set up as the office and then started for the rear of the house. "The stairs to the apartment are down this way."

Hunt followed her, glancing in the opened doors they passed, seeing little of interest until the last room on the right. It was a little girl's room, a fluffy confection of white eyelet and pink gingham, illuminated by the lamp burning on the bedside table. Intrigued, Hunt stopped. Locating the overhead-light switch, he turned it on and stepped inside.

Of course it was Melissa's room. Regardless of the fact that she was probably the last little girl to live in this house, Hunt would have known she slept here. The room had captured her fresh, sweet fragrance, and the pearls she'd worn at her throat last night were coiled on the dressing table, right beside a dog-eared teddy bear. Hunt picked up the stuffed animal, smiling as he turned it over in his big hands.

"Grandmother kept all my special friends for me," Melissa explained from the doorway.

Hunt put the toy back in place, realizing he had invaded her private space. "I'm sorry. This room just looked exactly the way I always imagined a little girl's room should." He paused as if searching for the words to describe it. "It's cotton-candy pretty."

Nodding in agreement, Melissa sent a fond glance around the room. "I loved it when I was ten. By the time I was sixteen, it had lost some of its charm. But Grandmother kept having the curtains and spread redone, and painting it the same old way. She was always encouraging me to grow up, but sometimes I think this room was the way she pretended I'd be a little girl forever, that she'd be alive forever."

Hunt didn't say anything, and Melissa looked up to find his solemn, sympathetic eyes on her. She tried to shrug off the melancholy mood. "She did the same thing in Edward's room."

"Edward?"

"My brother."

Melissa turned and left, and Hunt had no choice but to follow. The door at the end of the hall revealed a flight of stairs to the third floor's spacious apartment. A kitchenette was tucked under one eave, a sleeping alcove under another. On a sunny day, the dormer windows would probably flood the room with light, but today it was dark and glum looking. A door revealed a bathroom, which Melissa explained needed some minor repairs. She assured him that the fireplace really worked. "I had all the chimneys cleaned."

"You're sure you'll like it up here?" Hunt asked.

"Of course. As soon as I move up the furniture I want and get it arranged, I'll be snug as a bug in a rug. Face it, once everything gets under way downstairs, I probably won't have time to stay up here much."

Still, Hunt looked about him with concern. The whole thing reminded him of some Shirley Temple movie where the once-rich little girl was banished to a cold, barren garret. This time he couldn't stop the questions that sprang to his lips. "Melissa, are you sure about the whole thing?"

"What?"

"The restaurant."

"I don't know what you're talking about." There was genuine puzzlement in her voice.

"I mean," Hunt began patiently, "are you sure you want your home to be lost?"

"I'm not losing it."

"But it seems to me, seeing how much you obviously love the place, that perhaps your father might be able to help you keep it as a private residence." He could see the temper clouding her face, but he plunged ahead anyway. "I don't know what happened between you and your father—"

"Do you have to know that in order to be my business partner?"

"No, I—"

"Good. Because it's none of your business."

It was like a quick-freeze, the coldness that stole over Melissa and that she transferred to him. Gone was the teasing banter they'd shared over pizza. Gone was her compelling vulnerability. Gone even was the irritation with which she'd greeted many of his ideas for the restaurant. Eyes flashing, back practically arched, she was like a threatened cat. The claws were almost showing.

Curiously, her reaction made Hunt angry, too. Damn her, anyway, he thought. She crept under his skin and then turned on him when he exhibited nothing more than friendly concern. Oh, she was a sly one, all right. Soft on the outside, but inside, brittle enough to break a man in two.

"Fine," he said tersely. "I won't make the mistake of asking again." He glanced at his watch. "I have to go. I'll call you when the papers are ready, and I'll bring them down."

"Good." She started toward the door.

"I can let myself out."

She only nodded at his curt goodbye.

His footsteps echoed down the stairs, and Melissa crossed to the dormer window and moments later watched him get in his car and leave.

Why had she cut him off like that? There'd been no reason to be rude. He was a nice man, and he was curious. She should have given him the little speech she gave everyone about wanting to be on her own. That, after all, was the truth. Of course, that little speech didn't begin to convey the depth of her feelings on the subject, but most people weren't interested in looking beyond the surface meaning of her words. Most people...

She stopped to think. Maybe that was the problem. Hunt wasn't most people. Melissa sensed he didn't stop at the surface of any subject. He'd dig and dig until he pulled out all her secrets, all her insecurities and disappointments.

And, like most of the strong men she'd allowed to get too close, he'd use everything he knew as a weapon against her.

A fresh onslaught of rain hit the house, and the wind moaned around the corners. Melissa glanced about the attic room, feeling her aloneness keenly, wishing that any ghosts the old walls might harbor would come out and share their wisdom. But no specters appeared, and she was left with only the sound of the wind and the rain for company.

The rain stayed with Hunt throughout the hour and a half drive from Chattanooga to his parent's home in Athens. It slowed his progress not one bit. In fact, he barely noticed the slickness of the asphalt as his powerful car ate up the miles, first on the interstate and then on the back roads that took him home. Who could think about rain when a woman like Melissa filled your head?

He shouldn't have asked about her father. Hunt knew that with dead certainty. Now that he thought about it, aside from her grandmother, Melissa seemed strongly disinclined to mention her entire family. A family feud of monumental proportions, he decided, and what a pity. Here were people who had it all—money, education, advantages—but they invested their time and efforts in fighting among themselves. It was a waste.

He'd be better off leaving Melissa Chambers's private demons alone. Just doing business with her was going to be tough enough. Yet . . .

Hunt caught himself remembering the way the raindrops had caught in her hair, the excitement that animated her face when she explained her plans, the awareness in her eyes after she'd touched his arm and they'd stared at each other across the table. . . .

"My God," he groaned out loud. It was as if he'd spent the past twenty-four hours memorizing her every movement and reaction. The woman had bewitched him.

With impatience, Hunt realized he had drawn to a halt in his parents' driveway and was just sitting, the engine idling. He switched the car off and watched the light come on beside the front door, then smiled when he saw his mother's face peering out the window into the rainy night. It was nice to come home.

After grabbing his weekend bag from the backseat, Hunt ran through the rain to the house. Lois Kirkland greeted her son with a hug and an admonishment to get inside before he caught his death of cold.

A day spent in Melissa's big, empty mansion made Hunt's boyhood home seem a little cramped. The brick and frame ranch house was indeed small, and it was filled to capacity with homemade warmth. The living room was less than elegant, furnished with two worn recliners, a sofa and several end tables, all grouped around a television set. A black and white cat was stretched out on top of the TV. Another cat, smoky gray in color, lay curled on the lap of the big man who was leaned back in one of the chairs.

"We were about to give up on you, Son," the man said, not looking up from the action on the television screen.

"You hush!" his wife said indignantly. "I knew you'd be here when you could," she told Hunt as she bustled about, removing a basket of mending from the couch. Lois was small of frame, quick and efficient in manner and movement. Organized and cheerful, she was the kind of woman they always asked to head the fund-raisers at school and church. Hunt could remember her hosting his classroom parties and sewing costumes for the drama club plays. From the top of her iron gray hair to the bottom of her small feet, he loved her dearly.

"What you watchin', Dad?" he asked, dropping down on the couch. The black and white cat jumped from the TV and joined him.

"Some crazy movie he rented at the video place," Lois said before Bill could answer. She sat down in the other recliner and picked up her needlework.

"I think it's pretty decent." Bill sat up defensively. "This guy here," he pointed to the screen where Harrison Ford was helping build a barn, "he's hiding out with some Amish folks because he has some dirt on some bad cops."

"I've seen it; it's a good movie," Hunt agreed.

Lois looked up from her work. "I guess it's all right."

"Oh, shoot, if Hunt came in and said one of those skin flicks was good, you'd agree." Bill laughed good-naturedly.

"A skin what?" Lois asked.

Father and son looked at each other and grinned. Lois always pretended not to understand things of which she disapproved.

"You don't want to know, Mother," Hunt said with the ease of many year's practice. He changed the subject. "I'm going into business in Chattanooga."

"Oh, that's wonderful." His mother fairly beamed.

"So you got that pretty lady to see it your way, did you?" Bill chuckled and scratched his salt-and-pepper beard.

"What pretty lady?' Lois demanded, interest sparking her brown eyes.

Hunt groaned. In the past few years, his mother had jumped at even the most casual mention of a woman in his life. "She's my business partner, Mother," he explained. "Don't go getting any matchmaking notions."

"Well, who is she? I am allowed to ask that, aren't I?"

"Yes, Mother, that's allowed. You remember Congressman Chambers, don't you?"

Bill Kirkland snorted. "Why sure we do. He did a good job till he got too all-fired greedy and wound up in a mess."

"My partner is his daughter."

Hunt's father looked concerned. "I hope she's not a crook, too."

"Now, Bill," Lois exclaimed. "I don't think Hunt would go and get himself hooked up with the wrong sort of person. Would you, Son?"

"Melissa is not in the least crooked."

"Melissa, is it? Not Miss Chambers?" Lois's smile was hopeful.

"Oh for goodness' sake!" Hunt got up, disturbing the cat, who ran like a black and white streak out of the room. "What's to eat?"

"Coconut pie," Bill said, patting his ample girth. "I was thinking about having a third piece myself."

Movie forgotten, the three of them gathered around the heavy oak table in the small kitchen to eat pie and drink coffee, talking until nearly midnight. Hunt's parents wanted to know every detail about the new restaurant. Lois liked what Hunt told her about Melissa's ideas for fresh flowers and piano music in the foyer, and she loved the thought of a menu filled with traditional foods.

"It won't hurt you to do something a little different with this place," she said stoutly.

"I don't know if you want to tamper too much with success," Bill disagreed.

"You're just too cautious. I think this Miss Chambers has some really interesting ideas, Son. I'd like to meet her." Lois got up to stack their pie plates in the sink, avoiding her son's baleful look. "I could give her my cherry tart recipe. I've been wanting to see that on a menu for a long time."

"Now that's a good idea," Hunt said, barely suppressing a yawn.

Bill stood up. "You must be exhausted after haggling with an ex-congressman's pretty daughter all day. Let's go to bed."

Hunt really was tired, yet long after his parents had gone to their room, he sat in the kitchen, reveling in the easy familiarity of his surroundings, of the evening he'd just spent in their company. Homemade pie, rich coffee and good conversation with people you loved—he wondered if there was anything better.

He glanced about the simple room, noticing that his mother still hadn't painted over the door facing where they'd marked his growth from year to year. The curtain rod across the back window still sagged in the middle. The cabinet door to the right of the sink still had the dent he'd placed in it nearly twenty years ago with a baseball bat. There was comfort in the imperfections. This was a home, as dearly loved by his family as River Rest was loved by Melissa.

But while he had his parents, who was there for Melissa to sit with late at night? Who did she take her troubles to? Who shared her happiness over a success? The grandmother she'd loved was gone. There was Beau, of course, but Hunt wondered if even the gregarious redhead received many of Melissa's confidences. Who did she really rely on?

It was sad. His parents had been willing to risk everything to launch his dreams. They'd sold their own business and mortgaged this home and land in order to give him the money for that first restaurant. When things had been tight, his mother had cooked, his father had even bused tables and swept the floor. Their unconditional support had made success possible. And even if he had failed, Hunt knew they would still care.

Who cared for Melissa?

The gray cat wandered into the room and leapt nimbly from the floor to the cabinet, breaking Hunt's concentration. He glanced at his watch. It was almost one-thirty. Damn! Two nights in a row he'd sat up late thinking about Melissa Chambers. It was a habit he meant to break right now. Flipping off lights as he went, Hunt moved through the silent house to his bedroom.

Melissa had just fallen asleep when the phone beside her bed rang. It was storming again, and she waited for a streak of lightning to fade before she switched on the lamp and picked up the receiver. "Hello?"

"Missy, I'm coming to Chattanooga."

It was her brother, and from the slurred tone of his voice, Melissa knew the only place Edward needed to go was to bed to sleep it off. "No, Edward. You need to stay at school."

"But I hate it." He sounded like a spoiled child in the throes of a temper tantrum.

"Sooner or later there's going to have to be a school you do like."

"You don't understand...." His voice choked and faded.

"Edward?" Alarmed now, Melissa sat completely up in bed. "Edward, are you all right?"

She thought she heard him sob. "You do know what he's done now, don't you?"

"Who?"

"Father!" Edward spat out the word as one would a rotten piece of fruit.

Melissa sighed. Would her brother never stop blaming their father for it all? "No. What's he done now?"

"You mean he hasn't called to tell you?" The laugh at the other end of the phone was low and bitter. "God, I guess I should feel honored."

"Edward, just tell me," Melissa ordered.

"No, I think I'll let Daddy-dear deliver this message himself." He paused, and the bitterness was gone from his tone as he begged, "Missy, please let me come and see you."

"The semester has barely started."

"No one will miss me here."

"Oh, Edward." Melissa fought the sympathy that nearly pulled her in two. She wouldn't do him any good by being soft. "You know you can't mess this school up—"

"Watch me."

The line went dead, and Melissa sat staring at the receiver in her hand. What had her father done to set Edward off this time?

Chapter Four

River Rest was crawling with workers when Hunt returned to Chattanooga on Thursday. Cars and trucks lined the driveway. Painters were putting a coat of white on the columns, shutters and trim. He parked his car behind a pickup truck and went inside to find a crew of carpenters noisily stripping Sheetrock off the walls of the kitchen.

Hunt was amazed. How had Melissa managed to mobilize this kind of activity so quickly? He'd called Monday to tell her funds were being transferred into a Chattanooga bank and that she could get started on the renovations. She'd certainly been busy between then and now.

Two hefty young men came in from the back porch, toting a load of fresh lumber. Over the noise of a power saw, Hunt shouted, "Is Miss Chambers around?"

"Out back," one of them answered, nodding toward the porch.

Hunt stepped over building materials and debris to reach the door, spotted Melissa at the end of the porch and went outside.

Most of her blond hair was scooped back in a ponytail. The rest fell in disarray about her flushed cheeks. Her jeans were faded to white at the seams and ripped at the knee. On her feet were dirty white tennis shoes, and more dirt was smudged on her blue gingham shirt. She honestly looked a total mess, but when she glanced up at Hunt and smiled, he could have sworn his heart catapulted downward and used his feet for a trampoline. He steadfastly tried to ignore the feeling.

He'd sent their partnership papers down with a messenger and had only talked to Melissa twice this week. Each time, he'd wanted to apologize for prying into her private affairs and for leaving in a huff on Saturday. However, on both occasions she had acted as if they'd parted on the best of terms, and he'd been afraid to disturb the peace. Now, moving toward her on the crowded back porch, Hunt was glad he'd left the matter alone. It was better to slide back into the camaraderie they'd begun to establish before he'd overstepped his bounds.

"You've been busy," he said, stopping in front of her.

"You said to get started." Melissa grinned. "All I needed was money."

"But how did you find a crew able to start work so fast?"

"Luck." Looking past Hunt, Melissa called, "Hey, Cabot, come here."

Hunt turned to see a tall blond man in neatly pressed jeans and a plaid shirt coming up the back steps.

Melissa made the introductions. "John Cabot, I'd like you to meet my partner, Hunt Kirkland."

"Good to meet you," Cabot said, proffering his hand.

"Cabot's our lucky contractor," Melissa explained.

"Lucky?" Hunt echoed.

"Yes. Lucky for us, Cabot was available. He's the contractor I first talked to about the renovations, the one I really wanted. He just finished another job and the next one he had lined up hit a snag, so here he is."

"Then that is lucky for us," Hunt agreed. He looked at the contractor. "You do much renovation work like this?"

The man nodded. "Almost exclusively. Lots of people are choosing to redo older houses. I've taken on buildings in all kinds of conditions." He paused, and there was admiration in the glance he gave his surroundings, a glance that settled on Melissa. "But it's not often I get to work on a project this interesting."

Although Melissa seemed oblivious to the warmth in the man's eyes as she continued discussing the job, Hunt barely caught a word she said. Jealousy scraped his gut with a ragged edge, blocking everything else. Eyes narrowed, he concentrated instead on sizing up John Cabot.

The contractor was a tall man, well over six feet—several inches taller than Hunt. His hair was the color of wheat, his skin darkened by hours spent outdoors, his brown eyes framed with tiny squint lines. Hunt supposed lots of women would find John Cabot attractive in a basic, earthy sort of way. He found himself hoping Melissa wasn't one of those women.

His study of the man was cut short when Melissa demanded his attention. "Huh?" he said.

She gave him a puzzled look and tapped the blueprints laid out on a makeshift table. "Didn't we agree to put a new door for deliveries at the end of the kitchen?"

Melissa leaned over the plans in order to show Hunt the area in question, but he looked instead at Cabot. The man gave him a knowing smile, and it seemed to Hunt that Cabot was sending him a silent question—is she spoken for?

In answer, Hunt put a light, but possessive, hand on Melissa's shoulder as he bent close behind her, studying the plans. She glanced up at him, a faint, questioning line between her brows. But when Hunt gave her what he hoped was a friendly smile, she relaxed and turned back to the blueprints. Over the top of her head, Hunt nodded at Cabot's acquiescing salute.

It was some time later, when Hunt had followed Melissa inside to inspect her wallpaper choices that he realized the meaning of the little exchange with Cabot. He'd just laid claim to Melissa. Of course, the whole idea was absurd, like some ancient tribal rite. But he'd picked up on the other man's signals and had chosen to indicate a prior stake. Now why was that? Hunt was seized by a sudden urge to find Cabot, explain it was all a mistake, tell the man he had no personal interest whatsoever in Melissa.

But Hunt was beginning to realize that wasn't true. Certainly no business associate had ever occupied his mind in quite the way Melissa Chambers did. So instead of tracking her other admirer down, he stood beside her in the library, fascinated by the way the afternoon sun picked out the varying colors of blonde in her hair. She talked to him, but again he heard nothing she said.

"Hunt, is something bothering you?" Melissa finally asked when it became obvious he wasn't listening to her.

He blinked and smiled in a way that made her wonder exactly what kind of thoughts were going on behind his coffee-brown eyes. "I guess I'm just preoccupied."

"Business problems?" She led the way out of the room and into the foyer.

"A personal matter," he answered.

"Oh," Melissa murmured, oddly dismayed. When a man like Hunt had that kind of faraway look in his eyes, you could almost bet the object of his thoughts was a woman.

Now why did that bother her? Perhaps she'd been thinking about him too much.

Since she'd last seen him, there'd been plenty to occupy Melissa's mind. Her brother. Her father's latest news. The renovations. Yet she'd thought a great deal about Hunt, wondering how he'd act toward her when they met again. She was ashamed of the snappish way she'd reacted to his perfectly innocent question about her father, and she'd made an effort to be extra pleasant whenever he called. His casual, easy manner had been a relief. As business partners, they couldn't afford to waste time or energy on petty squabbles.

But business or no business, Melissa knew Hunt was on her mind entirely too much. And he simply wasn't the sort of man she needed to fill her thoughts; he was too strong. If she chose to allow it, he could too easily dominate her. She was not going to fall into that trap again.

"Come upstairs and see what I've done," she said briskly.

The upstairs as well as the downstairs had been stripped of the furnishings Melissa didn't want included in the restaurant. As she explained to Hunt, arrangements had been made to store the furniture even before they'd finalized their partnership. Some of the pieces had been sent to her mother in Nashville. "There were movers all over the place Tuesday and Wednesday."

"You were going to make this restaurant happen no matter what, weren't you?" Hunt commented, following Melissa through the upstairs hall.

"Yes, I was," she said bluntly as she turned into a room on the right.

The bedroom had been transformed into a workable office, complete with file cabinets, typewriter and two desks. Hunt recognized the comfortable love seat from the small sitting room downstairs, as well as the square oak desk from the library. Melissa showed him the neatly labeled folders containing receipts and purchase orders, the business checkbook and the petty cash box hidden in the back of her desk drawer.

Then, with a flourish, Melissa pulled the chair out from a rolltop desk. "Welcome to your Chattanooga office, Mr. Kirkland."

"For me?" Hunt said, genuinely amazed.

Melissa smiled at his pleasure. "This was my grandfather's desk. He kept it stuffed with letters and papers in an alcove downstairs. My grandmother was always after him to clean it up." She opened the top right-hand drawer and pulled out two candy bars. "He always had a treat for myself and Edward hidden here." She laughed and held one of the bars out to Hunt. "Have a seat," she invited. "You've even got your own phone."

Hunt's gaze flickered to the business phone on the desk. "Melissa, how in the world did you manage to get all of this accomplished in less than four days? An office, phones, the remodeling begun..."

"I've just always had a talent for organization, I guess," she said with a shrug. "Like my grandmother—"

"Pity I didn't inherit any of *that*, either," came a voice from the doorway.

Melissa's head snapped around, and Hunt followed her gaze to the door. "Edward," she murmured.

Even before she said the name, Hunt knew this was Melissa's brother. The slender young man's longish blond hair and dark blue eyes were very much like his sister's. In his lean, handsome face, there was more than a passing resemblance to his well-known father.

"Edward, where have you been?" Melissa demanded. "I was so worried when you didn't come home last night. I almost called the police—"

"Oh, Missy, don't fuss. You're just like Mother." Edward moved with catlike grace from the door to the love seat, sprawling across the cushions, putting his Italian leather loafers up on the arm. "I was out with friends."

Melissa seemed to have forgotten Hunt was in the room. She stalked toward her brother, angry color staining her cheeks. "And I'd like to know who you know that well in Chattanooga?" Unceremoniously she lifted Edward's feet from the sofa and dumped them on the floor.

"Some guys I used to run around with when I visited Grandmother." Edward sat up. "Is that okay?"

"Who are they?"

"Missy—"

"Who are they?" she asked firmly.

Anger flashed from Edward with the suddenness of lightning. "Just get off my case!" He jumped to his feet and glared down at Melissa.

His threatening stance made Hunt react. Hand clenching into a fist at his side, he took a step forward, his movement at last drawing the other two's attention.

"Hunt," Melissa began with a trace of embarrassment in her voice. "I'm sorry. This is my brother, Edward. He doesn't usually act like such a barbarian—"

"Of course I do," Edward disagreed brashly. He fixed his gaze on Hunt. "You the dude who's helping Missy get this restaurant started?"

"Yes. Hunt Kirkland." He stepped forward and extended his hand. Surprisingly, the young man's handshake was strong and firm. Political training no doubt, Hunt thought with a trace of distrust. No matter what, you always had a wide smile and a firm grip for the public.

Edward's eyes narrowed as he studied Hunt. "Do you really think this idea of Missy's will work?"

"If I didn't, I doubt I'd be willing to invest any money in it."

"Well, some people are always looking for tax write-offs. I wondered if that might be your game."

At her brother's caustic words, Melissa's glance flashed to Hunt's face. He could read the uncertainty in her eyes. Was she so unsure of him? He looked at her while he answered Edward's accusation. "I don't expect the restaurant to fail, so I doubt there'll be any write-offs." Bringing the look of relief to her face made him absurdly happy.

With a derisive sound, Edward sank back down on the love seat. "Seems to me the sensible thing would be to sell the place," he muttered, staring hard at the floor.

A sharp retort sprang to Hunt's lips, but he bit it back when Melissa frowned and shook her head.

Her tone was light when she spoke. "I was just showing Grandfather's old desk to Hunt. Remember how he always kept candy for us there, where Grandmother couldn't confiscate it." As she spoke, Melissa moved back to the desk and closed the rolltop. Edward didn't even look up.

"It's a fine piece of furniture, Melissa," Hunt said, filling the silence. "Thank you."

"Are you giving *him* the desk?" Edward's bitter voice snapped Melissa's head back around.

She sighed. Why did Edward have to be so impossible? "Hunt's just going to use the desk when he's in town."

"Maybe I'd like to have Grandfather's desk."

Hunt watched Melissa's expression soften. Her brother's interest really pleased her.

"Would you? You never said anything about wanting to keep the desk. If you do, I—"

"It'd probably bring a few bucks from an antique dealer, wouldn't it?" Edward asked coldly.

The blood seemed to drain from Melissa's face as she struggled with her fury. "You're not getting Grandfather's desk just so you can sell it."

"Why not?" her brother challenged, crossing the room. "You got the house."

Melissa sucked in her breath and then glanced at Hunt. She didn't want to air all her family's dirty laundry in front of him.

Though he was reluctant to leave her, he took the hint and excused himself, "I think I'll go downstairs and take a look at those blueprints again." Melissa thanked him with her glance. He nodded at Edward. "Nice to have met you."

"Likewise," came the gruff, almost rude, reply.

Hunt had barely shut the office door when he heard Edward's voice raised in anger. "Damn it, Melissa, I need the money!"

"I said no!"

"Melissa, I don't have a dime—"

Her next reply was quietly spoken, too low for Hunt to hear, and he wasn't about to lurk outside in the hallway trying to eavesdrop. Casting several worried glances over his shoulder, he headed for the stairs. The situation made him uneasy. He wasn't so sure Melissa was a match for her obviously troubled younger brother.

"Now, Edward," Melissa said in what she hoped was a soothing tone. "We've been through this at least ten times since you arrived Tuesday. I'm not going to give you any money. I'm not giving you anything to sell to make money. If you'd stay in school, you'd have all the money you—"

"But I hated the damn school!" Edward proclaimed bitterly. "I don't know why you all keep harping about college. It's a waste of time."

"And what do you propose to do without an education?" Melissa sat down in Hunt's desk chair and crossed her arms. "Tell me that."

"If I could just get my hands on my inheritance from Grandmother, I wouldn't have to worry about it." Edward flung himself down in the room's other desk chair.

"Go to college, concentrate, graduate, work a year or two, and when you're twenty-five the money is yours."

"But that's five years!"

Melissa rubbed at her throbbing temples. Was it only eight years ago that she'd been Edward's age and five years had seemed like an eternity to her, too? "Edward, if you'd just stay in school and find something you want to do, the time would pass quickly."

"That's really easy for you to say, considering that you got your inheritance."

Grasping the arms of the chair firmly, Melissa pushed herself up. "I'm not going to sit here and listen to this anymore. I told you when you got here that I was really busy and I didn't have time for your tantrums. Now, Father called this morning—"

"So?" Edward interrupted belligerently.

"He's worried about you. He wants you to come home."

Edward laughed, a mirthless sound. "Home? Now that's a joke. Did he say his precious Nadine wanted me there? I doubt that."

"Father didn't mention his wife."

"His wife," Edward echoed. "Do you realize you never even call her by name?"

Melissa swallowed. He was right. "I guess I never think about her very much."

"You should be happy you don't have to. You didn't have to live with the two lovebirds after the divorce when Mother was having a breakdown. You didn't have to be nice to Nadine's sniveling little brat.'' Edward's voice rose again in anger. "God, every time I think about her having another baby, I—"

"I know. I know you hate it!" Melissa shouted, losing her control. "Edward, I wish it could be different, but it just can't. Please, I just wish you'd accept that we can't go back."

Her words echoed off the walls, and Edward sat staring at her, blue eyes wide with shock, looking exactly like the hurt little boy his sister had always defended. In a quick movement, he swiveled the chair around and started to get up.

Melissa leapt forward, putting a detaining hand on his shoulder. "Edward, don't..." she whispered. "I'm sorry.... I guess I just don't understand."

"No, you don't. Nobody does," he muttered, sinking back in the chair, his back still toward her.

Leaning forward, Melissa looped her arms around his shoulders. "I try," she said quietly. "I try to put myself in your place, try to imagine what it must have been like to be barely sixteen with your whole family falling apart. I was older, Edward, but it hurt me, too—just not in the same way it hurt you. And I had other problems...."

"Michael," Edward supplied softly. He patted Melissa's hand in awkward sympathy, and her arms tightened about his neck.

"Yes...well, it never would have worked anyway." She allowed herself a sad little sigh. "I've put everything behind me, and that's what you have to do. And just because Father's started another family with Nadine, that doesn't mean you've been replaced—"

"You wouldn't say that if you'd lived with them!" Edward jerked out of Melissa's arms, out of the chair and across the room.

"He does love you," she insisted to her brother's retreating back, wishing she could believe the words. Sometimes she wondered if her father had resigned his love for Edward along with his political office. No, that wasn't true. He had to love him. It was just that he had no idea of how to show his feelings—especially to his son. Melissa had to make Edward understand that.

"Edward!" she said, but he stalked out of the room without turning around, slamming the door behind him.

What now? Melissa asked silently. It had been like this ever since her brother had arrived two days ago—one constant battle. He couldn't just stay here doing nothing. Yet he refused to go back to school, didn't want to see or speak with either of their parents. And who could force him to do anything? He was twenty years old.

Melissa was at a loss. Edward was too much for her to deal with, especially with all the work she had to do. If only she didn't worry so much about him, didn't feel so responsible. Wearily she sat down in her chair.

Four years ago, Melissa thought glumly, I should have worried about Edward instead of Mother. However, Jenna Chambers had been near collapse after the scandal of her husband's resignation. And when he'd asked for a divorce—well, that had been the final straw. She had fallen apart. Melissa had felt compelled to take care of her. They'd come here and stayed with Myra for a while then moved back to the family home in Nashville. It had been almost a year before Jenna pulled herself together. Then, of course, Melissa had started her own quest for independence. Edward had been lost in the shuffle.

Jenna had been in no shape to deal with a troubled teenager, but it had been a real mistake to leave the boy with his father and new wife. Nadine and Edward had clashed from the beginning, over his attitude, his friends, her son....

Melissa closed her mind to that line of thought. The past couldn't be changed. Somehow, her father and brother had to work out their differences. Then, and only then, would Edward get his head straight. Of course, her father's announcement that Nadine was pregnant hadn't helped matters. Even Melissa wasn't sure how she felt about that.

She remembered how pleased her father had been when she'd called him early Sunday morning. He'd told her his big news right away, sounding proud. Then Melissa had to tell him about the troubling phone call she'd had from Edward on Saturday night. He was upset, but like Melissa, like her mother, Malcolm Chambers didn't know what to do about Edward.

A soft tap sounded at the door, and Melissa looked up just as Beau stuck his head around the edge. "Is this the private executive suite of Melissa Chambers, famed restaurant tycoon?"

She managed a smile. "Semiprivate. Hunt's got a desk, too."

"So I heard." Beau came just inside the door, looking dapper as usual in a gray tweed suit. "Where's the brat?"

Melissa frowned at his description of her brother. "I think Edward is in his room. Why?"

"Hunt said he was giving you a hard time."

"Really?" Melissa's shoulders stiffened. The times she had with her brother, good or bad, were none of Hunt's concern. She folded her hands in front of her on the desk and looked down at them as she spoke. "I can handle Edward."

When she looked up, Hunt was standing behind Beau in the doorway. One eyebrow was cocked in a skeptical fashion, as if he doubted her words. Melissa raised her chin. "Did you want something, Beau?"

Beau chuckled. "Get off your high horse, Melissa. I brought a couple of bottles of champagne with me. I thought I'd go pick up some Chinese food and we'd have a celebration."

"Why?"

"Your partnership with Hunt, of course." Crossing his arms across his chest, Beau glanced from Melissa to Hunt and then back again. "You two aren't fighting, are you?"

"Not that I'm aware of." Hunt leaned against the door facing, his navy jacket slung casually across his shoulder, white shirt stretched taut across his broad chest. "Are we fighting, Melissa?"

"Of course not," she answered, truthfully. There was no reason to be angry with Hunt. After all, she and Edward had stood right here and argued in front of him. Naturally he'd told Beau. It was just that he was learning all her tightly guarded secrets. And she suspected those might be her only defense against his appeal.

Blushing at the thought, she busied herself by opening a desk drawer and pulling out a couple of folders. "We need to make some final decisions on fixtures, Hunt," she said.

"You two do that, and I'll see if I can talk Edward into going on a Chinese food run with me," Beau said.

"Is Cabot gone?" Melissa glanced at the small clock on her desk. It was nearly six o'clock. She'd wasted a lot of time arguing with Edward and sitting here thinking.

"Everyone's gone. We've locked the place up. See you in a few," Beau said, leaving.

Shadows spread through the room, and an hour passed while Melissa and Hunt worked companionably, pouring over price estimates. There was so much to buy—tables, chairs, refrigerators, stoves, freezers. So many decisions that had to be made quickly. Their target opening date was the week after Thanksgiving, and that left them just about eight weeks to get the restaurant ready.

"Are we cutting it too close?" Hunt asked once they'd gone down the list of all that remained to be done.

"You're the expert," Melissa chided lightly. "What do you think?"

He leaned back in the chair he'd drawn close to her desk and thoughtfully rubbed his jaw. Then he looked up at her and grinned. "I think Chattanooga just better get ready."

Melissa resisted the temptation to hug him. God, his confidence sounded good. "I don't suppose while you're feeling this congenial that you'd agree to refinishing the floors downstairs, would you?"

Hunt picked up a sheaf of papers. "Show me where to fit it into this budget, and I'll agree to it." He dropped the papers back to the desk.

Melissa gave him a shrewd look. "What if I did it myself?"

"You couldn't. It's incredibly hard work."

With the stubbornness he was getting used to, she pressed, "But if I did it myself, we'd save all that labor cost."

"True...."

"Ah-ha! So you think it's a good idea." She flashed a triumphant smile.

"If you want to kill yourself over a floor that looks fine right now, go for it." Hunt shook his head. "But if you get stuck, there's no money to call in a pro."

"I won't get stuck," Melissa said with confidence.

"Somehow I can believe that." Following the impulse he'd been trying to ignore all afternoon, Hunt reached up and wiped a smudge of dirt from her cheek.

Startled, she jumped at his touch.

"Construction dirt," he explained.

She rubbed at the spot he had touched. It seemed to tingle.

Hunt flexed his fingers. The feel of her skin lingered there. Soft. Smooth. Silence fell in the room, but he could almost hear the electricity crackling between them.

Melissa was grateful for the interruption when Edward came through the doorway.

"We're back with the food. Where do you want it?" True to character, all trace of bad humor was gone from his expression, a development that pleased Melissa. She wanted no more of Edward's temperamental displays in front of Hunt.

"Since the kitchen's demolished and the other rooms downstairs are practically bare, we'd better go up to my apartment." She stood and stretched.

"I didn't realize you'd already moved upstairs," Hunt said as they followed Edward out into the hall.

"Besides Edward's room, I only left one other furnished up here," Melissa said. "I thought it might come in handy. You could stay here instead of getting a hotel." She instantly regretted her invitation. She didn't want him here under the same roof at night. That sort of arrangement seemed entirely too intimate. Even with all the rooms in this house to separate them, she felt certain she'd be aware of Hunt's every movement.

The thought had a similarly disquieting effect on Hunt. With the amount of time he'd recently spent thinking about Melissa, the last thing he needed was to stay in this house with her. Knowing she was sleeping just a floor above him would do nothing for his already aroused interest.

Before the subject had to be explored, Beau appeared at the end of the hall carrying two large grocery bags and several champagne bottles. "Thanks for all your help, Edward," he complained.

"Hey, I got a load here, too, you know." Edward held up two bags overflowing with containers of Chinese food.

"What are we having, a banquet?" Melissa said, hurrying forward to rescue the champagne.

Hunt took one of the grocery bags. "You've got enough food here for ten people."

"I told Beau you hadn't stopped," Edward supplied. "He kindly bought groceries."

By the time they'd made it up to the third floor landing, all four of them were gasping for breath. Melissa opened the door, and Beau grumbled behind her, "Good thing you're going to have a restaurant downstairs. I'd hate to lug groceries up here all the time."

"You're just lazy and out of shape," Melissa said, secretly agreeing with him as she flipped on a light.

Beau gave a low whistle. Hunt paused in the doorway, amazed at the room's transformation.

Melissa deposited the champagne bottles on the small round table she'd placed near one of the dormer windows. She went about the room, turning on lamps, feeling pleased at the way her new home had come together.

The large room was furnished with her favorites from among her grandmother's many possessions. In front of the fireplace was the comfortable camelback sofa that had been in the back parlor. The leather wing chair beside it had always been in the library. She'd taken the round table from the small sitting room where she and Hunt had dined. The big oak bed in the alcove was from the corner guest room. With plants in the curtainless windows and the warm colors of an Oriental rug on the floor, the room was pleasantly inviting.

"Do you feel better about it now?" she asked Hunt, referring to his reaction to the room the last time they'd stood here together.

A grin tugged at his mouth as he remembered his concern for her living arrangements. It appeared he needn't have worried. The barren garret had become a comfortable, almost elegant, abode. "It'll do," he said finally.

"I thought we were going to eat," Edward complained.

Melissa's attention swayed reluctantly from Hunt's pleasant brown eyes. "Let's see what you've got in all these bags."

Hunt began unloading groceries and looked up to find himself the object of Beau's thoughtful gaze. He adopted what he hoped was a blank expression. He didn't need her cousin guessing the way he was beginning to feel about Melissa. It would be just like Beau to try and promote a romance.

And remembering his response to merely touching her cheek, Hunt wasn't sure he needed much encouragement.

The dinner was surprisingly congenial. As usual, Beau was full of good humor, regaling them all with his attempts to avoid matrimony to his latest lady love. Even Edward laughed.

Hunt found Melissa's brother to be much more intelligent than he initially would have guessed. Edward had an insider's knowledge of politics, a dry wit, and he talked a fair game of football. When the young man dropped his bored facade, Hunt actually enjoyed talking with him.

But what Hunt enjoyed most was Melissa. With her brother and cousin present, she was more relaxed than he'd ever seen her. She laughed a lot, tossing back her head so often that her sloppy ponytail finally gave up its tenacious hold, and her thick hair swung down on her shoulders. Any other woman Hunt knew would have retired to the bathroom to brush it out. Melissa merely raked her hands through the blond locks. He followed the movement of her fingers jealously. When had he last been so affected by merely looking at a woman?

Never, he thought with surprise, just as the clock on Melissa's mantel chimed ten.

"I think I'll hit the sack," Edward said, pushing back from the table. "I had sort of a late night last night." He grinned impudently at Melissa.

She tried to frown disapprovingly but found it impossible. Her brother could be charming when he wanted to. "Sleep well," she said, standing up to brush a kiss across his cheek.

Briefly, he touched his forehead to hers. "You, too, Missy," he murmured and then was gone.

Hunt studied the display of affection between brother and sister with some confusion. Just hours ago, the young man hard sparked Melissa's anger. Now all appeared to be forgiven.

After he was gone, Beau said quietly, "He told me Uncle Malcolm's news." Melissa's head swung around in surprise.

"He did?"

Beau nodded. "He's really upset."

"I know." Her voice was forlorn.

Beau leaned forward. "I think it's a damned shame your father didn't consider how Edward might feel about this."

"I guess the subject never came up. Father's very happy with Nadine. She's young; I suppose it's natural that she should want—" Melissa broke off, shooting a glance at Hunt.

Beau ignored her hesitation. "But still, Melissa, with Edward's history of problems, for them to be having a baby, I just—" He stopped, staring from Melissa's set face to Hunt's curious one. "Sorry," he mumbled to Melissa and changed the subject.

Hunt sat and listened with half an ear. So that was what was eating at Melissa's brother—his father's young wife was having a baby. Big deal, he thought. Beau had told him Edward was twenty years old. Wasn't that old enough to accept that your parents had lives of their own? It was certainly too old to be running to your sister with your problems. The little bit of sympathy he'd felt for the young man disappeared. All that spoiled rich kid needed was to grow up. He put Edward from his mind and rejoined the conversation.

It was almost an hour later when Hunt rose reluctantly from his seat. "I really need to be going. Thanks for dinner, Beau. Melissa, I'll be by in the morning before heading back to Knoxville. It looks as if you've got everything well in hand."

"Didn't I tell you she was something special?" Beau asked. "I think putting you two together entitles me to free dinners anytime."

Hunt smiled and left the two cousins haggling good-naturedly over who would get the last glass of champagne. His thoughts were centered on the restaurant as he started down the stairs. We've got a good thing here, he decided.

We. His choice of pronouns struck him just as he reached the second floor. He paused in the shadows of the doorway that led into the darkened hall. When had he given up the notion that Melissa would eventually tire of the project and let him buy her out? Several days ago, he admitted; ever since last Saturday, to be exact.

Maybe it had been when she'd produced all those detailed, carefully drawn plans. Or perhaps it was when she'd glided down those stairs, eyes shining, face filled with determination, to tell him every woman in town would want to come to *their* restaurant.

Yes, he thought, he'd accepted that the restaurant was going to be theirs, not his. So he might as well accept a few other things—like how much he wanted Melissa. Not *if* he wanted her, he repeated to himself, but *how much*.

Actually admitting that shook Hunt hard. So hard that he leaned against the wall and drew a deep, ragged breath. He'd known how she was affecting him. He'd known it from that night after they'd had dinner, when just the memory of her smile had kept him awake. Why did it seem such a shocking revelation now?

It was just that this wasn't part of Hunt's plans, this ache Melissa Chambers gave him. Oh, he wasn't opposed to a relationship. God knows, he was tired of the casual affairs he'd been playing at for too long. But Melissa? She was too independent, too complete unto herself, too vulnerable. He wasn't even sure he could explain the whole thing away as desire. When he looked at her, the attraction got all tangled up with tenderness. He should have known better than to become involved with her on any level, even business.

But how do you control the way your pulse accelerates when you catch the scent of a certain woman's perfume? Is there an explanation for the way your eyes linger on her mouth, the way you imagine her lips will feel as they part beneath yours...?

Hunt stopped just short of pounding his fist against the wall. And in that fraction of a moment, he watched a shadow slip through the dark at the other end of the hallway and into their office. He blinked. Who could be creeping around so suspiciously?

Without pausing to think, he crept down the corridor, hugging the wall, barely daring to breathe. The muted sound of Melissa and Beau's laughter filtered down from upstairs. Hunt passed what he thought was Edward's room, noting that no band of light showed at the bottom. He was probably already asleep. As Hunt hesitated, wondering whether he should rouse the young man, a light switched on in the office. He shrank against the wall, but when no one emerged, he inched forward again until he stood just beside the door.

Hunt felt perspiration bead his upper lip as he considered his options. One more step forward and he'd reveal himself to whoever was in the room. He listened as drawers were opened, papers rustled. He could take the chance that the prowler didn't have a gun and barge in now. Or he could wait here for the person to come out, and jump him when his guard was down.

The decision was made for him in the next second when the light switched off and someone came out of the room. Hunt sprang forward, slamming his body into the intruder's. They hit the floor with a loud thump, rolled against a table, sending a lamp crashing to the floor. Someone yelled and in that moment, Hunt knew he'd tackled Melissa's brother.

Before he could even let go of him, there were footsteps clattering on the stairs, the overhead light flashed on and Beau was yelling, "What the hell is going on?"

Edward struggled out of Hunt's grasp, got quickly to his feet. "He jumped me!"

A little dazed, Hunt rolled over, felt something beneath his cheek, and sat up. The floor was littered with money.

He knew Edward saw the cash in that same instant. His eyes, so like Melissa's, glittered with something akin to fear.

"You took it," Hunt said in a low, accusing tone. "You took this money from the petty cash box." Only after he said it did he see Melissa standing just behind Beau, one hand pressed to her mouth, blue eyes huge in her startled face.

"Don't be crazy, man. I didn't *steal* it!" Edward swung his gaze to Melissa. It seemed to Hunt he challenged her. "You told me to get the money, didn't you, Missy? I was going to pay you back when Father sent me a check. Isn't that right?"

Melissa hesitated. It was only a second's pause, but Hunt caught it anyway. And considering the bit of conversation he'd overheard this afternoon, with Edward demanding money and Melissa refusing it, the pause was damning.

But now she was sticking with her brother. "That's right," she agreed breathlessly. She flashed a look at Hunt and allowed her gaze to skitter away nervously.

"Then what were you doing sneaking around in the dark, Edward?" Hunt demanded, getting to his feet. He wasn't sure what made him more furious, Edward's stealing or Melissa's lies.

"Hey, I wasn't the one sneaking down the hall," the young man shouted, his face growing red with anger.

"Oh, come off it—"

"You come off it! I wasn't the one who tackled someone for no good reason. You're the one who has some explaining to do." Edward took a threatening step forward.

"That's enough!" Melissa shouted. All three men turned to stare at her. She took a deep breath. "Edward, obviously Hunt thought you were a prowler. Is that right, Hunt?"

He met her gaze steadily. "I was at the bottom of the stairs when I saw someone slip into the office. It never occurred to me it could be Edward."

"There. You see," she said, turning to Edward. "It was all a mistake. Let's forget it."

But Edward continued to glare at Hunt.

Beau stepped in. "Come on, guys. No harm done. Edward, let's get a broom and clean this glass up." He started down the hall. Edward glanced from Hunt to Melissa and then followed his cousin.

Hunt bent and scooped up a handful of bills. "Hey, Edward," he called. "Don't forget your money."

Melissa's brother turned and stared at the wad of cash in the outstretched hand. Full of resentment, his gaze locked with Hunt's, then flicked to Melissa.

"I'll get it later," he said carelessly and continued after Beau.

They had just disappeared downstairs when Melissa turned on Hunt. "That wasn't necessary."

"What?" he asked innocently, squatting down to collect the money.

"That last little remark."

"Oh." He stood, grasped her hand and closed her fingers around the cash. "Here's your brother's money."

Her chin lifted. "You don't believe I told him to get it."

"No, I don't." Calmly, Hunt stared down into her angry blue eyes. "He stole it."

"You have no right—"

"Don't I?" His brows lifted. "If I recall, it's my money, too."

Melissa swallowed her retort. "Just go," she managed to say at last.

With an impatient oath, Hunt grasped her shoulders and gave her a little shake. "You're something, you know that? You honestly think you can do anything on your own, don't you? From running a restaurant to dealing with a very, very troubled brother. You don't need any help, do you, Melissa?"

"I certainly don't need your help!"

He jerked her against him. She faced him without faltering. Their mouths were just inches apart; her soft breasts were pressed against his chest, but Hunt felt no stirring of desire, only anger.

"It must get damned cold in that ivory tower of yours," he muttered, before he dropped his hands from her shoulders, wheeled and walked away.

Trembling, Melissa waited until he was out of sight before she slumped against the wall. Damn him, she thought bitterly. *Damn him for making me feel so alone.*

Chapter Five

Melissa had hoped the morning would make the night's fiasco seem a little less traumatic. However, when she awoke, she still burned with shame over her brother's escapade.

Stealing.

She turned over in bed, pulling the covers high on her neck. When had Edward sunk to this level? How coolly he had lied in front of Hunt and Beau. How confidently he had assumed she would back him up. And, of course, she had. Backing up members of her family was what Melissa did best.

She sat up, clicked off the alarm before it could sound and got out of bed. Shivering, she crossed the room to close the window against the cool morning air. The sun was pushing fingers of rosy color across the sky, but a low-lying mist still clung to the ground, shrouding the trunks of trees which had

yet to take on their autumn colors. Melissa drew on her robe
and silently watched the day come to life.

What must Hunt think of her? He'd known she'd lied
about giving Edward permission to take that money. He'd
been disgusted by the whole episode, and the disdain on his
face had hurt her. Why? Why did she care so much what he
thought?

That wasn't a question she wanted to explore in depth this
morning. If she tried to examine the way she was beginning
to feel about Hunt Kirkland, she'd have to think about her
physical response to him. Like the way her pulse accelerated when he merely touched her cheek. Or how her legs had
trembled last night when he'd hauled her up against him in
anger. It had been more than fury that had raced through
her veins. And speculation about exactly what she had felt
scared Melissa to death.

"Forget it," she scolded herself, turning from the window. There wasn't time for romantic daydreams about a
business partner with entirely too much charm, even if his
brown eyes were the kind a woman could lose herself in.

With grim determination, Melissa flipped on her coffee
maker, took a shower and dressed in jeans and an old T-
shirt. Then, carrying a tray with two steaming mugs and a
plate of doughnuts, she made her way down to Edward's
room. She took a deep breath and called, "Edward, you
up?" At his mumbled, sleepy reply, she balanced the tray in
one hand and opened the door.

All that was visible of her brother was the blond hair
peeking out from the top of the covers. "Wake up, sleepy-
head," Melissa called, putting the tray down on the dresser
and pulling the curtains open. Bright sunshine flooded the
room.

"Go 'way," Edward mumbled.

"Get up. We have to talk." Melissa's no-nonsense tone must have made an impression on him because Edward lowered the edge of the covers and opened one eye.

"You're mad, aren't you?" he asked groggily.

"No, I'm humiliated, and that feels much worse." She went back to the dresser, picked up the tray and put it on the bedside table. Edward sat up and reached for the coffee.

"I'm sorry," he said. "I just really needed the money."

"Badly enough to steal from me?" Melissa had vowed she wouldn't let Edward see that he'd hurt her, but it was hard to maintain her composure. Picking up her own mug, she went back to the window and stood with her back to her brother as she continued, "I don't think I deserve what you did last night."

Edward was silent.

"If you need money that badly, you're going to have to work for it. I don't have it to give away." Melissa waited for the explosion she half expected, but it didn't come. So she went on, "I'm going to refinish the floor in the downstairs foyer and the library by myself. And you're going to help me."

"And you'll pay me?" Edward asked.

"Yes. Not much, but I'll pay you." Melissa turned around and gave him a steady look. "And after that, if you want to stay, I'll find some other jobs for you. When the restaurant opens there'll be plenty to do."

"You think your partner is going to go for that?"

Melissa had been avoiding that question herself. With a confidence she didn't feel, she said, "I can handle Hunt."

Her brother gave a short laugh. "I'm glad you're so sure of that."

"Do we have a deal or not?" Melissa pushed. "It's either this or back to school."

"I'll take floors over college or either of our parents," Edward retorted. "Deal."

"Good. Finish your coffee and let's get to work." Without pausing, she left the room.

During the long day that followed, Melissa had to give her brother credit for hard work. First they cleared the hall and library of all remaining furniture and blocked it off from the construction going on in the kitchen. They rented two upright sanders and set to work right after lunch. What at first looked like a small expanse of floor seemed to stretch for miles when they attacked it with the big, vibrating machines.

The construction contractor, Cabot, came in and gave them a few pointers, but the progress was slow. Even with both of them working, only the library floor and a fraction of the hall were sanded when Melissa called it quits that night. She had hoped to have done twice that much.

She and Edward were almost too tired to eat the quick supper she put together, and they went to bed soon after. Muscles aching, Melissa lay sleepless. All day long she'd waited for Hunt to show up so she could show him how hard Edward was working. Considering all that had happened the night before, she supposed it wasn't surprising that he'd chosen to stay away. But still, she thought as she turned on her side, he could have called. Then she could have at least told him Edward was helping her with the floors. More than anything else she wanted to show Hunt she was capable of doing everything she intended to do.

"Maybe he'll call tomorrow," she thought with anticipation. Then she lulled herself to sleep by devising several reasons she might have to call him.

On Saturday morning, Hunt appeared at his Knoxville restaurant. That in itself wasn't too unusual. The odd part was the way he found himself growling at anyone and everyone who crossed his path.

He stopped in the middle of chewing out the manager. "I'm sorry," he mumbled, looking around Mary Wade's neatly organized office.

"You should be," she said with the candor born of a nine-year-old friendship. Mary had started out as a waitress and had stuck by Hunt through thick and thin, working her way up to manager, a post she'd held for three years. "What's eatin' you?"

"Chattanooga." With a glum sigh, Hunt took a seat.

"Oh, the congressman's daughter," Mary said, nodding her head sympathetically.

Hunt shot his friend a suspicious glance. "Who told you about her?"

"Your parents were in for dinner Thursday night. Your mom told me all about your beautiful new partner."

"I wouldn't say she was beautiful, she's more—" Hunt began, then stopped, flustered.

Mary gave him a wise smile. "She's more what? Your mother didn't have all the details, since she's never met Ms. Chambers, but I got the impression a romance might be in the making."

"If I tell my mother a woman smiled at me, she makes it into a romance."

"Does Ms. Chambers smile at you?" Mary teased.

Melissa's well-remembered smile flashed across Hunt's mind. "Sometimes," he said, gazing at a spot just above Mary's shoulder. When she cleared her throat, he came reluctantly back to earth only to intercept a knowing look from her hazel eyes. "What?" he demanded.

"Oh, nothing," Mary said innocently, flipping her dark hair out from her collar. "I'd like to meet this partner who turns you into a grouch one minute and mooning teenager the next." Trying to appear all business, she picked up a folder, but her pixie eyes grinned at him over the top. "I never thought Hunt Kirkland would fall so hard."

"I didn't, either," he admitted ruefully. Ignoring the way Mary's expression changed from teasing to concerned, he left the office and was soon out of the restaurant.

He went home and made a few phone calls. Every woman he'd had a date with in the past six months was either not at home or otherwise occupied. He drove to his health club where an hour's wait for a racquetball court seemed entirely too long. Finally, exasperated, Hunt threw some things in a weekend bag and made the hour's drive to his parents' place.

"Why don't we go fishing?" he asked his dad upon arrival.

"At four in the afternoon?" Bill demanded, scratching his beard. "Your mother and I were planning on going to a covered-dish supper at the church."

"Oh."

"Come with us," his mother invited.

"I'll just stick around here."

Hunt settled on the couch to watch what remained of a football game. He couldn't concentrate on the plays. His parents left at six. He paced through the house for quite a while.

By seven-thirty, he was on the interstate, headed for Chattanooga. "Damn it, Melissa," he said aloud. "What are you doing to me?"

He still hadn't found an answer when he pulled to a stop in River Rest's driveway. Lights were burning on the bottom floor, so he knew someone was at home. Impatiently he rang the doorbell. No answer. "Damn bell's probably still not working," he grumbled, banging the heavy brass knocker. Still no answer. Smothering a oath, he tried the door. It opened. Stupid woman, he thought with irritation, anyone could walk in on her.

Only when Hunt stepped into the foyer did the loud drone of power equipment penetrate his preoccupied mind. He looked down at the floor. The old wax and stain had been sanded smoothly away. She really did it, he thought in amazement. He hadn't seriously thought Melissa intended to strip the floors herself. Shaking his head, he followed the sound of the sander to where a short hall branched off the main foyer.

Arms gripping the vibrating sander, head bowed, Melissa was intent on her work. Her tousled blond hair clung to her forehead and neck in damp clumps, and dark patches of perspiration stained her green T-shirt. She didn't look up and see Hunt, but as he watched she shut off the machine and leaned wearily against the wall. The hand she put to her forehead trembled.

"Melissa," he said softly when she looked up at him.

For a moment she merely gazed at him with weary blue eyes. Then she screamed.

"Melissa!" he yelled, stepping forward.

She shook her head, stared at him again and covered her face with her hands. "Oh, God, Hunt, you scared me."

"I'm sorry. I thought you saw me." He stepped closer.

She dropped her arms to her sides. "How did you get in?"

"The door was open. Not a smart move."

"I know, I know." Melissa bent down and unplugged the sander. She stood up quickly and blackness swam before her eyes. Her legs trembled as she backed up against the wall, searching for support.

"Melissa, are you okay?"

Her vision cleared, and she saw the concern in Hunt's face. "I'm just tired."

"Did you do all this yourself?" he asked, gesturing toward the floor.

Melissa bit her lip. "Edward helped."

Hunt's eyes narrowed. "Oh, really?"

She didn't even bristle at his skeptical tone. After all, Edward had deserted her. When she'd gotten up this morning, she'd discovered him gone, having taken from her purse the amount of money she'd agreed to pay him for yesterday's work. The only point in her brother's favor was that he hadn't taken more than he'd earned.

"He decided he didn't like the work," she explained.

"I bet," Hunt retorted sarcastically.

Melissa just looked at him, not rising to the bait.

"So you've worked yourself to death."

She shrugged. "It had to be done. I wanted it ready for finishing next week."

"Nothing interferes with your plans, does it?" Hunt was admiring her determination, but obviously Melissa misinterpreted the words.

"I'm not up to fighting with you," she said, squaring her shoulders with an effort. "I can see that, as usual, you want to criticize everything I do. Go ahead. Just don't expect me to argue with you." She started to walk away.

Gently, Hunt grasped her arm. "I'm sorry." She lifted her eyes to his. "Really," he replied to her unspoken question. "I'm out of line." His hand slid up to her shoulder. "You know, I should understand how you feel. When I want something very badly, I also do whatever it takes to get it."

It seemed to Melissa there was a meaning hidden in his quiet words, but though she searched his face, she couldn't fathom it. And she didn't care. Perhaps it was weariness, perhaps something more, but she found herself wishing that his arms would just close around her, that she could lay her head on his shoulder. She didn't want to think about the restaurant, her family, even about the disturbing effect Hunt had on her nerves. She just wanted to be held, and she wanted Hunt to do the holding.

However, he merely gave her a little push toward the stairs. "I think you need a hot bath and a good meal. Hungry?"

She nodded mutely.

"So am I. I'll cook. Get upstairs, and I'll make sure all the doors down here are locked."

Much later, when Melissa emerged from her bathroom wrapped in her blue robe, she was greeted with the sight of Hunt presiding over her stove in a white chef's apron. "Hamburgers and fries okay with you?" he asked easily.

"Perfect." Self-consciously, she slicked her wet hair behind one ear. "I'll dry my hair while you finish up." She slipped back in the bathroom, shut the door and stared at her steam-shrouded reflection in the mirror. It seemed stupid to be worrying about her appearance when Hunt had just seen her in grubby jeans and a sweat-soaked T-shirt, but nonetheless she frowned at her pale features. Makeup would seem obvious. So with a sigh, she plugged in her hair dryer and proceeded to make herself as presentable as she could.

Her trepidation was forgotten when she sat down to eat with Hunt. It seemed perfectly natural to be sitting in her old robe, sharing a burger with him. He made it easy, keeping the conversation general. Only when Melissa laughed at an outrageous joke did he get personal. "It's good to hear you laugh," he said, leaning his elbows on the table. "For a couple of minutes downstairs, I thought you were gonna pass out on me."

"So did I." Impulsively, Melissa put her hand on the curve of his arm. "Thanks, Hunt."

"For what?"

"Dinner." She nodded at the table, then met his eyes. "For being here. After Thursday night, I was..." She paused, swallowing. "I was ashamed. Edward took that money."

"I know."

"I shouldn't have lied."

"It made me angry that night, but he is your brother." Hunt's brown eyes crinkled at the corners as he gave a rueful grin. "I don't have a brother, but if I did I'd probably defend him, just as you did."

Melissa took her hand away from his arm and bit her lip. "Maybe we all need to stop defending Edward. Maybe then he'd stop forcing us to." She stood and started clearing the table.

"Uh-uh," Hunt said, stopping her. "I'll do this. Why don't you get us some brandy?"

"Okay." While Hunt stacked the dishes in the sink, she poured brandy into cut-glass snifters and put them on the coffee table. She turned on the radio, leaving the volume low on her favorite oldies station. All the while she steadfastly ignored the tiny voice inside that was asking why she was setting such a romantic scene. Curling her legs beneath her, she settled at one end of the couch.

Hunt took a seat at the opposite end and sipped his brandy. "That's good," he said with satisfaction. His denim-clad legs stretched out in front of him, and he leaned his head against the comfortable cushions.

For some time they sat in companionable silence, gazing at the empty fireplace opening.

Hunt was a bit reluctant to bring up the subject of Melissa's brother again, but since she had mentioned the young man earlier, he decided to dig a little deeper. He suspected her feelings for her brother would tell him a lot about the woman he'd felt compelled to see tonight. "I don't want to pry, Melissa, but I'm curious. Is Edward really so upset that your father and his wife are having a baby? Or is it something else?''

She didn't answer immediately, and he shot a glance at her face. Instead of anger he expected, Melissa merely looked thoughtful.

She answered him with slow, carefully chosen words. "It isn't the baby in itself which has Edward upset. He's never gotten along with my father's wife, Nadine.''

"Why?''

"It's not really so hard to understand, is it?" Melissa set her snifter on the coffee table. "To Edward, Nadine represents the end of our family.''

"Was she the end?''

Melissa didn't reply immediately. Crossing her arms, she pulled them against her chest, hunching her shoulders. A tiny frown creased the delicate arch of her brows. It was as if Hunt could see the struggle occurring in her mind. She was so intensely private; he felt like an intruder for asking these questions.

He started to give her an escape. "You don't have to—''

"No," she answered, blue eyes widening as she turned her gaze to him. "I don't mind telling you.'' The honesty of those words shocked her. She'd never wanted to tell anyone about the disintegration of her family. But talking to Hunt was so easy. Maybe too easy.

"I think my parents were unhappy for many, many years," she said. "Now, as an adult looking back, I can remember little warning signs that escaped me when I was younger.''

"You always looked like the perfect American family," Hunt interjected, thinking of the many newspaper and television stories that had been done on the congressman's family.

"It was very important to smile a lot. Father impressed that upon us. His press agent insisted on it. No matter what was happening to us, on the outside we had to look totally serene. Father was in politics from the time I was a little girl. I never questioned what I had to do even though I didn't always come through. I think Edward thrived on it."

"I can imagine," Hunt said dryly, thinking of the young man's easy charm.

"Edward always did what was expected," Melissa murmured. "I remember once when he was about eight, a reporter was coming to interview Mother. Photographs were going to be taken of the whole family. Well, our dog got hit by a car. I forgot my neat, clean clothes and rushed out and brought this bloody, dying dog into the house. Edward was trying not to cry. I was sobbing. Mother was having a fit. And the maid showed the reporter in."

"Great timing." Hunt watched Melissa's face closely.

She nodded. "Well, in the midst of the turmoil, Edward—little Edward—was the only one with the presence of mind to take over. He marched right up to the reporter and said, 'Can I show you the garden?'"

"A natural diplomat," Hunt said.

"Oh, yes," Melissa whispered. "A natural. Always being the perfect politician's son. Always mimicking the father he adored." She turned her gaze back to the empty fireplace and sipped her brandy, glad of the warmth it brought to her suddenly cold body.

"And what about your dog?"

"He died."

Hunt bit his lip. "Did Edward ever cry?"

"Of course. That night, out of everyone else's sight, he came and got in bed with me and cried himself to sleep."

"He always comes to you, doesn't he?"

Melissa nodded. "Except after the divorce. Then he stayed with Father and Nadine."

"You sound like that was a bad idea."

"It was a terrible idea." Her lips tightened into a thin line. "Edward should have been with me. Mother was going through a bad time, but I should have seen that Edward didn't have to stay with my father and the woman he'd been having an affair with for ten years."

"Melissa," Hunt chided gently, "you were pretty young. You couldn't be expected to take responsibility for a teenage brother. No more than you should have to take responsibility for him now."

"But I have to." Melissa's voice was firm.

"Why?"

"Everything changed for Edward when he was at a sensitive age. Someone has to help him."

"He's practically an adult. Maybe he needs to start helping himself." Hunt couldn't keep the impatience out of his voice.

It didn't matter that Melissa had said almost the same thing earlier that evening. She didn't need anyone telling her how to handle her brother. Her chin came up; angry color stained her cheeks. "I have to be there for Edward. The one time I wasn't, I let him down. I can't do it again."

Hunt made a short sound of disbelief.

"There are a few things you don't understand," Melissa said with spirit.

"Explain them."

"Edward and I worshiped Father, and it's very hard to accept when you find out your idol has feet of clay. I mean, first he uses campaign funds for personal investments. He has to resign. Then we find out about Nadine. And of course that wasn't all, there's—" Melissa choked on her words, tears filling her eyes. There were some things she just couldn't talk about. Not to Hunt. Not to anyone.

Hunt moved swiftly, so fast Melissa wasn't aware of his intentions until she was pulled up off the couch and into his arms. Amazingly, once her head rested against his shoulder, the tears that had threatened to overflow disappeared.

"I'm sorry," Hunt murmured low against her neck. "I don't know much about politics, or about growing up in front of cameras and the voters' eyes. I'm just a simple guy from a small town. When I was ten and my cat got flattened by a truck, my mother cried with me."

Unaccountably, a giggle formed in Melissa's throat, and she pulled away in order to smile up into his eyes. For a moment she lost herself in their velvety brown darkness. Then, quite naturally, she lifted her lips to his.

Hunt intended it to be a gentle caress, a friendly, comforting kiss. Instead, it was an explosion. The moment his mouth touched hers, desire danced through his body with all the grace of dynamite. It shattered his control, and he found himself greedily partaking of the lips she offered so freely. They parted under his not-so-gentle pressure, accepting his bold invasion while her arms stole up around his neck, her fingers cool against his suddenly flushed skin.

His right hand strayed down to the small of her back, pulling her closer against him while the fingers of his left hand threaded through her hair. It was soft. She was warm and willing, tasting of passion and untold delights. His mouth moved against hers, seeking a deeper intimacy.

It didn't occur to Melissa that she was acting without her usual restraint and coolness. Hunt's mouth, his touch, blasted through her reserve. She quivered with feeling, pressing her body to his, following the dictates of her emotions rather than her brain.

Melissa's heightened senses were aware of every input—the low hum of the Supremes' "Baby Love" on the radio, the gentle scrape of Hunt's beard against her cheek, the taste of brandy on his lips. But it was the desire within herself which overshadowed everything else, a desire as powerful as it was sweet.

Hunt took his lips from hers but didn't end the contact. Instead, he gathered her closer, pressing a light kiss on her temple. "I didn't expect this," he said softly.

"Neither did I," Melissa replied, her voice not quite steady.

"But I enjoyed it." Hunt turned his head to capture her lips again.

Lightning isn't supposed to strike twice, Melissa thought, as again the touch of his mouth sent arousal sweeping through her veins. Hunt's kiss made her weak. It was good just to follow his lead. She felt as if she could cling to him all night long.

A little alarm bell went off in her head. Melissa didn't want to *cling* to anyone, anytime. Hadn't she decided Hunt was exactly the sort of man she needed to avoid—too strong, too sure of himself and his own opinions? Why, then, was she kissing him?

Gently, she broke away. His arms held her too close to let her move very far, but she tilted her head back to look at him. "This is a mistake."

There was frost in her tone, ice in the blue eyes that just moments before had been warm with passion. How quickly she could change. Hunt's arms dropped from around her. He took a step backward, his gaze not quite meeting hers.

Afraid she had wounded his male ego, Melissa said quickly, "It's not that I didn't enjoy it, too."

His head shot up. "It's not?"

Melissa felt a flush stain her cheeks. "I just don't think we need to complicate our relationship. Do you?"

Hell, yes, Hunt wanted to say. He'd like nothing more than to spend the entire night complicating their relationship. And if he could but see beneath the cool exterior Melissa now presented, he was sure she felt the same way. After all, he'd felt her response to his kiss. Perhaps she just needed some gentle persuasion.

But no, Hunt thought, reconsidering. He knew Melissa well enough by now to know that pushing only made her resist harder. He'd bide his time and bet that the rewards would be all the sweeter for the wait.

"You're right," he said. "We're business associates. We don't need complications. A little brandy and soft lights just went to our heads. No problem, right?"

"No. No problem," Melissa echoed. Her brows collected in a frown as she watched him pick up their brandy snifters and carry them to the kitchenette. Maybe she'd expected him to try a little harder.

"I need to head out to the hotel," Hunt said, pulling his keys from his jeans' pocket.

"Stay here."

He sent her a surprised glance.

"I mean," Melissa said quickly, regretting the invitation. "Stay in the guest room. It's crazy to have all this space and make you go to a hotel."

"You really wouldn't mind?"

Mind? Melissa thought, glancing down as she tightened the belt on her robe. *Of course I mind; you make me feel things I don't want to feel. I want you a thousand miles away from me, not under the same roof.* But she couldn't say that. Instead, she managed what she hoped was a calm smile. "Of course I don't mind. Let me show you which room to use."

Later, after Hunt was settled on the second floor, Melissa returned to her apartment and hastily locked the door behind her. "Silly," she muttered and unlocked it just as quickly.

What was she afraid of? Hunt certainly wasn't going to sneak upstairs during the night and attack her. He was here at her own suggestion. Good grief, she'd asked him twice this week to spend the night here. At that thought, Melissa pressed her hands to burning cheeks. With those invitations and the way she'd melted into his arms tonight, he'd probably think she was trying to start something.

"Actions speak louder than words," she cautioned out loud, quoting her grandmother.

As she prepared for bed and flipped off the lights, Melissa resolved that no more romantic moments would be shared between her and Hunt Kirkland.

Yet she found the taste of him still disturbingly fresh on her lips. And with her heart pounding at the memory of Hunt's kiss, Melissa wondered how she would ever sleep.

Arms propped behind his head, eyes open to the unfamiliar room, Hunt found that sleep eluded him. Melissa was under his skin for sure. She was stubborn, a little mixed up and utterly adorable. She wasn't what he wanted; she was everything he wanted. The contradictions chased through his mind until his head ached. Only one thing did he know for sure; it had been a long time since anything had felt as good as kissing Melissa Chambers.

Melissa overslept the next morning, waking with a guilty start. Hunt was here; he'd need coffee and breakfast, and the only available kitchen was hers.

Pausing only to run a brush through her hair and throw on her robe, Melissa charged downstairs. An open door and neatly made bed told her Hunt was already up and about.

From downstairs came the low hum of power equipment. She hurried down to the foyer.

Hunt was working in the corner where she'd abandoned the sander the night before. He switched off the machine.

"Mornin'," he said with the lazy grin she was beginning to know very well.

"You didn't have to get up and do this. I'm the one who started it."

"There wasn't much left. Didn't take me long once I got the machine figured out." He stretched, and Melissa couldn't keep from noticing how his white knit shirt stretched across his chest. "I think it's ready for finishing once we do a little vacuuming," he said.

"I'm going to wait till tomorrow to start that." She almost shuddered, not wanting to admit how much she dreaded working any further on the floor.

"You're not doing anything else on this floor," Hunt said quietly.

She stiffened. "Yes, I am."

"We're calling in some professionals."

"But you said—"

"I was wrong," he interrupted. "This needed to be done. I can already see how great it's going to look. It's worth it to include it in the budget. Besides, you need to concentrate on more important jobs around here, like menus, employees . . ."

"Hunt, I can finish the floor." Shoulders set, eyes flashing, Melissa was ready for battle.

"I never said you couldn't," he returned, walking slowly toward her. "But I do think it's too small a concern to get yourself worked up over. You don't have to prove yourself on every point, you know."

She bit her lip. He was right. "If you think so," she began uncertainly.

"I know so." He covered the distance remaining between them and lifted her chin with his fingertips. "If you'd stop being so stubborn, you'd realize that you actually won another round against me, partner."

"So I did."

She laughed, and the merriment on her face was more than Hunt could resist. He pressed a feather-light kiss on her lips.

"Don't do that," she said, frowning.

"Then don't invite it."

"I didn't."

"But you liked it."

Unable to deny the truth, Melissa turned away. "I'm going up to put some coffee on."

Hunt's laughter followed her up the stairs.

The rest of the morning followed the same teasing pattern. They had breakfast, and Hunt insisted on helping her do the dishes, his body brushing against hers at every opportunity. They went downstairs to sweep and vacuum the foyer, and he chased her with the broom. He snuck up behind her and tickled her in the ribs. It seemed that everything they did and said was funny. Melissa laughed a lot.

And when she was trying to tell him he'd missed some dust near the far end of the hall, he kissed her again, then went about his work, whistling.

Melissa was at a loss. Last night he had agreed they didn't need romantic complications; today he seemed determined to capitalize on what had happened between them. She could either protest and make a big deal about it, or try to ignore him. If she didn't respond to his casual touch or kisses, then he'd get the message. She'd show him that they could be nothing more than partners and friends.

Outside, the autumn sunshine was warm, with just enough crispness in the air to make the day irresistible. After finishing their work, Hunt suggested they go out for something to eat.

"I've got a better idea," Melissa said impulsively.

Hunt gave her a suspicious glance. "I don't know if I should trust you when you have that tone of voice."

"Don't be silly. I can always be trusted."

After shopping to pick up drinks and barbecue sandwiches, Melissa's little red car took the twisting, turning road up the side of Signal Mountain. The higher they climbed, the freer she felt. All week long, she'd been wanting to come up the mountain, to see if the trees had begun to change colors at this higher elevation, to feel the cool rush of air against her face. Aside from River Rest, the mountain was her favorite spot in the world.

"Care to tell me where we're going?" Hunt asked when the car turned down a quiet, tree-lined street.

"A gorgeous place," Melissa said, flashing him a smile so brilliant Hunt was sure it touched his very heart.

He was still reeling from the impact of that smile moments later when Melissa pulled the car into a parking lot. She was out of the car quickly, bounding down a trail, pausing to look back at Hunt and call, "Come on." He quickened his pace and caught up with her just as she reached a low stone wall, the only barrier between her and a steep drop-off down the side of the mountain.

With a sigh of pure happiness, Melissa sat down on the wall. She could sense Hunt studying her and looked up at him with a sheepish grin. "I don't know why I love this view so much. It's not really spectacular, not like the view from Rock City on Lookout Mountain."

"Where you can see seven states?" Hunt said, thinking of Chattanooga's well-advertised tourist attraction.

Melissa nodded, turning back to the scenery. "Here I just like to look down at the river, and the mountain across the way, and the city in the distance.'' She paused. ''Grandmother and I used to come up here a lot. She was always trying to paint this view.''

Taking a seat beside her, Hunt could see the faraway look in Melissa's blue eyes, the soft smile that played about her mouth. Quietly he said, ''Loving this place has nothing to do with the view. We all tend to have a soft spot for the places we share with the people we love.''

''You're right,'' Melissa agreed, again turning her heart-stopping smile on him.

''She must have been some special lady, your grandmother.''

''Why do you say that?''

''Otherwise, you wouldn't have loved her so much.'' Hunt hesitated, then continued, ''I don't think you give your love too freely, Melissa.''

''I did once,'' she answered without thinking, then looked away from his perceptive brown eyes. Could he look deep enough to see the girl she'd once been, the girl who'd given her heart without a thought, who'd trusted her life to the dictates of other people? She hoped Hunt couldn't see that girl. For if he could, then surely he could resurrect that weak, malleable creature. Of that, Melissa was sorely afraid.

''Do you have a soft spot for a special place?'' she asked, more to move the conversation out of dangerous waters than from genuine curiosity.

''Yeah. It's a fishing hole on my parents' land.'' Hunt recognized Melissa's change-of-subject tactic. He'd let her get away with it—this time.

''What's special about it?''

''It's where my dad and I had all our serious talks.''

''About girls?'' Melissa teased.

''And football. And life.''

"I'm not sure what girls have in common with those other things."

Hunt laughed. "You need a game plan for all of them."

"Oh, really?" Melissa asked, amused. "Well, tell me, Mr. Kirkland, who's winning—you or the women in your life?"

Suddenly serious, Hunt brushed a lock of sun-kissed blond hair from her cheek. "It's halftime, and I'm mapping out my strategy for the third and fourth quarters."

Melissa didn't miss the meaning in his words, couldn't miss the thrill his touch sent through her veins. *I don't need this,* she thought. Avoiding his eyes, she scooted off the wall and headed back to the car. "Come on," she said over her shoulder. "Let's eat."

Finding a spot in the park to enjoy their meal proved impossible. Everywhere they went, a pesky group of yellow jackets followed. The swarming insects finally chased them back to the car, where Melissa and Hunt downed barbecue sandwiches, slaw and baked beans with much teasing and laughter.

The tension that had built between them on the wall was broken, and the rest of the sunny afternoon passed quickly for Hunt. They stopped at a roadside stand to buy some apples, and Melissa showed him some of her favorite houses on the mountain. He felt young and totally carefree.

As a matter of course, they talked about the restaurant. Melissa was pleased when Hunt agreed with many of the suggestions she made about special events and promotions. It occurred to her that the kisses they'd shared and the casually flirtatious relationship that was developing between them might be the reason he was being so agreeable.

The thought made Melissa pause. She'd never used feminine wiles to accomplish anything. She didn't like women who did.

Falling silent, she navigated her car down the mountain's "W" Road, so named because of its many hairpin curves.

"Something wrong?" Hunt asked when they reached the bottom without exchanging a word.

"No, I'm just tired," Melissa replied untruthfully. There seemed no good way to bring up what was troubling her. If she was wrong about the way Hunt had been acting all day, if last night's kiss meant nothing to him, if he treated all his friends who were women in this flirty fashion, then she'd be embarrassed about even mentioning the subject. In fact, who was to say that he didn't genuinely agree with most of her plans?

Late afternoon shadows were creeping across the front lawn when they returned to River Rest. Melissa wandered through the house to the front porch while Hunt gathered up his things. Carrying his small weekend bag, he came out the front door.

"Now remember, call someone tomorrow about finishing up the floors."

"I'm sure Cabot will know someone, or maybe his crew can take care of it," Melissa said.

"Maybe so," Hunt agreed. "And place an ad in the paper for staff."

"Will do."

"And call that Nashville chef who's interested in relocating."

"Yes, sir!" Melissa snapped to attention and gave a smart, teasing salute.

"Okay, okay," Hunt muttered, his dimple creasing his cheek as he grinned. "I'm giving orders again. I'm sorry."

"Just leave everything to me. I can handle it."

"I'm sure you can."

Melissa shifted nervously from foot to foot as Hunt stepped closer and studied her in silence.

"Thanks for the afternoon. I really enjoyed it," he said, not giving her a chance to reply before he kissed her.

He didn't touch her with his hands, didn't make a move to pull her body against his. Yet it was a searing kiss. Hard. Possessive. The contact lasted no more than a moment, but the feelings it aroused spread from Melissa's lips right down to her knees, leaving her weak enough to have swayed into Hunt's arms. However, he wasn't there to catch her. He was walking down the steps and putting his suitcase in the trunk of his car. Dazed, Melissa took a step backward and leaned against one of the porch columns, hoping he wouldn't notice.

Hunt closed the trunk with a snap. "I'll call you tomorrow, and I'll probably be back down later this week. We've got some work to do on the menu."

"Menu?" Melissa asked feebly.

"Yeah." Hunt rubbed his cheek. "I've been meaning to tell you all weekend. I looked over the list of food ideas you gave me. I've got to say, I think most of it's all wrong."

"Wrong?" Melissa said, beginning to come out of her haze.

"Yeah. I know we're trying to be sort of Old South traditional here, but I just don't know about butter beans and squash casserole."

Melissa's head cleared completely. "I suppose you were thinking about Buffalo wings and fried cheese sticks?"

Hunt put on his sunglasses. "How'd you guess?" He flashed a cocky smile as he got in the car. "We'll argue about it later this week, okay?"

The door shut, the engine roared to life and the Mercedes pulled away, leaving Melissa sputtering on the porch.

"Men!" she muttered. "Just when you think you've found one that's different, he does something typical!"

Chapter Six

Melissa's exasperated and totally adorable expression stayed with Hunt long after he drove away from River Rest on Sunday. In fact, it intruded on his thoughts over and over again during the next week. So much so that he called her—at least five times a day.

The calls weren't personal; he and Melissa were in the midst of a first-class battle over the menu. Hunt thought many of the dishes she wanted to include weren't sophisticated enough for the restaurant's atmosphere. Melissa disagreed, still clinging to her original plan to serve the foods her grandmother had loved.

Even though their conversations were all business, Hunt couldn't deny the pleasure that shot through him at merely the sound of Melissa's voice. His body would tighten at her breathless "hello." At times he lost track of the conversation because he was so immersed in imagining what she looked like at the other end of the phone. He could see her pale hair, her anger-darkened blue eyes, the pouty curve of her mouth. When he hung up, he would sit staring at the phone, searching for a reason to call her again.

By Thursday, he realized the situation was hopeless and called to tell her he was coming down.

"We're going to get this menu thing straightened out once and for all," he told her bluntly, although that was just an excuse.

"If you're not going to bring along an open mind, then don't bother," Melissa retorted.

"You might try some of your own advice." Hunt grinned at the sound of her smothered oath.

"You're impossible," she fumed.

"So are you. That's what makes us such a good team. See you tonight." He hung up with her protest ringing in his ear and a feeling of elation growing inside. He couldn't wait to see her.

Melissa replaced the telephone receiver in its cradle and propped her elbows on her desk, one hand cupping her chin. As infuriated as she was with Hunt over the menu, she really wanted to see him. It seemed like weeks instead of days since he'd stood out front and said goodbye, giving her that self-assured grin and that disturbing kiss.

She closed her eyes, remembering the feel of his mouth on hers. She'd been savoring that memory all week long. Even though she kept telling herself to forget it, Melissa found that she relived that moment over and over. Each time, the same undeniable desire would sweep through her. It was crazy. It was dangerous. Even if they weren't business associates, Hunt wasn't for her. She had to keep that in mind.

"Having a nice daydream?"

Melissa's eyes flew open at the sound of Beau's voice. Embarrassed color crept up her neck. "I was just resting," she snapped. "What are you doing here?"

"Goodness, where's that gracious Southern charm River Rest is going to be famous for?" The redhead took a seat on the office's love seat and regarded her with merry green eyes.

"People who sneak into other people's offices are not worthy of charm." Melissa opened the folder on her desk, trying to look busy.

"I didn't sneak. I think you were just too engrossed in your thoughts. They must have been pleasant—you were smiling." Beau flicked an imaginary speck of dust off his brown slacks. "Thinking about anyone I know?"

"Certainly not."

He laughed. "I suppose you were planning your next strategy in the continuing battle of the menu."

"So you know about that?"

"Of course. Hunt and I do talk occasionally."

"Well," Melissa said, shutting the folder with a little snap. "Maybe you can make the high and mighty Mr. Kirkland see the light. You don't serve sweet-and-sour chicken in a Southern mansion."

Beau laughed again. "I think you have a point about that."

"Of course I do." Melissa bit her lip and leaned forward. "Seriously, Beau, you've got to help me on this. Hunt is going to ruin my concept."

"I'm planning to help. That's why I came over here."

Melissa recognized the mischievous gleam in her cousin's eyes. "What's up?" she asked cautiously.

"I'll tell you soon. When's Hunt coming down?"

"Tonight."

"Perfect. Both of you are invited to my place for dinner."

"You mean I have to wait until Hunt's here to find out what you've got up your sleeve?"

"Exactly. That way you won't have so much time to mull it over in that busy brain of yours."

"What does that mean?"

"Oh, come on," Beau said, getting to his feet. "You know that if you have time to think about anyone else's suggestions, you'll decide they won't work."

"That's not fair—"

"You've carried this super independence attitude a bit far."

"Beau, I don't know what you're—" Melissa's words were cut short as the phone rang. "That's probably Hunt, calling to say he wants to put in a salad bar."

Ignoring her cousin's smile, she picked up the phone, her voice sharper than she intended as she said, "Kirkland's at River Rest."

There was a slight pause before Melissa's father replied, "That sounds very businesslike. When do you open?"

"Father," Melissa said softly. Beau let out a low whistle and sat back down on the love seat.

She cleared her throat. "What a nice surprise."

Malcolm Chambers chuckled dryly. "Yes, I'm sure you're surprised. Edward told me about the restaurant."

"Edward?" Melissa said, straightening. "Is he with you?"

"Yes. He went back to college to pick up his things and arrived here last night."

"I was worried. I . . . I tried to help him, Father. He just wouldn't listen. I'm sorry. I know you were counting on me—"

"You're not responsible for Edward. I don't expect you to be."

"But I've always been able to straighten him out—"

"Well, now it's his turn. It's time he started acting his age." Malcolm's voice was sharp. "Don't you worry about Edward, Melissa."

"But, Father. He's still so…" She fumbled, searching for the right words. "He still hurts so much."

"We all do."

Melissa caught her breath. Her father rarely admitted any feeling of sorrow, remorse or weakness. She held the phone, hoping he'd say more. Surely someday they'd have to explore their family's broken dreams.

But Malcolm's voice was brisk as he continued, "Tell me about this restaurant. How did you arrange financing?"

Slowly at first, but soon warming to the subject, Melissa filled him in on her plans and Hunt's involvement. Her father listened attentively, asking knowledgeable questions.

"It sounds as if you've put a lot of thought into this."

She swallowed. "Yes, I have."

He was silent for a moment. Then he murmured, "I would have helped, you know."

And turned it into your restaurant, Melissa thought rebelliously. She squashed the resentful words that sprang to her lips and said, "I know. I wanted to do it on my own."

"I wish you the best of luck." He sounded distant, almost formal. Then he quickly added, "Please, if you need anything, anything at all, please call me."

"I will, Father." Melissa was lying, and she knew that her father knew it, too.

"Well, goodbye. I'll tell Nadine you said hello."

Melissa paused. It hadn't occurred to her to send greetings to her father's wife, but she added hastily, "Yes, say 'hello.'" She hung up the phone, frowning.

"He really does a number on you, doesn't he?" Beau said sympathetically.

Melissa merely looked at him.

"Is Edward okay?"

She shook her head. "I don't think he's ever going to be okay, Beau. I really don't." She sighed sadly. "What can I do?"

Beau frowned. "You've done all you can. Stop feeling responsible for the whole world."

On one level, Melissa knew Beau was right, but on another... Lifetime habits die hard, she told herself. Throughout the afternoon her mind was busy searching for ways to help her brother.

The feeling of sadness must have lingered in her face because when Hunt arrived late that afternoon, he demanded, "What's wrong?"

"Nothing's wrong." Melissa stepped back, opening the door for him to enter. "And hello to you, too."

"I'm sorry. But you look worried." Hunt stepped inside. "Have you heard from Edward?"

He sees too damn much, she thought, hiding her face from him by closing the door. She pasted on what she hoped was a happy smile before turning around. "Edward's with Father. He's fine."

Hunt didn't believe that for a minute but didn't want to tell her that. "Good," he murmured.

They stood in the hall, scanning each other's faces until Melissa looked away, feeling uncomfortable.

"Did you notice?" she asked.

"Notice what?"

"The floor."

Hunt glanced down. The beautiful wood surface had been stained and finished. "That was quick."

"Cabot put a crew on it Monday afternoon," Melissa said. "Didn't I tell you?"

"No, the only things you've mentioned have been fried okra, creamed corn and sweet potatoes."

"Which I find infinitely more interesting than shrimp tempura and taco salad."

"Maybe *you* do, but you are not the only person in the world."

"You aren't, either."

"Melissa—" he began impatiently.

"Hunt—" she mimicked.

He put his hands on his hips, pushing back his navy blue blazer. His brows drew together, and his mouth thinned into an irritated line. Melissa decided the only thing missing was the thundercloud over his head.

"All right, let's just hold it," she said placatingly. "Beau has invited us to his place for dinner—"

"I hope he's not cooking—"

"—and he says he has a plan to solve our menu problems. I can't imagine what he has in mind, but I'm willing to listen." Her cousin's accusation that she didn't listen to other people's ideas had stung. She'd always prided herself on being open-minded.

"I guess it can't hurt to hear him out," Hunt agreed slowly.

"Until then, let's just talk about anything but the menu."

"Okay." Hunt dropped his arms to his sides. His eyes swept up and down her slender form. "You look nice."

Melissa glanced down at her slim blue denim skirt. She didn't think there was anything special about it or her long-sleeved pink sweater. "Thanks," she said, wishing Hunt would stop staring at her so intently. Nervously, she reached up to smooth her lace collar. "Why don't we go look at the kitchen? It's beginning to take shape."

"Fine," Hunt agreed, following her down the hall. The formfitting skirt showed off Melissa's small, rounded bottom. He enjoyed the view so much that he was smiling broadly when they reached the kitchen.

"What is it?" she asked.

"Oh, I just like the looks of things around here more and more," he answered, barely suppressing an impulse to pat her tantalizing fanny.

Keeping his mind on the renovations was almost more than Hunt could do. He decided quickly that he'd much rather be kissing Melissa than inspecting newly plastered walls. However, initiating the contact didn't come as easily as it had on Sunday. For Hunt knew he'd never be able to keep it light. If he kissed her now, with days of fantasies churning in his mind, he was afraid his control would slip. And then he knew she would run scared.

So Hunt held himself a little apart from her, hiding behind impersonal conversation. Melissa seemed to pick up on his reserve; she cloaked herself in a cool, polite facade. The atmosphere was heavy with the strain of their pretense, like the breathless pause between lightning and thunder.

They maintained that precarious posture for over an hour while they inspected the kitchen and drove the short distance to Beau's apartment. Melissa was glad to see her cousin; at this point seeing anyone else would have been welcome. Being alone with Hunt was almost unbearable.

Beau's home was in an apartment complex named for its perch high above the city, Cameron Hill. There were trendier places to live, all of which Beau could afford. But he preferred his two-bedroom apartment's view of Chattanooga. This evening Melissa could understand why.

Sipping wine, she walked out on the patio and watched twilight overtake the clear, autumn day. In the distance, Lookout Mountain stood sentinel over the city. Lights had begun to appear in buildings and on cars. There was peace to be found in the spectacle of day slipping into night. Melissa took a deep breath, letting that peace wash over her, eliminating the troubling tension between her and Hunt. She should have never let him kiss her. She should have stopped all this nonsense right then and there.

Behind her, she heard him say, "Don't tell me you're cooking?" She turned as her two companions emerged outdoors. Beau was carrying a platter of meat.

"Who can ruin beef like this?" her cousin replied, hoisting a steak onto the gas grill.

"You," Hunt said. "Step aside. I'll cook."

"Great." Beau moved out of the way, rubbing his hands together. "With two restaurateurs here, I don't see why I should have to trouble myself. Melissa, why don't you come do something with the salad?"

She laughed and followed him inside. Who could worry about anything with Beau around? They had a pleasant meal while he outlined his plan to settle their menu problems.

"You should hold a preopening party," he explained, looking immensely pleased with himself.

"Preopening?" Hunt echoed.

"How would that help?" Melissa asked.

Beau leaned forward, warming to his topic. "We'll invite only members of the media. They'll sample menu items that each of you submit, and then they'll vote for their favorites."

"It'd be great publicity," Hunt agreed cautiously.

"More than great," Beau corrected.

Melissa frowned, not sure if she liked the idea of showing off the restaurant before it was open to the general public. "Why would they come?"

Beau chuckled. "Why wouldn't they? They'll get a free meal and an advance look at what promises to be one of Chattanooga's hottest restaurants. Everyone is already talking about it."

"They are?" Melissa asked.

"Sure. I've told everyone I know."

Hunt gave Beau an approving slap on the shoulder. "The perfect public relations man."

"Just doing my job. I mean, I'm assuming you are going to let me handle your advertising, right?"

"Of course," Melissa told him. "But I'm still not sure about this party. What if these media people choose the wrong foods?"

"Meaning my foods?" Hunt said, grinning good-naturedly.

"Well—yes," she admitted, smiling back.

"We'll make it into a real competition, traditional Southern fare versus contemporary cuisine," Beau said. "It'll be lots of fun. You and Hunt can lobby for your favorites."

"I do know something about campaigning," Melissa said, with a sly look at Hunt.

"And my guess is that when they sit down to eat in that beautiful restored mansion, they're going to vote straight traditional." Beau shot Hunt an apologetic look.

"Hey, whose side are you on?"

"Sorry, friend. My money's on Melissa for this one."

Hunt laughed easily. "We'll see."

"It just might work, if the renovations are finished. I don't want anyone to see it till it's perfect," Melissa fretted.

"I don't think it would matter if all the furniture isn't in place, as long as the atmosphere is right. You told me today that the renovations will be finished within the month," Beau said.

"I bet we could swing it," Hunt murmured, his excitement showing in his face. "This could be a great party. We'd get terrific press."

"Do you think so?" Melissa couldn't help but catch his enthusiasm.

They spent the next several hours discussing timetables and construction deadlines. The menu had to be set at least three weeks before opening. That left them just about a month to complete the major renovations, furnish the place and hold the party. Who would prepare the food? Who would serve it? When did the invitations need to go out? There seemed to be a hundred and one questions demanding answers.

Earlier differences forgotten, Melissa and Hunt went over the details, sometimes arguing, often laughing. The more they talked, the more ideas they had, and the more problems they had to solve. Neither of them realized how late it had grown until Melissa noticed that Beau had slipped away from the table and was stretched out on the couch.

"Beau, how rude," she teased.

The redhead groaned and rolled over on his side. "I just wanted to see what you two thought of the idea. I didn't expect you to iron out all the details—tonight—in my apartment—when I need to rest up for a major presentation tomorrow."

Instantly contrite and reminded of his recent business setbacks, Melissa said, "How is business going anyway?"

He groaned and pulled the sofa's arm cushion over his face. "Don't ask."

"We'd better be going," Hunt said quickly.

"I'll do the dishes." Melissa got up and started stacking plates.

"No!" Beau said, lowering the cushion. "Dianne'll get those in the morning."

"Dianne?" Hunt asked.

"The maid. Simply gorgeous. She just loves to take care of me." The redhead's expressive eyes told the whole story.

"Fine." Melissa laughed and set down the stack of plates.

"Yeah, we wouldn't want to deny Dianne her pleasure," Hunt added.

"Good night to you both," Beau said pointedly. "It's almost midnight." He got off the couch and escorted them to the door.

Melissa had been up since six that morning and had put in a full day. She should have been tired, but her excitement over the preopening party precluded any thought of sleep. She and Hunt continued their discussion during the drive to River Rest.

"If we have this party around the last week in October, we could give it sort of an autumn festival feel," she said as Hunt's car drew to a stop in front of the house.

"Maybe," he agreed, getting out of the car.

Melissa joined him at the bottom of the porch's shallow steps. She pointed up at the sky. "If we could guarantee a harvest moon like that, we'd have it made."

Hunt glanced up. The moon hung like a fat yellow disk in the sky, touching the landscape with pure, fragile light. The air was cool, cooler than normal for early October in Tennessee. He looked back at Melissa. The faint breeze lifted the ends of her pale hair from her shoulders. She looks enchanting, Hunt thought, almost laughing aloud at his fanciful description.

In that instant, the desire started within him again. He'd successfully suppressed this kind of thought all evening. Now it was back, the simple need to hold her. He couldn't leave without touching her tonight.

"Let's walk awhile," he suggested.

She surprised him with her quick compliance.

They strolled down the driveway to the back of the house, continuing to talk about the party. Lights burned over the door of the garage and on the back porch, and in the distance moonlight glinted off the surface of the river. They were at the edge of the city, surrounded by other people, but it was very quiet.

"When I'm here, I feel as if I'm shut off from the rest of the world," Hunt murmured as they started back around to the front of the house.

"I like that feeling."

"So do I."

"My best memories are of this place."

They paused beside a tree that grew close to the front porch. Melissa leaned back against the trunk and gazed up through the night-shadowed branches.

"Edward climbed this tree once and got stuck halfway up, afraid to come down."

"Who went and got him?" Hunt asked, already knowing the answer.

"Me."

He was silent for a moment, considering his next words carefully. "How is Edward, really?"

"The same as always," Melissa replied without hesitation. "A mess."

"You know, maybe I could help him." The words were impulsive, but as soon as they were out, Hunt realized he meant them. However, it was really Melissa he wanted to help, not her brother.

"What do you mean?"

Hunt had moved closer to Melissa, and he could sense the way her body stiffened at his offer of help. How she hated the thought of even the smallest dependency. He forced his voice to remain casual. "It'd be no big thing. I could give Edward a job in one of my restaurants. The responsibility might be good for him."

"You'd hire a thief?" Melissa demanded, her voice full of scorn.

Hunt took a deep breath. "I'd hire *your* brother."

"I don't need favors."

A flash of anger, quick as a match strike, hit Hunt. "I wouldn't call it a favor."

"Then what would it be?"

He faltered. "Just something I'd do...something I'd want to do...for you."

"Sounds like a favor."

"No." He shook his head emphatically. "A favor is something you do for a friend of a friend, something they ask for. This...this is what you do for someone you care about." He held his breath, wondering how she'd react to his words.

Melissa stood ramrod stiff, caught between confusion and dismay. What was Hunt trying to say?

He took a deep breath and stepped forward, reaching up to trail his knuckles across her jaw. "I care, Melissa."

"Don't." She started to draw away, but his other hand closed on her upper arm.

"Why is it no one gets close?" he murmured. Without waiting for a reply, he drew her forward and touched her lips with his own.

The kiss was classic seduction. At first Hunt was gentle, seemingly content with the light pressure of his mouth against hers. As soft as the touch of a feather, he tricked Melissa, offering her tenderness where she had expected fire. When she relaxed under his sweetness he began to pursue her response, forcing her lips apart with steady persistence. Only then did she guess the strength of his need.

She barely attempted a resistance, though. Any protest was smothered deep in her throat, blocked by a desire that seemed to match Hunt's in urgency. One minute she was perched on the edge of passion. Then she was falling into it, pulled forward by a swell of powerful emotions.

Dimly, Hunt knew his control was slipping, sliding far from his command. Every second that his lips remained on Melissa's he walked a little closer to the point of no return. Arousal came fast. One hand encircled her neck, as if to draw her mouth even closer. The other moved down her slender back to rest on the delectable curve of her rear. Her body pressed against his, and Hunt hardened in response. He buried his face in her hair, murmuring her name. To kiss her again would be the cruelest form of self-torture.

Melissa fought her slow return to reality. It was madness. It was a deadly contradiction. But tonight, at this moment, she wanted Hunt as deeply as she'd ever wanted any man. The undiluted sexual yearning came as a shock, but she wanted to give in to its demands. Backing away from the temptation he offered took every ounce of strength she possessed. It would have been much easier to simply offer him her lips again.

"This has to stop," she managed to say, pushing against his chest.

"Why?" His voice was raw, as if even speaking was a struggle.

"Because it's crazy and foolish and irresponsible—"

"What's wrong with that?"

"Hunt—"

"Anything that makes you forget yourself, even for just a minute, has to be avoided. Right?" Hunt stepped away, thrusting his hands deep in his pockets.

His on-the-money assessment caught Melissa by surprise. She reacted with anger. "Don't try to pretend that you know me or what I want or what I think—"

"I found out more about you the first day we spent together than most people probably learn in a year. It's just that *way* between some people, Melissa." A trace of aggravation crept into his voice.

"Because we're attracted to each other, does that mean you know me? Because you get aroused when we kiss, is that significant? I'm not special—"

"Really?" Hunt gave a low laugh. "I'm thirty-three, and I've kissed a lot of women. I can assure you, not all kisses take me as far as I went tonight."

Melissa's face flamed, and she was glad of the darkness. "Hunt," she began, trying to sound calm and sure of herself. "We can't just follow our impulses."

"Why?" he asked yet again.

"Oh, don't be stupid!" she cried in anger. "This...this attraction between us in an unnecessary complication. I don't need it. I don't want it."

"But it's already here. Maybe you should just deal with it."

"Damn it, I'm already sharing my restaurant with you. What else do you want to take from me?"

Hunt fell silent. Her impulsive, angry words told the whole story—becoming close to someone meant she had to give up a part of herself. A wave of sympathy replaced his anger. Who had convinced her that relationships only worked one way?

"I don't want anything from you," he said quietly. "I wanted to give, not take. I'm sorry you misunderstood."

Melissa didn't answer. He sounded so sincere. But then, didn't they always? Making you trust them was just part of the ploy. Then, because they'd made you care, they sucked you dry.

He continued, "What would you like me to do, Melissa?"

The words slipped out before she could stop them. "Just be my friend."

Hunt took her hand in his. "Doesn't friendship seem a little bland?"

"No," she lied, to him and to herself.

He sighed. "You can't mean that. Who chooses a plain piece of cake when they can have the frosting, too?"

"Lots of sensible, smart people."

Did Hunt imagine it, or did Melissa's voice quaver ever so slightly?

"Someday you'll want the frosting," he predicted, his voice almost teasing.

She forced a lightness into her own tone. "Don't make book on it."

He laughed, almost but not quite clearing the air between them.

They strolled up onto the front porch. "Are you staying here?" Melissa asked cautiously.

In the faint glow of the light beside the door, he studied her face. She didn't want him here tonight. "No."

"Then I'll see you tomorrow." She inserted her key in the lock.

"I'll try," Hunt said, causing her to look up at him.

"What?"

"I'll try to just be your friend."

Melissa bit her lip as she stared into his brown eyes. Why did his words disappoint her? She forced herself to smile. "Thank you."

He leaned down and pressed a light kiss on her forehead, and his hand came up to smooth a strand of hair from her cheek. "Good night, partner," he whispered, then he turned and walked to his car.

Once inside the house, Melissa leaned against the door, wishing she dared call him back.

True to his word, Hunt tried to be just Melissa's friend. He thought he was fairly successful, considering the amount of time they spent together in finishing the renovations and

planning the preopening party. And he was downright
proud of his achievement in light of the way his attraction
for her grew with every moment he spent in her company.

There were a hundred times during the weeks before the
party when Hunt longed to forget his promise. Melissa
would turn to him, eyes full of excitement about wallpaper
or the delivery of tables and chairs or any one of a dozen
things, and it took all of his willpower to keep from kissing
her. She'd smile at him in the slow, steady way that was hers
alone, and he'd have to clench his fists to keep from reaching for her. If he touched her at all, it was light and impersonal.

He tried to understand why she stirred him so. Certainly
there had been women in Hunt's life who were more beautiful than Melissa. Yet he couldn't think of anyone who had
her freshness or charm, who brought such total enthusiasm
to any task. She would be directing the placement of furniture in the foyer one minute, going over party invitations the
next and moving just as quickly to fix peanut butter sandwiches for lunch. She did most everything with a smile, even
something as unpleasant as haggling with a florist over
prices. Hunt's admiration for her grew.

She's something very special, he thought, watching Melissa's face while they went over the newly completed kitchen
with the contractor. She was beaming with pleasure.

"I love it," she said, running a hand along the gleaming
aluminum table in the center. "Don't you?" She looked
expectantly at Hunt.

He started. Once again, he'd been so busy admiring Melissa that he had lost track of where he was. Now he glanced
approvingly at the streamlined efficient kitchen.

Aluminum racks waited to be filled with pots and pans.
Refrigerators, freezers and storage bins were ready to be
stocked. The ovens and grills stood poised for use. It was the

perfect restaurant kitchen, large enough for comfort, small enough for convenience.

Hunt smiled at Melissa. "It's great," he agreed.

Full of excitement she hugged him. Then, evidently regretting the impulse, she almost jumped away.

Damn, he thought with irritation, even an innocent hug puts her on edge. He glanced up and met the contractor's interested gaze. There was a speculative gleam in Cabot's eye.

"Of course, it's not totally complete," the man drawled, opening a door on the right. "We've got to get the dishwashing setup put in here." He turned back to the left. "But the good news is that the back porch is finished, and the bar will be ready for next week's party."

Melissa trailed after Cabot, studiously avoiding Hunt's eyes. She hated the way she had been overreacting to his slightest touch. And it wasn't as if he'd been making romantic overtures. She told herself to be grateful that he was sticking by his promise to be nothing more than friends. Yet, conversely, she kept wishing he'd kiss her.

There were times when Melissa thought Hunt was barely holding himself in check. Sometimes she thought she saw a yearning look in his brown eyes, but the expression was always quickly masked, maintaining the friendly harmony between them.

So why did she find herself daydreaming about those moments in his arms out under the stars?"

I've got to stop this, she chided herself, as she followed Cabot into the almost-completed bar. Together, she and Hunt had worked hard to plan the upcoming party. They'd hired a chef who would be here this weekend. Melissa had even gone up to Knoxville to talk with the cook and the waiters and waitresses Hunt was planning to bring down just for the party here in Chattanooga. And even though the entire event was supposed to be a contest, they'd worked together to select the wide, varied party menu. Melissa had to admit they were a great team.

And the last thing they needed was romantic complications, she thought firmly, turning her attention to the bar.

This was the room she had fought Hunt hardest on, but now she was looking forward to seeing it completed. They'd turned the back sitting room and the sunroom into one large area. The walls facing the river and the backyard were glass; on the floor were wide pine planks and ceiling fans had been installed above. True, the feeling was contemporary, but Melissa was sure that when the wicker furniture was in place, the room would look a lot like a traditional Southern porch.

"You can start stocking the bar as soon as we finish the floor in one corner," Cabot told Hunt. "Everything else is in place." He tapped the brass-trimmed bar. "I think it looks great."

Melissa and Hunt quickly agreed, and Cabot left.

"Well, partner," Hunt said, leaning against the doorjamb. "We've come a long way in a month."

"But we've got a long way to go," Melissa reminded him. "The party is Thursday. This is Friday. We've got to get this room finished, set up the buffet tables, arrange for someone to play the piano, order flowers, get the linen service started, get our new chef settled, and—"

"And we can do it all," Hunt interrupted. "Relax," he said, just as he'd done a dozen times over the last few weeks. "Don't you know? We can do anything." He took her hand and gave it a little squeeze, adding again, "Partner."

Melissa didn't even try to fight the trill of pleasure that went through her. God, but the man was dangerous. Who was he that a touch of his hand could put butterflies in her stomach? It wasn't rational, but she couldn't run from it any longer. As he said, she had to deal with it.

So she left her hand in Hunt's grasp and forced her voice to remain light. "Well, *friend*, if you say we can do it, I know we can."

Hunt didn't miss her emphasis on the word "friend." Nor did he miss the way she trembled just slightly at his touch. A triumphant little grin tugged at the edge of his mouth. "Let's get back to work, pal," he said, dropping her hand.

But as she turned away, Hunt made himself a promise: *Sometime very soon this friendly pretense is going to end.*

The day of the party dawned cool and rainy, and Melissa fretted over the weather until around three, when the clouds began to clear. By the time she had dressed and checked the tables for the umpteenth time, the day had given way to a crisp October evening.

"Melissa, you look gorgeous."

She looked up from the flowers she was fussing over as Beau strolled down the foyer, looking terribly correct in his dark blue pin-striped suit.

"Do you like the dress?"

"Very much."

Melissa gave a nervous laugh and dropped a teasing curtsy for her cousin, holding the full skirt of her tea-length bronze dress in one hand. She hadn't wanted to overdress, and the simple yet shimmery silk dress had seemed the right choice. "You'll notice I'm wearing Grandmother's pearls," she added, touching the necklace that encircled her neck.

"Most appropriate," Beau declared, laughing as Melissa executed a neat model's pirouette to show off her dress some more.

She laughed, too, grinning over her shoulder until she caught sight of Hunt at the end of the stairs. He was leaning against the newel post, watching her with those dark, knowing eyes of his. Melissa's laughter died in her throat.

Following her gaze, Beau turned around. "Hello, Hunt," he said. "I didn't hear you come down. Doesn't Melissa look gorgeous?"

Hunt nodded, overwhelmed. He'd gotten used to seeing Melissa in jeans and T-shirts, with no makeup and her hair caught up in a scraggly ponytail. He found her fresh-scrubbed naturalness very appealing. But this Melissa, this carefully made-up beauty in the shining dress—this was a woman who could take his breath away. She'd looked like this the first night he'd come to dinner here, when he'd felt that first tingle of attraction. The tingle was now an ache.

He stepped forward and took her hands. "You are beautiful," he said softly.

Melissa couldn't quite fathom the look in his eyes. She quickly freed her hands. "Come take one more look at everything with me. Everyone will be here soon."

Hunt followed her into the kitchen, ignoring Beau's inquiring glance.

The party was soon in full swing. Beau had done his job well. Members of the Chattanooga media filled River Rest. Newspaper reporters mingled with radio and TV personalities, sipping their drinks, sampling the food and good-naturedly falling in with the challenge of voting for their favorite dishes. A television crew wound through the crowd, taping the event for a feature story.

One buffet table was loaded with Melissa's traditional favorites, including fried chicken, shrimp creole, carved roast beef, baked ham and a big selection of vegetable dishes. On Hunt's side were items like beef kabobs, sweet-and-sour chicken, blackened redfish, fried cheese and potato skins. The waiters and waitresses were busy circulating champagne and keeping the tables filled. Mary, Hunt's

Knoxville manager, was supervising the work, leaving him and Melissa free to mingle with their guests.

Keeping it light, Melissa lobbied for her own dishes, playing up the contest. This was nothing new to her. She'd been trained to be a hostess, on constant public display. The only thing that bothered her was Hunt.

He watched her steadily. Melissa would look up from a conversation or move from a group and find him standing to the side, gazing at her. Even when he was talking with someone, which was often, it seemed that his eyes were always trained on her, following her across the room. Despite the noise and the crush of people, an awareness vibrated across the space that separated them. It sent tingles up and down Melissa's spine. She found herself looking for him.

Of course the press wanted pictures of them together. They posed all over the house, smiling for the camera while Melissa shivered at the light touch of Hunt's hand on her back. She was so keyed up that she wasn't ready for the one question she'd known was coming. In a room full of reporters, someone had to mention her father.

Hunt and Melissa were posing on the stairs for a picture when a pretty blonde asked, "Does your father have an interest in the restaurant, Miss Chambers? Is he planning to move back to Chattanooga with his wife, who I understand is pregnant?"

Hunt glanced sharply at Melissa's suddenly drawn face.

Her poise slipped a little. It had been a long time since she'd been questioned about her father. "No," she answered, her voice brittle. "My father does not own any part of this restaurant. This is my business. My house. My restaurant. Got that?"

"Then he's not moving back?"

"No," Melissa said fiercely.

"And he's not involved in the restaurant at all?" the reporter pressed, scribbling on a small notebook.

"No, he is not. Didn't you hear me?" Melissa snapped, surprising Hunt. The reporter stopped writing and stared at Melissa, her eyes narrowing. Clearly, she smelled a family quarrel.

To throw her off the trail Hunt cut in, "Mr. Chambers doesn't have a financial interest, but of course he's giving his daughter his support. This restaurant is important to Melissa. She's worked very hard to make it happen." Hunt grinned. "I'm just happy that she allowed me to become her partner. After all, this is something she could have done on her own."

His comment drew the reporter's interest, allowing Melissa time to regain her control. My goodness, she thought, what's wrong with me? I know better than to answer a question in that way. Thank God Hunt is here.

Thank God Hunt is here? The words echoed through her head. Just weeks ago she'd been cursing his interference. Now he had so woven himself into her life that she actually couldn't imagine not seeing him nearly every day.

That realization astounded Melissa. When had Hunt Kirkland changed from a necessary inconvenience to someone whose presence she enjoyed? The knowledge should have frightened her, but instead it filled her with relief.

She moved down the stairs, talking with another reporter. At the bottom, she glanced back up at Hunt. In his dark gray suit, he looked quietly handsome, reassuringly solid and dependable. His gaze, steady and direct, caught hers. He grinned in that slow teasing way of his. She had grown used to that smile. In fact, she'd miss it if he left.

Something effervescent—was it anticipation?—stirred within Melissa, and she was suddenly impatient for the party to end.

Chapter Seven

Untying her chef's apron, Melissa gave the kitchen one last glance. The party had wound down about two hours ago, and the clock on the wall said it was almost one-thirty. Working together, she and Hunt and the crew from Knoxville had managed to quickly clear up the mess. He'd just sent the others off to the motel where they were to stay the night.

It was a great party, Melissa thought, switching off the kitchen light and starting down the darkened foyer. If they got the kind of coverage she hoped for, the town would be eagerly awaiting the opening. Even the voting for favorite foods had gone well. As Beau had predicted, her traditional fare had taken top honors. However, some of Hunt's dishes hadn't done too badly. Maybe they could reach a compromise. She smiled, wondering why she couldn't have been so accommodating earlier.

A movement on the stairs caught her eye, and she paused on the bottom step.

"What do you think, partner?" Hunt asked softly.

"I think we're a hit." Melissa leaned against the newel post, smiling at him. Sitting on the stairs with tie loosened and collar undone, Hunt radiated boyish appeal. She stepped up and sat down beside him, her full skirt spreading out around her.

"We're probably going to have more business than we know what to do with," he murmured.

She settled back against the stairs and expelled a satisfied sigh as she crossed her arms. "I think we can handle it."

He leaned back also, smiling down into her eyes. "We'll manage."

Their laughter mingled comfortably.

"I want to thank you for rescuing me," she said. "I really lost it with that reporter who kept asking about my father."

Hunt shrugged. "She was looking for trouble."

"No. I was." She returned his steady look. "Thank you again, especially for all the nice things you said about me."

He paused, considering his words. "You know, I think your losing your cool like that really showed me how much doing this on your own means to you."

"You didn't realize that before?" Melissa was a little surprised.

Hunt smiled ruefully. "I know you've shown me your determination all along, but tonight I think it finally hit me just how much it all means to you, how important it is to you to do it on your own. I really respect that."

"You do?" The compliment warmed her.

He nodded. "I mean the easiest thing would have been to just go to your father and ask for the money. You didn't take the easy way. You had the gumption to try something else—even putting up with an opinionated so-and-so like me."

They both laughed. Then Hunt's voice lowered, and his eyes became serious. "I admire you."

"Thank you," Melissa said softly, sitting up. "You don't know how good that makes me feel. I know I've been difficult. I've fought you on a lot of things. But this is my dream. It's something I have to do. Some people would think it was silly, but I—"

"I don't think it's silly. I don't think you're silly." Hunt eased forward until he was beside Melissa. He took her hand. "In fact, I think you're a pretty incredible person." Their eyes met again.

Melissa couldn't think of anything to say, and though she wanted to look away and break the disturbing contact with Hunt, she couldn't. His arm came around her shoulders, and she closed her eyes as he drew her against him and rested his cheek against her hair.

"Tell me I'm not crazy," he murmured. "There's something here between us, isn't there, Melissa? Something more than friendship or business?"

There seemed no reason to protest the obvious. "Yes," she whispered and turned her head so that their lips could meet.

Passion, sweet as spring rain, poured through Hunt. It was both demanding and subtle. And, as always, the want quickly grew.

She drew away, and in the soft light he could see that her blue eyes were troubled. "This isn't what we should be doing," she said.

"Why?" he asked. "What makes you afraid?"

She fumbled for a explanation. "It just never works out.... I can't... I'm not good at being close."

"But you've never been close to me." Hunt brought her hand to his lips and pressed a kiss in her open palm. Then, placing that hand against his chest, he said, "This is me you're dealing with, Melissa. I'm not the same person as those others, whoever they might have been. There's just me and you and here and now. We don't have a history. And I'm not looking to hurt you."

Through the thin shirt beneath her hand, Melissa could feel the warmth of Hunt's skin. Her fingers slid upward until they rested against the pulse that beat at his throat. There was so much honesty in his voice, a light in his eyes that seemed to beg her to believe his words. Would he hurt her? And if she didn't unbend enough to find out, wouldn't she always wonder what she'd missed?

"Part of me says I shouldn't trust you," she whispered. "But part of me wants to—very badly."

"Maybe I just need to be a little more persuasive." Hunt stood, drawing Melissa up with him. He kissed her with an ill-concealed intent, his tongue probing, demanding that she respond.

Soon there was only one answer Melissa could give. She was going to forget yesterday and tomorrow and seize the moment, hold on to what she felt right now. She broke away and started up the stairs, her hand reaching back for Hunt's. "Come with me."

In her apartment, there was a moment of awkwardness for Melissa, a feeling that they were moving too fast. When Hunt began undoing the buttons that ran up the front of her bodice, she stepped away, toward the sanctuary of the bathroom.

"No," he said, gently drawing her back into his embrace. "I don't want you out of my sight. Not for a minute. Here, if you're going to be modest . . ." He turned off the lamp which burned on the table beside her bed.

The moon filled the room with silvery light, but Melissa forgot her shyness in the wonder of her response to Hunt.

His hands were gentle, guiding her dress from her body, helping her slip out of delicate lingerie. When she was naked, his fingers lightly traced a line from her throat to the valley between her breasts, and desire scorched her skin in the wake of his touch.

His lips were warm against hers. They whispered along her neck while he pressed her smoothly, tenderly onto the bed. Her fingers tunneled through his dark hair, holding him against her as his mouth covered her breast. The light, liquid contact sent raw need pulsing through Melissa's body. His tongue dallied, and she arched upward. Heat seemed to swirl in ever-widening circles from the juncture of her thighs. Hunt's mouth moved to her other breast, and she gasped in pleasure.

Laughter, low and pleasingly male, rumbled in his throat. He kissed her lips again, hard, before he stood to toss aside his jacket and tie.

Naked and curled on the bed in the moonlight, Melissa was a temptress. Through the shadows Hunt could see that her eyes were closed and her lips were pouted, as if waiting to be kissed again. Light brushed across her small breasts, revealing rosy, erect peaks. Desire squeezed impatiently at him, and he fumbled with the buttons of his shirt.

Melissa opened her eyes and watched him silently for a moment. Then she sat up, smiling. "Let me," she said and knelt in front of him, pushing his hands aside, making short work of the troublesome buttons.

The shirt fluttered to the floor, followed shortly by everything that kept them apart. Even in the joy of flesh meeting flesh, a tiny voice of reason filtered through the haze of Melissa's desire.

"Hunt," she whispered, shivering as his big hands curved over her bottom, molding her close. "Hunt, I'm not prepared.... We have to—" She stopped, embarrassed as he drew away to look at her.

"Precautions?" he asked softly.

"I'm sorry," she murmured, not anxious to destroy the mood but unwilling to take a risk. "This isn't something I planned, and I just—"

He silenced her with a kiss. "No problem." He fumbled in the pants which were pooled on the floor.

"Are you always prepared?" Melissa teased, half-serious.

Hunt correctly read the uncertainty in her voice. "No," he answered. "But when a man's been hopin' and wishin' and prayin' that a certain lady would give him a certain smile—"

"What smile?" Melissa asked breathlessly, reassured by his fervent words. Her mouth curved into a grin.

"That one," he whispered, claiming her lips again.

Spellbound by his touch and his voice, Melissa allowed the rest of the night to unfold like a cherished dream. He was her long-awaited perfect lover, rock-solid masculinity tempered with silken tenderness. He was bold—guiding her hand to encircle his hardness, pressing his lips between her legs. He was gentle—kissing the curve of her thigh, trailing feather-light fingers up her spine.

His touch brought her to one earthshaking climax, and before she could fall from that peak, he slid deep inside her. His own satisfaction came like a cloudburst, and she soon followed him into the storm.

Melissa was like lightning in Hunt's arms, pure, electric passion. He'd known of course that her cool exterior hid unfathomed depths. He hadn't known how quickly she would open them to him. And to his surprise, pleasing her was more important than being pleased himself. That unselfishness was new to him.

They talked in the intimate calm that followed the loving. Limbs entwined, weary beyond measure, they resisted sleep, sharing the kind of lover's secrets that darkness and sexual fulfillment tend to encourage.

Once or twice, Melissa wondered that she should be lying here with Hunt. Steadfastly, she refused to consider all that she was revealing about herself. For right now, the only thing that seemed to matter was Hunt—his gentleness, his kindness and the breathtaking way he could make the world disappear with the touch of his hand.

Just before dawn that touch again drew them to the edge of passion and beyond, and finally, they slept.

The ring of the telephone woke Melissa the next day. Unwilling to open sleep-clouded eyes to the sunny room, she groped for the receiver. "Hello," she mumbled, smiling as Hunt's warm body curved around hers.

"Are you still asleep?" Beau asked cheerfully. "It wasn't *that* good a party."

"Uh-huh," she agreed. Hunt's hand cupped her breast.

"Who is it?" he whispered against her ear.

"Beau."

"What?" her cousin said, obviously thinking she was talking to him.

"Nothing," Melissa said into the phone.

"Well, are you awake enough to tell me if Hunt stayed there last night?"

"Yes, he did." Without thinking, Melissa handed the phone to Hunt. Then realizing her error, her eyes flew open. She grabbed for the phone, but he was already answering.

"This is a hellacious hour to be calling, Beau."

"Well, well, well," Beau said, chuckling. "It certainly didn't take Melissa long to track you down, old buddy. You must have been close by." Far from disapproving, Beau sounded downright pleased.

Hunt grinned, ignoring the frantic signals Melissa was sending his way. "Did you want something important?" he asked Beau.

"No. Just wanted to tell you to look in the paper. They did a great story on the party."

"Super. Is that all?"

Beau laughed. "I'll talk to you later when you're thinking straight."

"Do that," Hunt said and reached across Melissa to hang up the phone.

She groaned. "I guess Beau knows."

"Were you hoping to hide our new status?" His hand threaded through her gilt-blond hair.

"No, I guess not."

He kissed her nose. "Then what's wrong?"

"Nothing."

With his fingertips, he drew circles around the hardening peak of her breast. "Then good morning, Miss Chambers." His lips paused just a fraction from hers.

"Good morning, Mr. Kirkland." His kiss smothered her giggle.

Several moments later she said, "We need to get up."

"Why?"

"Because it's after ten."

"So?"

"We have work to do."

"It'll get done." His hand slid from her breast across the flat planes of her stomach. She drew in a sharp little breath. "We'll work later," Hunt murmured, drawing the covers down and sliding his body over hers.

His mouth was hungry; his hands were strong. Under their pressure, Melissa stopped worrying about work or her cousin or anything except the need Hunt aroused in her. In the warm, sun-dappled bed there was nothing more appealing than making love with him again.

Shyness forgotten, Melissa was glad it was light. It pleased her to watch the flicker of emotions across Hunt's face. Passion. Fulfillment. Tenderness. She saw them all in his eyes. She enjoyed the masculine lines of his body, the perspiration that beaded his forehead, the dark growth of beard on his cheeks.

As his body surged into hers, she wondered why she'd ever hesitated over something that now seemed so right, that felt so good.

Around noon they finally got out of bed and showered, taking turns in Melissa's small bathroom. The sight of Hunt shaving in front of her mirror, his lower body draped in a towel that barely met on the side, seemed almost natural to Melissa. She stood in the doorway and admired the firm muscles of his broad shoulders, thinking that getting dressed with a man was almost more intimate than making love with him. In the mirror their gazes met. He smiled, and a warm, happy feeling coursed through her.

I could get used to this, Melissa decided. She turned away, telling herself not to get serious. Nothing good could ever last. It never did.

While Hunt cooked breakfast Melissa went down to pick up the paper. Back upstairs, she read aloud the story about the party.

''It says here that 'The lovely Melissa Chambers, daughter of ex-congressman Malcolm Chambers, has joined with well-known restaurateur Hunt Kirkland to combine all the right ingredients for Kirkland's at River Rest. It's sure to be a winner.'" Melissa tossed the paper aside and gave Hunt an impulsive hug. "Isn't it wonderful?"

He placed her breakfast on the table in front of her. "Yeah, it's great. It'd be better if we had a menu."

She groaned. "We still have to do that, don't we?"

"Yep." Hunt slid his omelet onto a plate and took a seat across from her. "Let's get to work, partner."

They didn't argue—much. And what disagreements they had were good-natured. Based on the voting and the comments of the night before, it seemed sensible to Melissa to devise a menu that combined the best of the traditional and contemporary. Hunt was pleased by her suggestion. By late afternoon, they'd made their choices, dividing the menu into sections called "River Rest Favorites" and "Kirkland's Best." They set the prices and jotted down some ideas for Beau's agency to use in coming up with the menu's design.

"There's not much left to do," Melissa commented as she walked with Hunt to the door. "The rest of the furniture will be here next week."

"And we'll be ready to open the Friday after Thanksgiving."

"Uh-huh." Melissa looked at the floor. "Do you really have to go?" It required a lot of effort to ask that question. She didn't want to cling, but the day had been so nice and the night before so wonderful, she really didn't want him to go. So much had changed.

Hunt drew her into his arms, resting his chin on her soft blond hair. Damn, but he wanted to stay. He'd like nothing more than to carry her back to bed and spend the rest of the day and night making slow, sweet love.

"I haven't been to my office since Monday," he said, pulling back to look down into her face. "My mother called last week and told me she was beginning to forget what I look like."

"So?" Melissa said, kissing his chin.

"So they're getting on in age, and occasionally they do want to gaze at their only son and heir. After all they've done for me, it's the least I can do for them."

"You're lucky. You know that, don't you?" Melissa asked, thinking of her own parents.

Hunt kissed her intimately, mouth open, body straining against hers. "I feel damn lucky right now," he murmured fiercely.

"Hunt—" Melissa warned, uncomfortable with the seriousness of his words.

"I know, keep it light."

As always, she was amazed by the way he read her thoughts.

He laughed against her hair and brought her mouth back up to his. Several moments later he stepped back and picked up his suitcase. "I really have to go."

"I understand." The pout on Melissa's mouth belied her words.

Hunt groaned. "Please don't look like that, Melissa."

"Like what?" she asked innocently, blue eyes widening.

"Damn." He dropped his suitcase. "Like that." Grasping her hand, he pulled her after him up the stairs. "Come on, I don't think I can make it to the third floor."

They made it to their office.

"Your grandfather would be shocked," Hunt said as Melissa eyed the rolltop desk wickedly.

She unbuckled his belt, giggling. "I won't tell him if you won't."

"My lips are sealed," Hunt said, lowering his mouth to hers again.

* * *

In the next few weeks, the November air grew cooler, and the brilliantly colored leaves began dropping to the ground. It was Hunt's favorite time of year, a season of foggy mornings and smoke-scented evenings. Yet for all the notice he took, it could have been spring. The only thing that mattered was Melissa.

He couldn't stay away from her, and consequently he spent a lot of time traveling the interstate between Knoxville and Chattanooga. There'd be one day spent in his office, frantically plowing through paperwork, then two days spent with Melissa. Two days there, one day here. Back and forth he went.

They had plenty of work to do. The rest of the restaurant fixtures arrived, and they spent days arranging and rearranging tables. The staff was hired. Waiters and waitresses were trained. Test dinners were prepared and served. Tables were set and reset. Recipes were adjusted. Supplies were stocked. River Rest buzzed with activity.

But in between the decisions, after the training, the preparations and the adjustments, Hunt and Melissa found time for each other. Time for candlelit dinners and twilight walks. Time to share their thoughts. Time for Hunt to lose himself in the magic of her laughter or the beauty of her smile.

They were drawing closer, coming to depend on one another. Yet every day Melissa cautioned herself to think no further ahead than tomorrow.

One night they decided to case the competition and set out for drinks and dinner at a restaurant on Chattanooga's entertainment strip, Brainerd Road. Yet they forgot to judge their waitress's performance, ignored the quality of their wine and barely touched their meal. It seemed enough to sit in a quiet, darkened corner, holding hands and gazing into each other's eyes.

Melissa acknowledged that Hunt was courting her. She knew she was experiencing every cliché associated with infatuation—sweaty palms, accelerated heartbeat and that curious, empty feeling that comes from waking up alone when you'd rather have someone beside you.

Oh, she fought the feelings, but they still didn't go away. And always, no matter what, she stopped shy of admitting to herself that she might be falling in love. This was attraction. It was a sexual awakening of some sort. But it had nothing to do with her real emotions. Melissa didn't need Hunt. Certainly it was nice having him around; she admitted that freely. However, she could make it without him.

Sometimes at night, when he slept beside her, his arm curved around her body with hand resting lightly against her breast, she wondered what she'd do when it was over. It never occurred to her that it would last. Melissa felt compelled to let Hunt know that she hadn't any big expectations.

Late one night after lying awake thinking about the situation for hours, she woke him up. "Hunt, we need to talk."

He came groggily awake. "Huh?"

"I think we have to get a few things clear."

"What are you talking about?" He rolled over and glanced at the alarm clock. It was after three.

Melissa took a deep breath. "I just think you should know that I'm not expecting any kind of earth-shattering declaration from you."

Hunt sat up and switched on the bedside lamp, blinking in the sudden light. Running a hand through his tousled hair, he sent Melissa a perplexed look. "What in hell does that mean?"

She swallowed nervously. Perhaps this nocturnal conversation wasn't one of her better ideas. "I just don't want you to feel obligated. I mean, just because we're sleeping together..."

"Do you wish we weren't sleeping together?" Hunt demanded, trying to clear the cobwebs from his brain.

"Of course not." Melissa gave an exasperated sigh. "For heaven's sake, I just wanted you to know that I'm not waiting for you to tell me you love me." She turned her back to him and lay down again, pulling the covers up around her shoulders. "Now go back to sleep."

Hunt sat silently rubbing his chin, staring at the tiny bit of her blond hair that showed at the edge of the sheet. What in the world was she talking about? He hadn't even thought about telling her he loved her. Sure, he cared about her; he desired her. She filled half of his waking thoughts. But love? Was the little speech she'd just given some sort of perversely feminine way of saying she wanted him to love her? He switched out the light and lay down again. Damn, but women were complicated.

"Melissa?" he ventured a few moments later.

"Yes."

He took a deep breath. "If you're not worried about whether or not I love you, why did you bring it up?"

She bit her lip. Why did he have to be so perceptive, even at three in the morning. "I just wanted to let you know how I felt, so you wouldn't feel pressured or anything."

"Oh." He lay still, considering her answer. "Do you?"

"Do I what?"

"Feel pressured—" his voice deepened "—to love me?"

Melissa shut her eyes. She should have known better than to start this. "No."

"Good," he said, scooting closer to her. "I don't want to pressure you." Gently but firmly his hands turned her around to face him. "Let's not worry about things like this. Not now." His lips settled on hers.

"But Hunt—" Melissa protested against his mouth.

"Ssshhh," he said, his hand tracing circles ever lower across her stomach. "Let's just enjoy ourselves. Okay?"

Her body was already telegraphing her assent.

Taking his advice, Melissa tried not to worry about love. In fact, she tried erasing it from her thoughts. It crept back at times—like when Hunt laughed or she unexpectedly caught his clean, masculine scent. At those moments she might question whether or not it was love she was beginning to feel for him. However, the thought was quickly put aside. She busied herself in preparations for the opening.

The days ticked by quickly, and soon it was the day before Thanksgiving, two days before they would open their doors for business. Late Wednesday afternoon, Hunt and Melissa headed to his parents' for the holiday.

"Are you sure this is a good idea?" she asked as Hunt's car turned down a narrow, rural road.

"Of course. Mother and Dad have been wanting to meet you."

"But aren't they coming to the opening?"

"Yes, but you won't have any time to talk to them then." Hunt glanced at her quickly. "Besides, you need to get away for a day."

"I suppose you're right." Still, Melissa battled the nervousness that rose within her. What would Hunt's mother and father think of her? From what he'd said, his parents were as different from hers as night from day. He'd been raised in warmth and security. Why, this holiday demonstrated their differences all too well. Her father and his new family were in London. Her mother had taken Edward to the Bahamas to visit some family friends. She doubted any of her family would come close to even the smell of pumpkin pie.

And that was exactly the aroma which greeted them when Hunt and Melissa arrived at his parents' home a short while later.

"Mother," Hunt called, leaving Melissa in the small, comfortable living room. "We're here."

Melissa was surprised by the tiny woman who soon followed him through the doorway, wiping her hands on her apron. She looked small next to her son and older than Melissa had expected, with completely gray hair. But her eyes were like Hunt's, a sparkling dark brown.

"Melissa Chambers, this is my mother, Lois Kirkland."

"Oh, Melissa," Lois said eagerly. "I am so happy to meet you at last."

Melissa smiled. "It's nice to meet you, too. Hunt's told me a lot about you."

"Well, I wish I could say the same about you. But my son never tells me anything." The woman tsk-tsked, while Melissa shot Hunt an amused glance.

"Well, maybe I can fill in the details."

"I certainly hope so," Lois returned with spirit. "Now you just come with me. I'll get you settled in the guest room. Hunt's father is out getting a load of wood."

"Wood?" Hunt asked, following the two women down the hall. "It's not cold. What does he need wood for?"

"Now you know as well as I do that your father insists on having a fire in the fireplace at Thanksgiving. It may be eighty degrees, but Bill Kirkland *will* have a Thanksgiving fire. Tomorrow, we'll just have to turn on the air conditioning—just like we did last year." She laughed, Hunt joined her, and soon Melissa was chuckling, too.

"What's so funny?" a voice boomed.

They turned as a big man came down the hall. He was taller than Hunt, with a full salt-and-pepper beard and hair to match. An outdoorsy scent clung to his jeans and flannel shirt. "Well? What are you all laughing at?" he demanded.

"You and your fires," Hunt said.

"Some people have no respect for traditions." The older man shook his head and turned to Melissa. "You must be Miss Chambers."

"Just Melissa," she said.

"Well, Melissa, we're pleased to have you here. I must say you're much better lookin' than any of Hunt's previous business partners."

"Bill!" Lois admonished.

Hunt only smiled, and Melissa laughed, feeling completely at home.

It was a warm, comfortable evening. They ate homemade soup and sandwiches around the table in the kitchen. Then Melissa helped Lois prepare the stuffing for tomorrow's turkey while Bill puffed on a pipe and recounted Hunt's glorious career on the football field.

"You could've made the pros, Son."

"In your dreams," Hunt returned, stroking the black and white cat, which had settled on his lap.

"Bill was the one who wanted the football career," Lois explained to Melissa. "I do believe he saw every game Hunt ever played in. He'd get so keyed up, he couldn't sleep the night before."

"And then he'd pace the floor and wake everyone else up," Hunt added, grinning.

Melissa stood to the side, watching and listening, letting their easy camaraderie wash over her. Does he know how special they are? she wondered, looking at Hunt. She and Edward had felt privileged if their father had made an appearance at one school play or ballgame out of twenty. Oh, what she'd give to be able to sit around with her family like this, reminiscing.

While his parents chattered on, Hunt noticed the pensive expression that stole over Melissa's face. He put the cat down and crossed the room to stand beside her. "Something wrong?" he asked softly.

"No." She smiled up at him. "I'm having a wonderful time. They're good people."

"The best."

"Treasure them, Hunt," she whispered, a fierce note in her voice. "Not everyone has people who love them no matter what." She turned quickly away, asking his mother a question.

Her sadness tore at Hunt's gut. God, how he'd love to get hold of that sainted father of hers. And her mother? She seemed to have forgotten she even had a daughter. Melissa never mentioned her, had refused to invite her to the restaurant's opening. Hunt wished he could shake some sense into the two of them.

He turned back to the kitchen as his mother said, "Now, Bill, you absolutely cannot smoke another pipe in this house. We'll all smother to death tonight if you do."

"Oh, all right," the man grumbled. "Come out on the porch with me, Son. Fill me in on the business."

Father and son stepped out on the back porch into the cool evening air. Bill squinted up at the stars. "I guarantee that this time next week it'll be ten to fifteen degrees cooler."

"Think so?" Hunt answered absently, his mind still on Melissa. He leaned his back against the cedar porch rails and gazed at the house. Through the kitchen window, he could see Melissa's blond head bent close to his mother's gray one. The sight pleased him.

"You and Miss Chambers..." his father began.

"Yes?" Hunt said, turning to face him.

"You've got more than a business going, don't you?"

Hunt smiled. He'd never been able to put anything past this man. "How'd you know?"

"You're not trying to hide it, are you?"

"No sir."

"How does she feel about it?"

"I don't know. We're taking it slow."

Bill chuckled.

"What's funny?"

"Son, you've never done anything slow in your life." Bill struck a match and lit his pipe, puffing on it while he regarded Hunt in the dim porch light. "I like that girl. You'd be making a mistake to let her get away."

Hunt was silent, considering the words.

Bill hitched up his trousers. "Now, I'm going down to the barn to check on a sick cow. You're welcome to come along, but if I were you, I'd invite my woman out to look at the moon." He patted his son's shoulder and was gone.

Hunt stayed on the porch, thinking. It seemed as if that was all he'd done since Melissa had awakened him last week with her questions about love. Instead of relaxing and enjoying himself as he'd advised her to do, he'd been agonizing over the state of his own emotions.

Love. How does a man know when it's real? It was more than great sex. Hunt was experienced enough to know that much. But then, sex with Melissa was terrific. Was it companionship? God knew she was wonderful to be with, to laugh with. When there was pain at the thought of not being with a person, was that love? The idea of never seeing her again certainly hurt.

Shivering in the light breeze, Hunt thrust his hands into the pockets of his jeans. Melissa's laughter mingled with his mother's and danced across the crisp air. He could picture her animated face and the way her eyes crinkled at the corners when she smiled.

"I'm not ready to put a label on what I feel for her," he said out loud. "But I'm willing to spend a lot more time finding one that fits."

The next day was a typical Tennessee Thanksgiving, a little too warm and somewhat overcast. Inside, Bill built a fire and Lois ran the air conditioner while she heaped the dining-room table with enough food for an army of people.

By now Melissa felt she'd known Hunt's parents for years. They were endearing people, and it was pleasant to observe the love they had for one another and their son. Though she cautioned herself against feeling so comfortable, she liked being part of their circle.

Over their pumpkin pie dessert, Lois started asking about the restaurant. "You know Melissa, I really liked the ideas you had that Hunt told me about."

"Which ones?"

"The piano music in the foyer."

"Well, we're going to have that on weekends. But Hunt thought it might be a little too much every night of the week."

Lois frowned. "That's too bad. I liked the idea. I hope you're still going to have fresh flowers."

Melissa shifted in her chair, glancing at Hunt. "No, we've got silk arrangements for the tables. There'll be fresh flowers in the hall, though."

"When did we decide that?" Hunt asked.

"It was one of our compromises." She laughed. "We've had to make quite a few of those," she explained to his parents.

"Well, you just watch that, Melissa," Lois warned. "Hunt is just like his dad. He'll compromise you right into doing everything he wants if you don't watch it."

"Oh, come on," Hunt protested, laughing.

"But it's true," his mother persisted. "Even as a boy, Hunt let nothing stand in the way of something he really wanted. He can be real hardheaded when he wants to."

The simple words, innocently spoken, struck at the heart of Melissa's vulnerability. While the other three chuckled, she stared down at her plate. Damn, but she'd known it from the beginning. Hunt Kirkland was a man who got his way, no matter what. Hadn't she seen that in him from the moment they'd met? How many of her ideas had she shoved aside during the last few weeks? She frowned at that disturbing thought.

"Something wrong with the pie, Melissa?" he asked.

Her head jerked up. "No, the pie's terrific. I'm just full."

"You can finish it up after we watch some football," Bill told her.

"I think Hunt and I probably need to get back to the restaurant this afternoon," Melissa said quickly.

"You do?" Lois sounded disappointed.

"I thought we were going back tonight?" Hunt said, looking puzzled.

"I've changed my mind." Melissa's voice was cold, her blue eyes colder still.

Hunt frowned. What was wrong? He cornered her in the kitchen after the meal.

"Are you upset about something?"

"No," she lied. "I just want to get back to the restaurant and make sure everything is set for tomorrow."

"You know it is."

"Then just humor me, okay?" she snapped, turning away.

"Wait a minute." Hunt took hold of her forearm, holding her beside him. "What is wrong with you?"

Melissa could see the genuine concern in his brown eyes. He honestly didn't know, and if she tried to tell him he wouldn't understand. Hunt was simply Hunt. Trying to get his own way was just part of his nature, the same as the tender way he held her and the intelligent, analytical way he approached a problem.

Of course she'd come to appreciate his intelligence. As for the way he held her, well, Melissa wasn't so sure she was ready to give that up. But he was not going to dominate her. He had said he respected her for trying to start the restaurant. Maybe it was time he started proving it. She knew she couldn't change him, but she had to stop allowing her own desires to take a back seat to his. If she didn't, pretty soon there'd be nothing left of the way she'd originally planned to run the restaurant. And standing up for herself was her problem, not his.

Right now nothing was to be gained by getting angry. "I'm sorry," she said. "I'm just feeling nervous about the opening. I really want to go home."

"Okay," Hunt agreed. "I just thought you were mad about something."

"I'm not mad."

"Good." He drew her close, his voice dropping to a seductive whisper. "It might be nice having a whole evening to ourselves."

"Yes," Melissa agreed without hesitation, raising her lips for his kiss. Would maintaining her identity mean keeping Hunt out of her bed? I hope not, she thought, I don't know if I'm that strong.

Chapter Eight

The opening weekend crowds started on Friday at lunch and continued unabatedly through Sunday night. At times it seemed to Melissa that everyone in Chattanooga was trying for a taste of Kirkland's at River Rest. No one was turned away, even though getting a table required as much as a two-hour wait.

She was proud of the staff's performance. The activity was frantic in the kitchen, but tray after tray of delicious, attractively prepared meals disappeared through the swinging doors and onto elegantly set tables. The waiters and waitresses hustled without appearing too harried, their courteous smiles always in place.

Unforeseen problems cropped up here and there. Orders were mixed. They ran out of pecan pie late Saturday night. An exhausted busboy dropped a loaded tray. But overall, their performance couldn't be smoother.

It helped that the weather cooperated, remaining unseasonably mild. The bar did a steady business with the crowd that waited in the foyer and spilled over onto the back porch and the terraced deck that had been added to the sloping backyard.

Hunt and Melissa tried to be everywhere at once—assisting sometimes overwhelmed hostesses, preparing salads, soothing patrons who were a little anxious about the long wait. He had to repair the dishwasher. She had to unclog a drain in the ladies' rest room. Every time they turned around there was a question, a problem, a dilemma. Somehow, they did it all.

And from everyone there was praise—for the food, the service, the atmosphere. Over and over Melissa greeted people who said they'd known her grandmother or mother, who'd worked for her grandfather. There were a few comments about her father, sly remarks about his early "retirement" from Congress. She ignored them, never losing her cool.

Hunt's parents were there on Friday night, nodding, smiling and approving of it all. Even Melissa's family was represented. Her mother and father both sent impressive congratulatory flower arrangements, and Beau proved his loyalty by coming every night, escorting a stunning blonde who turned out to be Dianne, the maid. That, of course, explained the disapproving glares he earned from his mother, Melissa's socially conscious Aunt Martha. But even Martha couldn't fault the restaurant.

Happiness should have been unqualified for Melissa, but she couldn't help wishing the success were hers alone. She knew it was a selfish feeling, that Hunt had worked as hard as she, that he was taking a huge financial risk and deserved to share the glory. However, logic has little to do with emotion, and she couldn't help resenting his presence. This was supposed to have been her restaurant. Now it was theirs. It didn't help matters that he constantly vetoed her decisions.

As expected, one customer didn't care that they'd just opened and that there were a few bugs to be worked out. He thought he'd been waiting too long for his dinner.

"He's really mad. What should I do?" the frantic waitress asked, catching Melissa in the beverage center.

"Tell him the meal is on the house," she answered quickly, moving toward the kitchen to check on the long delay on another meal.

Hunt appeared at the waitress's side. "No," he said. "Offer them a free dessert. They'll order the most expensive one on the menu and be just as happy."

"But—" Melissa started to protest.

"We want to be courteous, but we don't want to be pushovers. Everyone's waiting a little longer than normal for their meals," Hunt reasoned.

The waitress glanced uncertainly from one to the other.

Melissa sighed. "Do as Mr. Kirkland says." When the girl was gone she turned to protest the action, but Hunt was already gone, his attention demanded elsewhere.

Behind the scenes, a waiter angrily asked a hostess why another waitress had been given one of his tables. Melissa stepped in, trying to reason with the two.

Hunt issued a succinct command. "Get back to work. We'll discuss the problem, *if* there is one, later."

He and the employees quickly scattered, leaving Melissa simmering in resentment.

She asked a waitress to help bus some tables; he pulled the girl off the job. When there was a problem with a bill, Hunt took the figures out of her hand, adding them quickly, finding the mistake. On Sunday night, when the ice machine went on the blink and Melissa was valiantly trying to find the problem, he gently pushed her to the side. She decided she'd had enough.

"Mr. Kirkland, when this is fixed, could I see you in the office?" she asked, whirling away with a swish of her blue satin dress before he could answer.

He was in the office in a matter of minutes. "Something wrong?"

"Why won't you let me do anything?" she demanded.

"Huh?"

"Don't play dumb, Hunt. For the past three days you've been coming along behind me, counteracting my every move. I *have* run a restaurant before, you know."

He was silent, regarding her flushed, angry face. Was he guilty of acting as she accused? Surely not. "I think you're being oversensitive."

"No, I am not," she denied hotly and recounted the instances in question.

"I thought you needed help," Hunt said, spreading his hands wide.

"Well, I don't. And I've told you that from the beginning." She crossed the room and grasped the door handle. "I wish you'd remember that it's my restaurant, too." The door closed behind her with a firm little bang.

"I'll be damned," Hunt said, taking a seat at his desk. He hadn't once considered that he was being overbearing. In fact he was sure he hadn't. Melissa was just tired, and she wasn't thinking clearly. They'd all been working like fiends for the past few days. With the opening weekend behind them, things would settle down. When she had time to really think, she'd realize how much she needed his help.

Later that night in the apartment as they both got ready for bed, Hunt tried to reason with her. "Melissa, I didn't realize I was running over you."

"I know you didn't. It just comes naturally." She was trying to keep a lid on her frustration.

"What does that mean?" He paused in unbuttoning his white shirt, a line of irritation beginning to show between his eyebrows.

She hastened to explain. "You're so used to being in charge of your own restaurants that you can't stop being the boss. But you're not my boss. We're supposed to be partners."

"And I try to compromise with you on the things that you want." He tossed his shirt over the chair beside the bed. "But it just so happens that I do have more experience than you."

"And that means I can't correctly add a customer's check?" Melissa returned, aggravation growing as she stepped out of her dress.

"Of course not."

"Then why did you grab it out of my hand?"

"I just thought there was something else you'd probably rather be doing." Hunt's pants followed the shirt to the chair.

"Well, there wasn't. And if you weren't here I'd have to do it myself. I wish you'd back off." She hung her dress in the closet.

"If I'd back off, you wouldn't even be in business," he tossed back, irritation giving way to genuine anger.

"Don't be so sure," she snapped.

Hunt drew in a deep, calming breath. What were they doing? They'd just had the most successful opening he'd ever had any part in, and they were fighting. They should be celebrating.

"Why are we arguing about something so minor and petty?" he said softly.

"It isn't petty or minor to me!" Melissa whirled around to face him, breasts heaving under her delicate silk and lace slip.

Fury slapped him hard, and Hunt reacted with a string of curses. "You are being ridiculous," he added, pulling back the covers on the bed. "And I'm not going to discuss it with you."

"Yes, you are!" she insisted, crossing her arms firmly over her chest.

"Oh, hell." With vicious swipes, Hunt plumped up his pillow. "Maybe you're right. Maybe I have been trying to run the show. But damn it, Melissa, that's what I do. I'm not used to having a partner. I'll try harder. Why don't you give me a break?"

"I'm trying to. That's why I brought the whole thing to your attention."

"Good. Now that I know everything I'm doing wrong, maybe we can get some sleep."

She turned away. "I don't know that I want to sleep with you."

He was beside her instantly, hand grasping the soft skin of her upper arm, wheeling her around to face him. "You're not going to do this, Melissa. We're not going to bring what happens down there," he pointed to the floor, "up here to our bed."

"I thought it was *my* bed," she said, instantly wishing she could take back the words.

As if burned, his hand fell away from her. "Well, pardon me. I thought what happens here was one thing you didn't mind sharing with me. If you resented it, you sure could have fooled me."

"Hunt—"

He silenced her explanation with an impatient wave of his hand. "I'll go sleep downstairs."

"No!" she protested. "I don't want that."

His brown eyes, which could be so warm, were cold and dark with anger. "Make up your mind. I've never stayed in a woman's bed when she didn't want me."

Melissa shut her eyes. What did she want, anyway? She looked up at him again and took a deep breath. "Don't you see that one part of our life is inevitably going to affect the other?"

He was silent.

"If I'm angry about something you do in the restaurant, I can't just come upstairs and shut the door on my emotions. And it would help if you didn't just brush my concerns aside."

"I didn't," Hunt protested, his voice still tinged with anger. "I told you I would try and curb my tendency to take over. What else do you want from me?"

Wearily, she sank down onto her side of the bed. "I don't know."

Over her protests, he sat down and pulled her onto his lap, his arms hugging her close to his solid chest. Melissa silently berated herself for feeling so at home.

"Why can't anyone help you?" Hunt whispered. "Why is it that every time anyone tries to do something for you, you resent it?"

"But you weren't 'doing something for me,'" she protested, drawing away. "You were taking away my authority."

He didn't answer her immediately. His fingers threaded gently through her hair. It was silky to his touch and as pale as moonlight. His eyes strayed to the heavy blunt-cut ends as he considered her accusation. Very softly, he said, "I was just trying to do everything I could to help you—to help us—have a successful opening. If I overstepped my bounds, I'm sorry." His gaze lifted to meet her again.

His sincerity was real, although the apology didn't erase the way he'd acted; it didn't solve the problem. But Melissa found it hard to remain angry when she was locked in Hunt's embrace, her breasts hardening traitorously against the silken barrier that separated them from contact with his skin.

She bowed her head. Perhaps he really could change. Perhaps she could learn how to accept his help without feeling threatened. Whatever the case, her anger and frustration were quickly giving way to the one aspect of their relationship she had no doubts about. "Take me to bed," she told him huskily.

Dipping his head, Hunt's mouth met the lips she offered so freely. "We're already in bed," he reminded her a few moments later.

"Then just take me," she murmured, already drawing him back for her kiss.

He fell back across the bed, holding her body on top of his while they kissed. Mouths open, greedy for the desire that grew with each thrust and parry of their tongues, they kissed for what seemed like an eternity of yearning. Melissa's soft hair fell like a curtain on either side of her face, and Hunt allowed his fingers to tangle in its silken tendrils.

He lost himself in the fragrance of her—the unique, utterly fresh scent that was Melissa's alone, that lingered in his mind when they were apart. Was it roses or violets or merely a mixture of everything that was sweet and pure? He didn't know. Didn't really care. What made it special was that it was her perfume, as delicate and feminine as the woman herself.

Her smooth skin warmed under his touch as the wispy apricot slip was drawn upward and over her breasts. Legs straddling his hips, she sat up in order to pull the garment over her head and unhook the lacy, matching bra. Hunt sat up, too, his lips unable to resist the temptation of her small, pink-tipped breasts.

Melissa closed her eyes, and her neck arched backward as the languid movement of his mouth spread an ache of pure need through her body.

"Ahh, Melissa," he murmured as she drew his mouth once more to hers. He pulled away. "At this moment you could do anything with me."

"That sounds very promising," she whispered, wiggling her lower body suggestively against his.

"Anything," he repeated as they fell once more to the bed.

Melissa felt daring—free. Here, there was nothing that stood between her and Hunt. Here, they were equals. There was power in that knowledge. She smiled.

"Something amusing?" he asked.

She shook her head. "I like making love with you," she said, amazed at how easy the words came.

His chest vibrated with laughter. "Do you really? I never would have guessed."

Light as butterfly wings, her fingers traced the strong contours of his face. He was becoming so familiar, so increasingly dear. Was that too dangerous? Melissa shied away from the thought. Somehow she had to stop worrying about all the tomorrows.

Bracing herself off the bed, she allowed her body to slide downward over his. His briefs were skimmed off hastily, tossed to the side, and his breath caught in sharp surprise as she took him into her mouth.

The strength momentarily left his limbs, but it returned quickly when he drew her lips once again to his own. He reversed their positions, pressing her into the softness of the bed with the movements of his mouth and body. Her legs wrapped comfortably around his hips.

"You could almost make a man lose his head," Hunt groaned, rolling away to find the necessary protection in the nightstand drawer.

"Thank you for remembering," she whispered.

And in moments they were joined, walking on the clouds, caught in mindless, unquestionable passion.

The climax left Melissa with barely enough strength to crawl under the covers. She certainly didn't have enough energy to worry about their business relationship. In fact, she thought as sleep overtook her brain, who cares?

The morning brought a sharp return to reality. There was no time for cuddling in bed or playing lover's games. To be ready for lunch, the restaurant had to shift into high gear by 7:00 a.m.

There were adjustments to be made in the table arrangements and supplies to be ordered. Hunt was on the phone with his other restaurants for part of the morning. Melissa spent an hour working with a couple of the less experienced waiters. By the afternoon, they'd already had three calls about reserving rooms for holiday parties. Then Hunt had to leave.

As they said goodbye outside the side entrance to the kitchen, Melissa had mixed emotions. Yes, she'd miss him. But no, she wasn't sorry to have the restaurant all to herself.

"I really do have to go, or I wouldn't leave you," he said, drawing her close.

"Don't be silly. I can handle it." Melissa fingered the lapels of his gray tweed jacket and gazed steadfastly at his tie. It wouldn't do to let Hunt see that she was even the tiniest bit pleased about his impending absence.

As usual, she couldn't fool him. Hand under her chin, he tilted her face up to his. "I know you secretly wish I'd never come back."

"Oh no," Melissa denied emphatically. His words started a hollow ache inside her. "I'll miss you terribly."

"Terribly," he echoed, smiling. His lips touched hers in the softest of kisses. "That goes double for me."

"I hope everything is fine with the Atlanta restaurant and that you'll be back soon," Melissa said.

"I'm sure it is, but it'll be Friday before I'm back. I'm going to be at the Birmingham restaurant on Wednesday afternoon and Thursday. It's been way too long since I visited either place."

"Just be careful." Melissa kissed him again.

"I will," he said, released her and started to leave. Midway down the steps, he stopped and turned back. "Don't make any decisions about booking parties upstairs, okay?"

"But, Hunt," Melissa protested. "This is the party season. What better time to start?"

He shook his head. "I just don't think we have the staff for it yet."

"I disagree."

Hunt sighed. "Okay, let's at least put off arguing about it until I get back."

Stubbornly, Melissa didn't answer. If he thought she was backing down, he could just think again.

Hunt gazed at her set face and decided not to push it. Just as he'd promised her last night, he was trying hard not to play the boss. "I'll call you tonight," he said finally.

Melissa summoned a smile. "Great."

"Goodbye."

Though the November breeze had turned cool, she stood on the side porch and waved until Hunt's car disappeared from view. After he was gone, she watched drying leaves dance across the lawn, and a quick glance at the gray, wintry sky told her the weather was changing. However, the shiver Melissa felt was from anticipation, not a chill. She hurried back inside.

Throughout the days that followed she barely had a moment to herself. Business was so brisk that she had to call in some of the weekends-only employees. It was obvious that more staff was needed, at least for the holiday season, and she placed a want ad in the classifieds.

Inquiries continued to pour in about private parties. Finally, when a call came from a friend of her grandmother's, Melissa relented and booked a luncheon. Then she booked a few more for throughout the holidays. The rooms upstairs were already furnished and were just sitting idle. As long as the parties were for during the day when they weren't as busy, she couldn't see the harm. Putting aside a ridiculous feeling of guilt, Melissa refrained from mentioning the special bookings to Hunt when he called.

Busy as she was, the work exhilarated Melissa. The people working for her were mostly young, and almost all were even tempered and energetic. There seemed to be few personality conflicts. In fact, everything was running as smoothly as cream, something she *didn't* fail to mention in her phone conversations with Hunt.

"I can do it all—all on my own," she said aloud as she locked up late Thursday night. She resisted the thought that she was trying to prove anything to anyone other than herself.

On the personal side, Melissa missed Hunt, missed his sleepy smile in the mornings, missed the way his warm body enfolded hers at night. *If only we could separate our relationship from the restaurant,* she thought. Then she'd be completely happy.

But she didn't feel sorry for herself for long. Melissa had only to think of her brother to consider herself lucky. Edward had called Thursday morning. He was unhappy with the job her father had found for him with a Washington brokerage firm.

"I'm nothing more than a gofer," he complained.

Melissa sighed in exasperation. "What did you expect? To be chairman of the board?"

"You just don't understand. You've got it made. Your own business, your own money," the young man said hotly. "And you've never had to live with *her*."

Melissa knew he meant their father's wife. "What's she done now?" she asked, although she already knew the answer. Anything the woman did was wrong to Edward.

"Nothing out of the ordinary. She just runs all over town buying presents for her little brat."

"You mean the baby."

Edward snorted. "No, I mean her other brat."

"Perhaps you need to look at Joey in another light," Melissa suggested tentatively. "I mean, he is our—"

"Perhaps you should practice what you preach," Edward retorted. "Why don't you come up here and try living with it all?"

He's right, I've never had to face it firsthand, Melissa thought, the old guilt returning. "I offered to let you stay here and work."

"Is your partner still hanging around?"

"Of course."

"Then, no thanks."

"Edward—"

"I gotta go, Missy. My boss is giving me dirty looks. I hate this crummy job, but it's all I've got. Dad isn't handing me an allowance like he did you."

"I stayed in school," Melissa reminded him sharply. "Why don't you go back?"

"You've got to be kidding." Edward's laughter was brittle. "See you—"

"Edward—" she began, not wanting to end the conversation on a sour note.

"Huh?"

"I love you, and I miss you."

He was silent for a moment, but his voice was softer when he answered. "Yeah. I miss you, too. Goodbye."

Troubled, Melissa hung up the phone. No, compared to her brother, she had no problems at all.

As luck would have it, everything that had gone right during that week went wrong on Friday night. They again had a capacity crowd, but now that it was too cold for everyone to wait outside the foyer and bar were jam-packed, making it seem even more crowded. The ice machine broke down again, and two waiters called in sick with the flu.

Melissa rushed all night long. From the hostess desk to the kitchen to the bar, she virtually ran, always feeling just a step behind. Despite the problems, the diners seemed to be having a good time and orders were being taken and filled as quickly as possible.

By nine o'clock, she was glancing at her watch every five minutes. Where was Hunt? Melissa worried, though she hadn't time to waste on the thought.

In the room just outside the kitchen she cast a critical eye on the plates a waitress was loading onto a tray. "Wait a minute," she said. "Those vegetable portions are a little small, aren't they?"

"Yes, but we're running low—"

"Running low?" Melissa groaned and said, "Wait here," before stepping through the double doors to the kitchen.

"Why are we running out of vegetables?" she demanded of Walter, the chef they'd hired from Nashville.

The tall, thin man shook his head. "I don't know why, but everyone's ordering the asparagus and the cauliflower tonight."

Noting the interested looks of the pastry chef and the kitchen assistants, she drew Walter to the side. She wouldn't embarrass him in front of them. "Are more being prepared?"

"Yes, of course—"

"Can you use the microwave?"

The man frowned. He liked preparing his food the old-fashioned way. "If I had to, I suppose—"

"Do what you have to do, but don't cut portions," Melissa told him firmly.

"But it was only a little—"

"Not even a little," Melissa insisted.

"Miss Chambers," a voice called insistently from the doorway. It was the waitress she'd left standing outside. "This food is getting cold."

"Add what vegetables you can," Melissa instructed, taking the tray of food and passing it to Walter. "And zap the plates in the microwave for a few seconds." She turned back to the waitress. "I know you're behind now. What can I do to help you catch up?"

"Table twenty's food is ready, too."

"I'll take it out myself."

"It's these two plates."

Just as Melissa loaded a tray, another voice called from the doorway. "Miss Chambers, now the ice machine is making too much ice. It's all over the beverage station floor."

"Get a broom and a couple of buckets from the utility closet and clean it up."

"But I've got customers," the waiter protested.

"Then grab a busboy."

"They're all busy."

"Oh, for heaven's sake." Melissa lifted the loaded tray. "I'll get it myself in a minute."

She forced herself to smile as she went through the doors and ran right into Hunt.

"Whoa, there," he admonished, steadying her tray before it could tip over. The dimple appeared in his cheek as he grinned. "Hi, partner. Waiting tables, too?"

Melissa's heart lurched at the sight of him, complexion ruddy from the brisk night air, eyes sparkling with good humor. Why was she so happy to see him? And why, oh why did he have to arrive just as everything fell apart? "There're a few problems—" she began.

"Just a few? On a Friday night?"

"Yes, but I've got everything under control."

"Miss Chambers!" came a voice from behind Hunt. "Now the ice machine is spitting cubes in the air."

"Oh, damn," Melissa muttered.

The hostess hurried into the room. "Miss Chambers. Rudy isn't keeping up with his customers, but he got mad again when I gave one of his tables to Clair—"

"Okay," Melissa said, handing the tray to the hostess. "You take this to table twenty. The man got the sirloin. I'll get the ice machine."

"No, I'll get the ice machine," Hunt said with authority. "And you send Rudy in to see me in the beverage center," he told the hostess as he moved toward the door. Still smiling, he glanced over his shoulder at Melissa. "I thought you said everything was going fine."

"It was," she said just as the door shut behind him. Unreasonable anger uncoiled within her. Here he goes again, she thought. He walks in the door and tries to take over—

"Miss Chambers?" The voice penetrated Melissa's preoccupation.

"Yes?" She looked up to see another waitress bearing a loaded tray.

"Could you carry a stand out for me to put this tray on while I serve?"

"Sure," Melissa said, quickly following the girl out of the room. But even though she concentrated on the tasks at hand, her thoughts were still with Hunt. *We're going to talk again,* she promised herself.

However, there was no time for talk in the next few hours, and Hunt didn't interfere again. But Melissa's anger grew. She knew that if he hadn't spent the entire night fixing the cantankerous ice machine, he'd have been right in the thick of things, once again shunting her to the side.

By the time the restaurant was empty and they were in their office running the night's totals, Melissa was more than ready for a fight. She was just about to let Hunt have it when the front doorbell pealed through the house.

He got to his feet quickly. "I'll go see who it is."

Just a few moments later, the phone on Melissa's desk buzzed. "Your brother's here," Hunt said tersely.

There must be trouble, she thought, hurrying through the hall and down the stairs. With Hunt standing beside him, Edward sat with head bowed on a sofa near the front door. He glanced up, and Melissa gasped when she saw his face. "My God, what happened?"

Edward's right eye was swollen shut and surrounded by angry, purpling bruises. His nose was covered by a bandage. There were stitches in his puffy lower lip.

"I'm not going back," he said gruffly. "So help me, Melissa. I'll never go back."

Hand pressed to her throat, Melissa merely stared at him. Hunt repeated her question, "What happened, Edward?"

The young man shot him an angry look. "Not that it's any of your business, but I got into a fight."

"That much is obvious," Hunt returned dryly.

Melissa dropped to the couch beside Edward. "Are you in pain? Do we need to call a doctor?"

He shook off the hand she put on his arm. "No. I saw a doctor last night."

"Where?" Hunt asked.

"In Washington."

"How did you get here?"

"I drove. How do you think?"

"But Edward," Melissa protested. "If this happened last night, you must have been on the road ever since. What did Father—"

Edward interrupted her angrily, "Our dear father no longer has anything to say about me or my life. I've declared my independence."

She gave him a long, steady look. "What did Nadine do?"

Hunt glanced at her sharply. Nadine was their father's wife. How did Melissa know this had anything to do with her?

"I owed some money to a friend. He came around to the house last night to pick it up, and I didn't have it, and—"

"Money for what?" Hunt asked, unable to contain the question.

Edward scowled at him.

"And then what happened?" Melissa pressed, shaking her head in warning at Hunt.

"Then we got in a fight. Nadine called the cops. My friend—"

"Some friend," Hunt interjected.

"—he ran away. And Nadine starts screaming at Father that I've got to be sent away for good. That I'm going to get her and her precious little Joey killed—"

"And what did father do?" Melissa asked.

Edward's voice shook. "He told me to get out."

"For the night?"

He stared at the floor. "For good."

Melissa slumped against the back of the sofa. "I wonder why Father didn't call me?"

"Oh, I'm sure he didn't want to trouble you," Edward said scathingly. "He's told me several times in the last few weeks that I'm not to call you with my problems. That I'm to leave you alone so you can just get on with your life. 'Poor Melissa' he says, 'she's finally doing something for herself. We're not going to bother her.'" Edward got to his feet and paced back and forth. "Well, what about me? What about my life? It's always been everyone but me."

As the boy's self-pitying speech continued, Hunt watched its effect on Melissa. Guilt seemed to smother her features. It's not right for her to sit here and take the blame for this mixed-up, foolish kid, he thought, growing angry.

"Stop it," he said sharply. "Edward, just stop it right now."

"Hunt—" Melissa protested.

"No," he snapped. "He's trying to make you feel responsible for his own stupidity. Don't you see that?"

"Hey," Edward began, stepping forward.

"Hey, what?" Hunt jabbed a finger in the boy's chest. "You really enjoy making her feel terrible, don't you? You enjoy calling her up and crying on her shoulder because she sympathizes with you, because she loves you so much she can't see what a rotten little bastard you've become—"

"Hunt!" Melissa shouted now, jumping to her feet.

He ignored her, continuing to talk to Edward, his voice rising. "You make me sick, you know that? You've got everything—everything—and you don't even know it!"

"You don't know anything about me," the young man protested. "And even if you did, what gives you the right—"

"Yes," Melissa added hotly. "What gives you the right to say a single word to him?"

"I thought what we had between us gave me the right to care when someone's hurting you," he answered, flashing a look at her tense face. "I'm not going to just stand by and watch him inflict this little guilt trip on you."

Before Melissa could reply Edward said sarcastically, "So you and the good Samaritan here have something more between you than this old mausoleum?" The eyes he turned on her were full of betrayal.

She stepped forward, pleading, "That has nothing to do with you, Edward. Hunt has nothing to do with you."

"No, he doesn't, Missy. But perhaps you should have explained that to him. He seems to think that what he says matters to you." He turned to the door. "I can see I'm not welcome here."

"Yes, you are!" Melissa said, going after him. "You're staying here. We're going to work everything out." She grabbed hold of her brother's arm. "Stay here, Edward. I don't want you to go."

Over her head, Edward's gaze met Hunt's. Then he laughed, a bitter sound. "No thanks, Missy. I just left Father. Why would I want to stick around when you've found a man who's just like him?"

Shaking off her detaining hands, the young man flung open the door and ran outside. Melissa followed him, begging him to stay. But in a few minutes, Hunt heard the roar of an engine and the screech of tires as a car tore off into the cold night.

"You had no right," Melissa said, slamming the door behind her as she came back inside. "You couldn't keep out of it, and now he's taken off for God knows where. If anything happens to him, Hunt—"

"Oh please," he said, stopping her tirade. "Don't try to put any blame on me. You're much better at just taking it on yourself."

"Why couldn't you keep your mouth shut?" she demanded.

"I told you. He was trying to make you feel guilty—"

"So what?"

"So I don't like seeing you made to feel that way. It's not right, Melissa—"

"And who appointed you keeper of what's right and wrong?" She ran a hand through her blond hair. "Oh Lord, Edward is so right. How did I end up with someone so much like Father?"

"I don't think—"

"Of course you don't think," she said. "You just do. You push and you pull and you take over everything. You're just like him."

Hunt stared at her. "I don't understand this obsession you have with people trying to run your life."

"Because that's what they've always done, Hunt. I've always been just a pawn in someone else's game. And I'm not going along with it anymore."

The undisguised pain in her voice tore at Hunt. He grasped her arms. "Melissa," he implored softly.

"Oh no," she said, twisting away. "You're not going to sweet-talk me. That's what he used to do. You're not going to get your way like that."

"Don't you think you're being a little melodramatic?"

"No, I don't." Melissa paced to the bottom of the stairs, her blue eyes snapping with anger. "I spent my whole life doing everything to please my father. I was a little blond-haired doll he could put on display for his constituents. I used to wish I were ugly. Know why? Because I thought that way I'd find out if he loved me for myself."

"But, Melissa," Hunt protested. "He has to love you. You're his daughter."

"Oh, he loved me. He smothered me with love," she said, her eyes filling with tears. "He chose my school, my friends, my job, even the man I was going to marry. I built my whole life around my father. And what does he do? He resigns, to marry his mistress."

Shocked, Hunt stared at her. "But I thought he resigned because—"

"Misuse of campaign funds?" Melissa laughed, though tears were running down her face. "Why do you think he had to steal money to invest in that resort? I mean, my father wasn't exactly poor. But he was running two households, keeping up five houses. Keeping two women in diamonds and furs."

"My God," Hunt murmured.

"I'm not saying my mother didn't deserve it, Hunt. She's not the easiest person in the world to love. But why did he have to hurt us all like that? Nadine was a twenty-year-old student when they started having an affair. She's only five years older than me."

"I had no idea."

"Well, let me tell you something else you probably had no idea about. Few people do. My father and his sweet little Nadine have a son."

Blank with shock. Hunt's mouth dropped open.

"Oh, yes," Melissa said, correctly guessing the direction of his thoughts. "My half brother, Joey, is eight years old, born well before my parents were even contemplating divorce."

"That's incredible. I mean there was no hint of this in the newspapers."

"Joey and Nadine were kept well away from the press. It was Edward and Mother and I who had to face all the questions. Joey gets plenty of my father's love and devotion. Unlike myself, and especially unlike Edward, who gets nothing but Nadine's contempt and father's misguided attempts at discipline."

Melissa sank down onto the sofa again, covering her face with her hands. "I know Edward's confused. I know he's troubled. But he's my brother, and most of the time I'm all he's got, Hunt." She raised her tear-streaked face to him. "Just me."

Without hesitation Hunt was beside Melissa, gathering her close, allowing her to cry against his chest. Her explanation told him so much about her. Her father had taken all her love, all her devotion and repaid her with disillusionment. No wonder she had grown fierce in her independence. What else could you expect from someone who'd spent her whole life bowing to someone else's wishes? Once free, caged birds rarely wish to return to captivity.

But I don't want to capture her, Hunt thought. If I can just make her understand that.

"Melissa, listen to me," he said when her tears seemed to have subsided. "I'm not trying to run your life." With his fingers, he gently wiped the moisture from her cheeks.

She sighed. "I know you don't think that, but—"

"Sshh." He pressed a finger to her lips. "I know I'm hardheaded and opinionated, but I wouldn't try to dominate you. I respect you."

"No, you don't," Melissa denied. "If you did, you wouldn't walk in and take over like you did tonight in the restaurant, and you'd have let me handle Edward."

"But—"

Melissa pulled out of his embrace. "Don't you see, Hunt? You're already taking over my life. First it was *my* restaurant—now it's ours. Then you swept me off my feet and into bed."

"You seemed to want to be swept," he pointed out.

"Maybe I did," she agreed. "But the point is that my whole life is starting to revolve around you. You want to do everything for me."

"Is that wrong?" he asked, clearly confused. "I've spent my whole life thinking it was right to want to do things for people you care about."

She shook her head sadly. "You just don't understand."

"No, I don't."

"I have to be my own person," Melissa said, grasping his hand.

Hunt stared down at their joined hands for several moments. A week ago he'd stood and looked at the stars and wondered if what he felt for Melissa was love. Now he was sure. With every second he'd spent away from her this past week, he'd grown more certain that he loved this stubborn, sweet woman.

Why couldn't that be the end of it? Once, long ago, he'd thought that when you finally found that one special person to love, your problems ended. Now with Melissa, he was afraid loving her was just the beginning.

He dared to look into her deep blue eyes. Can't she see the love inside me? he asked himself. *Can't she see I'd never hurt her?*

"Is it written somewhere that being your own person means being alone?" Hunt asked sadly.

Melissa's hand withdrew from his. "I hope not," was the only answer she could think to give.

Shaking his head sadly, Hunt got up and walked out the door.

Chapter Nine

Y ou know her better than anyone I know. What should I do?" Hunt turned from gazing out the window and faced Melissa's cousin.

Beau didn't answer immediately. Tapping a finger thoughtfully against his chin, he poured himself another cup of coffee and propped his elbows on his dining room table. He'd been listening to Hunt talk about Melissa since a little after four in the morning. It was now seven o'clock.

"Well?" Hunt prompted, taking the seat opposite him. "Tell me what you think."

Beau sipped his coffee before speaking carefully. "I think you should have known better than to interfere with Edward."

"But damn it, I care about her. I couldn't just sit there—"

"But you had to have known she'd react like a cat guarding a kitten."

"Yes, but—"

"But what, Hunt?" Beau shook his head. "Face it, you screwed up."

Hunt expelled a long breath, stood and went back to gazing out the window. Morning was spreading across the city, but all he could see were Melissa's eyes—eyes full of anger and hurt. After leaving her last night, he'd driven around for hours before landing on her cousin's doorstep. All he wanted was to figure out what she expected from him.

"Do you think I'm like her father?" he asked quietly, not turning from the window.

"To a degree," Beau answered. "But Melissa's exaggerating. I mean, you and her father are both successful, determined men. But her father is—or I should say was—ruthless. I don't think you are."

"She acts as if I intend to take the restaurant away from her."

"Don't tell me the thought never crossed your mind."

Hunt started guiltily at the words. Making the restaurant his own had been his original scheme. "That was before I realized what the place meant to Melissa, before I fell in love with her," he protested, turning back to his companion.

"But you've never quite trusted her abilities, have you?"

"Of course, I . . ." Hunt began and faltered. Despite his words to the contrary, did he really respect Melissa professionally? He admired her as a person, yes. But he'd never even considered that she could run the restaurant without him. Throughout the past week when he'd been in Atlanta and Birmingham, he'd worried about it constantly.

Beau gave him a triumphant look. "Don't you see? You two are involved on two different levels, personally and professionally. One relationship can't help but affect the other. And because Melissa is the way she is—independent to the point of contrariness—she feels like you're closing in on her."

"She told me that," Hunt said thoughtfully.

"Then why didn't you listen?"

"I guess I thought she was just overreacting. And until last night, I didn't really understand the degree to which her father had dominated her. She told me, of course, but I..." Hunt railed off, guilt sweeping through him.

"But you just didn't think it was that significant," Beau completed for him. "It sounds as if Melissa's been trying to tell you how to treat her all along and you just haven't been paying attention."

"I guess I haven't," Hunt agreed ruefully. "What should I do?"

"Well, I'd start with an apology."

"It'll take more than that."

"Then why don't you give her some space?"

"But I don't want to be apart from her. Damn it, I love her."

"And that means you can't give her the room she needs?" the redhead asked incredulously.

"Of course I don't mean that."

"Melissa spent years trying to be what everyone else wanted her to be. She won't do that anymore."

"But that's not what I want—"

Beau cut in sharply, "But if you push her too hard for any kind of commitment, she's just going to pull away. You know that about her. Think with your head, not your heart, man."

Hunt groaned. Damn, but it was all so complicated.

"Listen," Beau said as he got up and stretched. "I can't solve your problems for you. You've got to do that yourself. But if you love Melissa the way you say you do, you'll back off." He started through the living room. "You're welcome to crash on the couch or the extra bed. It's Saturday, and I'm going back to bed.''

Hunt sprawled in a chair at the dining room table and watched the early December sunrise. He hadn't really needed any advice. He had come here hoping to prove himself wrong. It had been obvious last night that he needed to distance himself from Melissa. It was even clearer this morning.

Yet how could he? Being away from her for just four days had been sheer hell. He had ached to hold her, to see her smile, hear her voice. Being with Melissa had simply become a necessity. How was he supposed to give that up?

Besides, he told himself, they were business partners. They had to make decisions about the restaurant. He couldn't just disappear. He had to help run the place....

But I don't, Hunt thought in a sudden burst of inspiration, *I don't have to run the place.* He sat up, considering the possibility, rejecting it, considering it again. Maybe there was a way to give Melissa the room she needed and yet still be with her. Maybe it was time he became the partner she had always wanted.

Hunt poured himself more coffee and rubbed his unshaven cheek. The mug went untouched as he stood and paced the room, thinking. Would Melissa go for it?

"There's just one way to find out," he said out loud, fishing his car keys from his pocket. Quickly he moved through the apartment and slammed the front door behind him as he headed for his car.

Melissa had never felt less like working. The early morning tasks of getting Kirkland's at River Rest ready for another day of business seemed almost more than she could face. She was worried about Edward, worried about Hunt and worried most about herself.

What was she going to do if Hunt had walked out of her life? That question had hammered at her brain throughout the sleepless night. She admitted that the man made her furious, that his interference was unwelcome and aggravating. But did she want him gone? No. She wanted him to change, and she knew that was unrealistic.

Don't ever expect a man to change. Weren't those words emblazoned across everything she'd ever read about psychology or relationships? There was no way a thirty-three-year-old man was going to alter his basic personality so drastically. For heaven's sake, even his mother admitted that he always had to be the one in charge.

But he can't run my life, Melissa told herself firmly. If she had to spend the rest of her days without Hunt Kirkland's smile, without the feel of his strong, hard body against hers, she wasn't going to back down.

With that thought firmly in mind, she finished the paperwork on her desk and headed down to see how things were progressing in the kitchen. Yet even three cups of strong coffee and the staff's constant questions didn't push Hunt from her mind. Melissa found herself watching the door for him.

He appeared a little after ten—unshaven, wearing the same clothes as the night before and looking as if he hadn't slept at all. Melissa had to restrain herself from touching the lines of weariness beside his mouth. It was an effort to remain calm as she faced him across the kitchen. "Want some coffee?" she asked.

"No, thanks. I've had too much already."

"Oh."

He glanced around at their busy employees. "Can we talk?"

She swallowed nervously and nodded, not trusting herself to speak. Silently, they mounted the back stairs and walked down the hall to their office.

The curtains were open at the long, narrow windows, and light spilled into the room, emphasizing the pallor of Melissa's skin and the deep shadows beneath her blue eyes. She looks fragile, Hunt thought, longing to touch her. He resisted the urge, taking a seat at his desk instead.

It seemed best to get right to the point. "I've decided to let you run the restaurant."

He heard her sharply indrawn breath.

"I realize that I've been acting unfairly. When we made our original agreement, I said you'd be left in charge when I was confident of your abilities."

"But you're not."

There was an edge of anger to her voice that surprised him. Hunt glanced up at her face. "What do you mean?"

"I mean," she said carefully, "you don't really trust me."

"Of course, I do," he returned evenly.

"You didn't last night. Why the sudden change?"

"Last night caused the change." Hunt stood and shoved his hands deep in his pockets. "I did a lot of thinking. I realized that I barely even said hello before I started taking over last night. Then I interfered in a private family matter. I shouldn't have, and I'm sorry."

"Apology accepted," Melissa murmured, watching him pace back and forth. "But what does that have to do with you turning the place over to me?"

"Everything," he said, coming to a stop in front of where she stood. "All the different parts of our lives are tangled up together. You've said that yourself."

"True," she agreed.

"And right now our personal life is most important to me."

Melissa turned away, fighting the anger that rose within her. "What you're saying is that since we're lovers and you don't want anything to interfere with that relationship, you're willing to let me run the restaurant."

"Right," Hunt said, not realizing the implication of her words until she whirled around and he saw her angry blue eyes. "I mean...no...that's not what I mean...."

Her hands clenched and unclenched at her sides. "If we weren't lovers, you wouldn't dream of putting me in charge."

"That's not true," Hunt protested. How does she always see through my words? he thought. He'd been positive that she'd be so eager for this chance that she'd jump at it, no questions asked. And by separating at least one aspect of their lives, he hoped to give her the independence she craved without sacrificing the feelings that were growing between them. It looked as if he'd need to do a first-class acting job to convince her that he thought she could run this place.

Wearily, he pushed fingers through his hair and then spread his hands wide, imploring her. "Look, I was gone almost all of last week, and things went just fine. You've proven yourself."

"But you called every day, and last night you certainly didn't act confident."

"Force of habit."

"Do you call the managers of your other restaurants all the time?"

"No," he hedged, "but they're not managing new restaurants, and besides, when I called I just wanted to talk to you—"

"I don't believe you," Melissa said bluntly, moving away.

Hunt caught her by the shoulders, forcing her to look up into his face. "I want you to be in charge here. No reservations. No questions asked. All I want to hear about is the bottom line. We'll even put the arrangement into writing if you want.''

She searched his face, trying to decide if he was telling the truth. She hoped so, desperately she hoped so. She wanted this opportunity so much. This way, she could prove to herself and to him, once and for all, that she could make this place a success. She couldn't quite believe that he trusted her, but she was going to win his approval. And with that settled, perhaps they could figure out what was happening between them. In essence, maybe they both wanted the same thing.

"Okay," she agreed at last.

He sighed in relief.

"But I do want it in writing," she said. "We'll draw up a contract."

"Fine." His hands tightened on her shoulders, and he drew her close. "Melissa, I just want things to work out between us. I want to make you happy."

She allowed herself to relax against his strength. It felt good just to be held. "I missed you this week," she said softly.

"I missed you, too."

She lifted her lips for his kiss. As always, warm sweet desire swept through her.

His deep brown eyes smiled into hers. "Why don't we go upstairs and get reacquainted?"

It was tempting, so tempting. Melissa would really have liked nothing better than to lock the apartment door and spend the rest of the morning in bed with Hunt. But she couldn't.

"We could have the bar send up a bottle of champagne," he suggested, nibbling at her ear.

Melissa wavered.

…unt's mouth was hot and demanding against the pulse that beat at her temple. "The chef could send up some quiche."

"Ummmm," she sighed, sorely tempted.

His hand cupped the fullness of her breast, his thumb brushing across the hardening peak. "And maybe we could have some pecan pie."

Their mouths met in an ever-deepening kiss that almost destroyed Melissa's resistance. But finally, gently, she pulled away. "I'm sorry, Hunt, but I've got work to do."

"A good manager delegates," he murmured, edging her back into his arms.

"I don't think so." Melissa disentangled herself from him gently. "You look like you could use some rest. Why don't you go upstairs and get a little sleep?"

"That bed'll be awfully lonely."

"You'll manage." She laughed and headed for the door. "Maybe I'll join you when the lunch crowd dies down."

"I'll save your place," he promised, smiling as he watched her leave.

It's going to work, he thought happily. He'd let Melissa run the restaurant, and they'd concentrate on making each other happy. He only hoped he could keep his promise and not interfere. He wished he felt a little more confident about her abilities. Could she run this place alone? It was a risk he had to take.

Melissa never found the time for Hunt that afternoon. The flu had spread to another waitress, and the lunch crowd was huge, swelled by holiday shoppers who'd decided to make the day an occasion by dining out. Melissa was surprised. They were a long way from the malls, and downtown's shopping appeal was dwindling. However, from talking with their customers she discovered that River Rest's reputation was spreading. She was pleased that people thought they were worth a special trip.

The lunch rush blended into dinner, and Melissa virtually forgot about Hunt until she saw him coming down the back stairs.

"You stood me up," he said, only half teasing.

"I'm sorry," she said. "We've been busy all day."

Hunt had to bite back an offer to help. He'd promised to stay out of the way. "You have to eat. Why don't you order something and we'll share it upstairs?"

"Oh, Hunt. I just don't think I can leave it down here, but I can send something up for you."

He hid his disappointment. "I'll go to the kitchen myself. Is that okay?"

"Of course it is," Melissa said with a stiff little laugh. They were acting so formal with one another.

He shifted from foot to foot, feeling useless. "After dinner, maybe I'll call Beau and see if he's got plans."

"Great. I'll see you later."

Hunt ate a solitary meal and then joined Beau and Dianne at a comedy club. It should have been a relaxed evening, but he couldn't help wishing he were at River Rest helping Melissa get through a busy Saturday night. Staying out of the business was going to take some getting used to.

It was very late when she came to bed, and she was plainly so exhausted that he didn't even think of making love. Instead, he held her while she slept, more than a little frustrated.

By the time Hunt left for Knoxville on Monday a pattern had been set. Melissa worked, and he waited. It was torture for him to be around and not participate in the decisions. As for his plans for romantic interludes free of business tension—there was no time. Melissa was simply too busy for him. It was better to stay away.

Yet that, too, was difficult. No matter what else he was doing, his mind was with her. He couldn't call too often for fear she'd think he was checking up on the restaurant, but he had to talk to her.

So he'd telephone her late at night, scrupulously avoiding any mention of business except, of course, the bottom line. They were bringing in money. Melissa finally told Hunt about the holiday luncheons she was booking. She casually mentioned plans for a New Year's Eve party and special incentives to bring people in after the first of the year. Hunt disagreed with some plans, agreed with others, but he kept his feelings to himself. That she was managing so well without him was both pleasing and deflating. He realized he'd been sure she'd be calling him for help.

Because they mainly avoided business discussions, they were forced to find other things to talk about. The result was finding out they had a great deal in common. How else, Hunt wondered, would he have discovered that they both liked *Star Trek* reruns, Carly Simon's early albums and Stephen King novels? It took separation for them to get better acquainted. Up to this point, their shared time had been spent putting together menus and quenching their physical desire for one another.

It was that desire that sent Hunt back to Chattanooga on Saturday. He had to see her. And staying away seemed worth it when he saw the way her face lit up when she saw him. She found time for him that night.

And that night, losing himself in her welcoming depths, he wondered how he was going to leave her again.

As Melissa stood waving after his disappearing car on Sunday afternoon, she prayed for the strength to make it through the coming week without calling him.

With the first blush of accomplishment wearing thin, she was discovering it was no picnic to carry the responsibility of the restaurant alone. In Nashville, though she'd been in charge, the owners had been right there to use as a sounding board. Here, there'd always been Hunt. Now she had to make all the decisions. She hated to admit it, but she missed him.

Although there were no major problems, she missed Hunt's input on the day-to-day decisions involving supplies, personnel and schedules. And above all, Melissa missed sharing the excitement. Someone would compliment a dish or the service or the decor, and she'd instinctively want to tell Hunt. At night when the restaurant was empty and silent, she'd sit impatiently waiting for his phone call, yearning to tell him all that happened, but afraid to share too much lest he find something he had to criticize.

During the day she missed him as a friend. At night, alone in her suddenly too-large bed, she missed him as only a lover could.

Was this love? she asked herself often. She still stopped just short of giving an answer. Love would make her vulnerable. Melissa knew from experience that loving someone gave them power over you. She wasn't yet ready to trust Hunt with that power.

December wore on, and the days grew shorter. With holiday anticipation filling the air, River Rest's party rooms were booked almost every day for Christmas luncheons. Melissa worked hard, and Hunt stayed away.

He called late Friday night on the weekend before Christmas. "Keeping busy?" he teased.

"You should know," she returned. "How's it going up there?"

"I've got a problem."

"Oh?" Melissa asked lightly, not wanting to press. Hunt never talked to her about his other restaurants.

"Yeah." All day long he'd wanted to call and ask Melissa's advice, but now he felt strangely reluctant. Finally, he plunged ahead. "I'm losing a manager. Mary's leaving me."

"You're kidding?" Melissa said, thinking of the pert brunette who had helped with the preopening party. "I thought she was a Kirkland's employee for life."

"Me, too, but her mother, who lives in California, is ill, and Mary's going to move out there to care for her. There's no one else to do it."

"I hate to hear that."

"I'm thinking of just managing the restaurant myself." Hunt paused. "What do you think?"

Pleasure uncurled in Melissa's chest. Hunt was asking her for advice. "Are you sure you want to be tied down like that?" she said.

"Well, I've got a good assistant manager. I really wouldn't be too locked in."

"If the assistant's so good, why not promote him?"

"It's a her."

"Well?"

Hunt sat and considered. "I guess I don't really have a reason why. I've been feeling a little bored, and I thought I might like the challenge of the day-to-day grind again."

Melissa laughed. "You. Bored? I can't imagine."

He joined her laughter. She was the reason for his boredom. He was as restless as before they'd become partners. He'd counted on the River Rest project to keep him occupied, but here he sat—twiddling his thumbs in Knoxville.

She continued, "Aren't you afraid of losing that assistant?"

"She seems to like her job."

"But she's probably expecting to move up. When she doesn't, she might leave. There goes a good employee. And you may send the wrong kind of signals to your other staff.

The ambitious, bright ones may think there's no opportunity to advance."

"You're right." That was one angle Hunt hadn't even thought of. "Thanks. I really wanted to know what you thought."

"You're welcome," Melissa said, more pleased by this compliment than any he could have given her. Suddenly she missed him more than ever. "When are you coming down?"

"When will you have time? These days before Christmas are always busy."

"I know."

"Are you going to spend time with your family?"

"No." Her voice was firm.

Hunt took a deep breath. "Is Edward okay?"

"He's with Mother in Nashville. He'd doing all right, I suppose." He wasn't, of course. Melissa's mother had called to report that he was out of control, running with a wild crowd and driving her crazy.

"I hope he'll be fine," Hunt said with all the genuine feeling he could muster.

Melissa was touched by the effort. "Thank you."

"So how about if I come down the day before Christmas Eve? Mom and Dad would love to have us both for dinner on Christmas Day."

"I'd like that," she said, pleased.

They said goodbye, and Hunt replaced the receiver feeling happier than he had in weeks. He'd begun to think that Melissa could get along without him in all areas of her life. Tonight, she had been warm and receptive and obviously flattered that he had wanted her advice. And darn good advice it was, he added to himself.

He pulled into River Rest before five o'clock on the day before Christmas Eve, and in his eagerness to see Melissa, he didn't even think of using the side entrance.

She was standing beside the hostess desk. In a pale pink sweater dress that hugged her slender body, with blond hair gathered in a bun at her neck, she looked cool and sophisticated. The image was quickly dispelled when she looked up and their gazes collided. The light in the depths of her eyes was anything but cool.

"Hunt," she said softly, taking a step forward.

He ignored the early diners crowding into the foyer and gathered her into his arms. "You look so damn good," he murmured against her cheek.

"So do you," she answered, surprising him with the kiss she pressed on his lips. "I'm glad you're here."

"Can you come out to the car and help me carry presents and suitcases upstairs?"

"I think they can spare me for a little while."

After making two trips apiece up and down the back staircase, both Melissa and Hunt were out of breath. She was staggered by the pile of brightly wrapped packages he put on the tiny table in the apartment.

"You must have bought out several stores. I don't have nearly this much for you," she said, shaking one of the larger boxes.

Behind her, Hunt's arms stole around her waist, and he pressed his cheek against her hair. "You can be my present."

Smiling happily and forgetting her reserve, Melissa turned around. "Okay. Do you want me wrapped or unwrapped?"

"Wrapped. I like untying bows."

The telephone interrupted their kiss. Melissa talked just a moment before she sent Hunt an apologetic smile. "I'm sorry. There's a problem downstairs."

"That's okay. I was going to stop in the office and look over the books, anyway. Your reports on the phone have been terrific. It sounds as if you've got everything on track."

Melissa was still glowing with pleasure over Hunt's casual compliment when she started down the main staircase. An agitated hostess waylaid her at the top with an urgent whisper, "Beth isn't here yet."

"That's the third time she's been late this week," Melissa murmured.

"And we've already got a crowd. The reservation list alone is a mile long," the hostess wailed.

"I'll help," Melissa soothed, starting down the stairs.

Beth, the other hostess, showed up soon after Melissa reached the hostess station. "Miss Chambers," the girl began.

"No excuses," Melissa said quietly. "I told you yesterday this couldn't happen again."

"But the babysitter was late—"

"Let's go up to the office, Beth. I want to get this cleared up right now."

Apologizing to the other hostess, Melissa led the way upstairs. She'd forgotten Hunt was in the office until she opened the door and found him sitting at his desk.

He glanced from Melissa's set face to that of the other girl. "Want me to leave?"

"No," Melissa said. There was no reason he couldn't be present while she talked to the girl. She took a seat behind her own desk and asked Beth, "Why can't you get to work on time?"

"I live with my mother who babysits for me. She works, too, and by the time she gets home, sometimes I'm already late. I'm sorry, Miss Chambers. I'm trying, and I really need this job."

"And I need you here at five o'clock."

The girl stared glumly at the floor, and Melissa tapped a pen impatiently against the desk. She didn't want to fire Beth. Once the girl got here she was energetic and organized. "Would it help if your mother could pick up the baby here? The problem's not transportation, is it?"

"Oh, no." Beth's face was brightening. "It would be easier if she came here, but I figured you'd be upset if I showed up with a baby."

"Well, I'm not ready to run a day-care center yet, but as long as your mother is here by five, I won't mind."

The girl expelled a long sigh of relief. "She'll be here. Thank you so much, Miss Chambers. I really appreciate it. I'll get back to work right away." She escaped through the door, obviously happy to still have a job.

Melissa pushed away from the desk and caught Hunt's eyes on her. "What are you smiling about?" she asked him.

He leaned back in his chair. "That was a very astute thing you just did. You held on to a good employee by helping her solve a problem. And you were smart enough to have the girl bring the baby here to wait on her mother. That way she'll actually be getting here a little early."

"We hope," Melissa said. "Who knows? I may have created a new problem."

Hunt shook his head. "I don't think so." He got up, crossed the room and perched on the edge of her desk. "You know something, Miss Chambers, you're very good at this. I was wrong to think you couldn't handle it."

She couldn't help smiling. "Are you really pleased?"

"Everything's running smoothly. We're making money. Your decision to go ahead and book parties really paid off, even with the extra staff it took to do it. No one could have done a better job."

"It means so much to have you say that," Melissa whispered.

Hunt took her hand. "Well, I'm really happy with the restaurant. More than that, I'm glad you're happy."

"Of course, we've only been open a month. I might sink the ship yet."

"I don't think so."

They smiled into each other's eyes.

"Shouldn't we get back to work?" Melissa asked.

"What's this 'we' bit? I don't work here."

She laughed. "You do tonight. I could use the help."

"I do believe those are the nicest words you have ever said to me," he returned. "I'd love to help you."

Melissa actually had fun working with Hunt. Maybe it was that his attitude toward her was different, or perhaps it was she who had changed, but she no longer felt threatened by his presence. They acted as a team instead of two people trying to outperform each other.

The restaurant cleared out early, and Melissa and Hunt were able to slip upstairs sooner than they'd expected. There they trimmed the small tree Melissa had placed in one of the dormer windows. She'd used most of her grandmother's ornaments on the big tree downstairs in the foyer but had saved her favorites for this tree. Every Christmas ball and star had a story she shared with Hunt.

They left the tree lights on when they went to bed. And in Melissa's mind everything ran together—the softly colored twinkling lights, the deep timbre of Hunt's voice, the gentle touch of his hands, the taste of his mouth. Like a spinning top, the colors and sounds went around and around and around, whirling to a peak and then slowly, slowly fading as her body accepted ecstasy and then slipped into sleep.

In the morning, Hunt was beside her—warm, disconcertingly familiar. On his cheek was early morning stubble; his hair was adorably mussed, his eyes full of sleep. Melissa lay curled at his side, watching him come slowly awake, thinking she was surely stealing a glimpse of heaven.

Heaven was shattered when he was fully awake. With that slow sleepy grin that creased a dimple in his cheek, he murmured, "I love you."

And for all the same old reasons, all Melissa could feel were the same old fears. There was no happiness, no instantaneous yearning to say those same words to him.

Love has a price tag, the little voice inside her head reminded. *Are you ready to give up part of yourself again?*

Yet it hurt her more than words could explain when the expectant, happy look in Hunt's eyes gave way slowly to disappointment.

"Damn them!" he exploded, tossing back the covers and getting quickly out of bed. "Damn all the hurts you can't seem to forget!"

The bathroom door slammed behind him, and Melissa rolled onto her side, body folded as if to block out the pain and eyes filling with angry, frustrated tears.

Chapter Ten

Y ou fool,'' Hunt told his reflection in the bathroom mirror. He should have known better than to announce his feelings to Melissa like that. What did it matter if last night felt like magic? So what if they seemed to have at long last worked out their business relationship? She was still running from the demons in her past, and he shouldn't have forgotten.

He switched on the shower, stepped into the stall and let the hot water pound against his body, hoping it would wash away his resentment. For Hunt resented Melissa, resented the way she could twist him in knots with just a smile and wound him without a word. She always has the upper hand, he thought, reaching for the soap.

Somehow, someway, he had to find it within himself to back off. Everything had happened so fast; Hunt knew that Melissa hadn't been expecting the impatient, furious kind of involvement he was offering. She wanted it slow and steady with gradual changes, gradual demands.

"If that's what it takes, that's what she gets," he muttered, turning off the water. It could be a long time before Melissa was willing to share more of herself than Hunt had already claimed. He would wait. Grimly, he pulled a towel from the rack beside the door. Determinedly, he forced himself to smile.

"Got any coffee?" he asked, emerging from the bathroom.

Startled, Melissa turned from the kitchenette. She'd been expecting hurt, fury or even an ultimatum, anything but the pleasant, even-tempered lòok now on Hunt's face. Her movements jerky, she poured him a mug of coffee.

He accepted it with one hand while the other rubbed a towel across his wet hair. "The bathroom's yours," he said casually, turning away.

Staring at his broad back, Melissa stood perfectly still. He was acting as if he hadn't uttered one word about love. Could she blame him? She'd practically tossed the words back in his face. Who would want to risk that again?

"Thanks," she murmured, scampering to the relative safety of the steamy bathroom.

Nothing changed over the next few days. Like neighborhood cats, they merely coexisted. Wary. Distant. Robbed of spontaneity. Hunt tried hard for outward holiday cheer, but underneath he was cold and depressed. Even spending the day with his parents brought no warmth. As he and Melissa drove back to Chattanooga that night, each wrapped in silence on opposite sides of the car, he wondered what she wanted from him. If she didn't love him, had no hope of loving him, then what in heaven's name were they doing?

There were no answers to be found in their faultlessly polite responses to each other. Hunt had planned to stay in

Chattanooga through New Year's Day, but he didn't know if he could keep this cheerful, undemanding facade in place that long.

They worked side by side in the restaurant. At least there Melissa felt they were able to recapture some of the warmth that had disappeared from their relationship. It wasn't that Hunt was exactly cold. Just guarded. And she hated knowing it was all her fault. She'd flung the barriers up between them.

"I'm the one who ruined it," she murmured aloud to the small storage room on the second floor.

She'd come up here to check through the boxes of hats and noisemakers she'd ordered for tomorrow night's New Year's Eve party. Outside it was cold and gloomy, and inside business was slower than usual. Hunt had disappeared into the office with the closed expression on his face Melissa was beginning to know and dread. There was no particular reason for her to get back to the restaurant, so instead she sat down on the trunk in the middle of the floor. She needed some uninterrupted time in which to think.

She glanced around. Most of the room's walls were covered in shelves. One side was filled with restaurant supplies. The other held some items that had belonged to Melissa's grandmother. On impulse, she pulled from the shelf a box marked "photos."

The albums inside were old; the pictures they held were a little faded. Yet the faces were still vibrant enough to bring a smile to Melissa's lips. Her grandparents' love of life and each other seemed to shine from the pages she turned.

How did she stay so strong? Melissa wondered as her fingertips traced the outline of her grandmother's picture.

Myra Delacourt had been just twenty years old when she'd married Jonathan Lewis. He was thirty-four and had already made a fortune in the shipping business. She was the debutante daughter of a wealthy family; his father was a poor farmer. Myra bore her only child, hosted dinners and parties, did all the things which were socially acceptable for a wealthy man's wife. Then, when he fell ill, she stepped in and ran his company. She did it so well that after recovering he still turned to her for advice.

Melissa knew that her grandparents had fought over politics and social issues. Jonathan had been none too happy to have his wife marching in a Vietnam War protest. She'd objected to his conservative stand on many an issue. Yet through it all they'd maintained their love, each respecting the other's right to an opinion.

"Love and respect," Melissa murmured. "That's really all it takes." Deep in thought, she closed the photo album and hugged it close to her chest, thinking about her relationship with Hunt. Did they have anything in common with her grandparents? Melissa had earned Hunt's professional respect; she felt sure she'd always had his personal approval. He said he loved her.

As for her feelings for him? Well, Melissa thought, I respect his integrity, his honesty, his love for his parents, and . . .

"Do I love him?" she said softly, sitting down on the old trunk again. How she longed to talk to her grandmother.

But you did talk with her about love and commitment, Melissa thought, suddenly remembering a conversation she'd had with Myra. It had been over four years ago, just before Melissa had become engaged to Michael Billings. Now that Melissa thought about it, her grandmother's words came back loud and clear.

"Does he listen to you?" Myra had asked. "Does he share his thoughts with you? Can you not imagine spending your life without him at your side?"

Naive and hopelessly fooled by Michael's smooth talk, Melissa had of course answered yes.

Then her grandmother had continued, "Before you marry someone, Melissa, I think you have to be certain that you are the person you want to be. Any relationship requires you to make changes, perhaps even to set aside some of your own dreams. But if you're complete unto yourself, if you're strong, the sacrifices and the compromises won't erode who you really are." Myra had smiled then, her eyes soft with memories. "On the other hand, when you truly do love someone, you're never really complete without them again."

Perhaps because Melissa hadn't really loved Michael, the words had rolled right by her. Strange how they made so much sense now.

Was she the person she wanted to be? Melissa asked herself. The answer had to be yes. She'd supported herself without help from her parents for over three years now. She'd earned the respect of her employers in Nashville. She'd found a way to have her own restaurant. She was what she'd set out to be: independent.

There's no one who can change how good I feel about myself now, Melissa told herself—not her father and not Hunt.

And what about Hunt? Was he the person she could spend her life with? He certainly satisfied her grandmother's first two requirements. He'd listened to Melissa's plans and schemes from the very beginning. He might have been hardheaded and a little skeptical, but he had tried to understand what she wanted and needed. By the same token, he'd shared his dreams with her. And he'd done everything he could to change for her.

And as for spending her life without him, Melissa could barely stand to entertain the thought. Maybe that hollow, empty feeling was exactly what her grandmother had meant about not being complete without that one special person.

"I love him," she said softly, savoring the words. She waited for the old fears to rise within her, but they didn't. Melissa felt only joy. Just as her grandmother had always told her, the answers to her questions had been in her heart. When she'd stopped being afraid to explore exactly what she felt, admitting that she loved Hunt was only natural.

"I have to go talk to him," she murmured and dropped the photo album back into the box, raising a little cloud of dust. As she started for the door, it opened and her cousin's red hair appeared around the edge.

"They said you were up here," Beau said. "What are you doing?"

"Party favors," Melissa said, holding up one of the noisemakers. "I was just going—"

"But I have to talk with you," he said, taking a seat on the trunk she had just vacated. Beau's expression, normally so jovial, was serious. He stared down at the floor and shook his head.

"Nothing's wrong, is it?" Melissa said, taking a step forward. "It's not Edward. He hasn't—"

"No, it's not Edward. It's Hunt."

"Hunt," she echoed, frowning. "What about him?"

"He's miserable," Beau stated flatly.

"I know. I was just going—"

"And you've got to do something about it," he added, ignoring her words.

"I agree—"

"I mean, it's all well and good to want to be independent, Melissa, but you're going to extremes. Hunt's a wonderful guy. He's crazy about you. Loving him isn't going to interfere with who you are or what you want. What are you waiting for?"

"I'm not. I—"

Beau still wasn't listening. "I know your father gave you a bad time. I mean I was there when he'd start pulling the old strings. But Hunt's not like him. You've got things all mixed up in your head."

"I did, yes, but—"

"No buts, Melissa," Beau said firmly. "Hunt probably did overstep his bounds with Edward. However, men in love are known to do foolish things. You need to forgive and forget—"

"You're absolutely right," Melissa said, finally managing to capture the redhead's attention.

"I am?" he asked, sounding surprised.

"I'm going to talk to him—"

Another knock sounded at the door, and Hunt stepped into the room. "What are you two doing in here?"

"Just talking," Beau supplied, while Melissa merely smiled, momentarily robbed of speech.

Maybe it was the knowledge that she truly loved him, but Hunt seemed suddenly so handsome. There was something about his square, smooth-shaven jaw, something in the broad set of his shoulders, something so completely appealing in his rather sad brown eyes that she had to force herself to listen to what he was saying.

"I just talked to the Knoxville restaurant. They're having a going away party for Mary, and I feel like I should be there. I'm going to leave right now."

"But you can't!" Melissa protested, earning a puzzled look from him. "I mean, what about the party tomorrow night?"

"I'll be back for that," he promised, searching her face intently. There was something different about her. Her eyes looked bright, almost feverish. "Are you okay?" he asked.

"Of course," she lied. Actually, Melissa felt as if she were about to burst with the feelings that were crowding her heart. Maybe it would be better to wait and talk with him tomorrow after the party. Telling Hunt that she loved him sounded like the best possible way to start the new year. The knowledge within her had been a long time in coming. It could wait one more night to be told.

"Go on to Knoxville and have a good time. Tell Mary good luck for me," she told Hunt.

"I will," he said, still staring at her. "Are you sure you're okay?" His hand brushed across her cheek.

His touch left Melissa feeling slightly giddy. "I'm really fine," she managed to say. "Just be careful, and make sure you're back for the party." Already her mind was racing ahead with plans for a late supper by the fire in her apartment tomorrow night.

"Okay, I'll see you both tomorrow night." Hunt nodded at Beau and closed the door behind him.

Melissa clasped her hands together in excitement and whirled around, momentarily forgetting that her cousin was still perched on the old trunk, watching her.

"I don't know how you can be acting so silly when Hunt's so unhappy," he said shortly. "You saw him. The guy is just about the saddest individual I've ever seen."

Melissa sat down beside him and forced herself to sigh sadly. "You're right. What should I do?"

"Come to your senses. Tell him you love him. I know you do."

"You're right."

"I know...I mean, I am?" Beau's green eyes widened in amazement.

"As I've been trying to tell you, I'm going to tell him tomorrow night."

"You mean I've really convinced you?"

Melissa laughed. "Well, you helped."

"Gee, that was easy."

Melissa laughed harder at the sight of her cousin's almost comical expression of relief.

"I mean," he pointed out, "I try not to interfere in other people's lives."

"Oh, really? Then what were you doing when you brought Hunt Kirkland into my life in the first place?"

Beau smiled and put an arm around her shoulders. "I just thought you two might hit it off."

"I knew it," Melissa returned, feigning disapproval. Then she kissed his cheek. "Thanks, cuz. Maybe someday I'll return the favor."

New Year's Eve didn't begin the way Melissa had planned it. The head chef called in sick, and she and Hunt had to alternate in supervising the kitchen staff. And then there was the crowd. It was huge, even larger than she'd expected.

"Aren't any of these people going to home to their TV and watch the ball drop on Times Square?" one of the waitresses complained.

Melissa laughed. "Don't worry. At midnight we'll serve free champagne. That'll run out fast, and they'll leave soon after. The bar is closing at one o'clock sharp."

She silently prayed it would be that easy. Actually, if she had it her way, they'd just close the restaurant right now. She couldn't wait to be alone with Hunt. He'd returned to Chattanooga early this afternoon, but they'd been too busy to really talk. Despite the fact that she had dinner reservations to unravel and larger than normal parties to accommodate, Melissa thought the hands of the clock were moving slower and slower. About eleven o'clock she slipped away to put a bottle of champagne on ice and lay a fire in her fireplace upstairs.

As he worked in the kitchen, Hunt tried not to think about Melissa. He was completely fed up with their friendly little charade, and he'd been happy to get away from it for a while. He'd even considered staying in Knoxville. Like a magnet, however, he'd been drawn back again.

Smothering a frustrated oath, he dumped a bowl of breaded shrimp into a basket and lowered it into the deep fryer. A hostess pushed open the kitchen doors. "Has anyone seen Miss Chambers?"

"Nope," Hunt answered, turning back to the shrimp.

"Well, there's a phone call on line one for her. The guy says it's urgent, and I can't find her."

"I'll take it. It's probably just someone who *urgently* wants a table for tonight." Hunt impatiently wiped his hands on the long chef's apron he'd put on over his tuxedo. Stepping into the little vestibule off the side entrance to the kitchen, he picked up the phone.

"Hunt Kirkland here. Can I help you?"

"Oh damn. I said I wanted to talk to Melissa."

Hunt instantly recognized the voice. It was Edward.

"Sorry," he said steadily. "She's occupied right now. If you'll give me a number, I'll have her call you."

"That would be a little difficult." The young man hesitated.

"Oh?"

"I'm at the city jail. I need to be bailed out."

Closing his eyes, Hunt leaned against the wall. This kid was just trouble on its way to happen. "What'd you do?"

He heard Edward take a deep breath. "I don't think that's any of your business. Just tell Melissa to come and get me."

The phone clicked off, and Hunt lifted the receiver away from his ear and stared at it for a long, silent moment. The sensible thing would be to find Melissa, give her the message and let her handle it. But he really didn't want to send

her down to that police station. He could go with her, of
course, but he didn't think he could bear to watch the disillusionment on her face. Facing her brother would surely be
worse in those grim surroundings.

Mind made up, Hunt slammed the phone down and returned to the kitchen. "I've got to leave," he said quickly,
addressing the assistant chef. "You're in charge. If you need
help, find Miss Chambers. Tell her I've had an emergency,
and I'll be back soon."

Praying he wouldn't run into Melissa, he ducked into the
bar and found Beau holding court with two beautiful
blondes at a table in the corner. "I need your help," Hunt
said grimly.

Frowning, Beau was on his feet instantly, excusing himself to the ladies and following Hunt out on the porch and
into the cold night air. "What's wrong?"

"Edward's in jail. Do you know where your father is?
Can he help?"

"Sure," Beau answered. "I'll call him right now. What
does Melissa want me—"

"Melissa doesn't know," Hunt snapped.

"Doesn't know?" The redhead's eyes widened. "Hunt,
I think you should—"

"I'm not telling her," Hunt insisted.

"There'll be hell to pay."

"You let me worry about that. You just tell me how to get
to the jail, and then get hold of your father. I don't know
what Edward did, but it's a sure bet that he needs a good
lawyer."

"Okay," Beau agreed, and quickly gave directions to the
downtown jail.

Hunt paused midway down the back steps. "Tell Melissa
I'll be back soon. And call her father."

"What!" Beau shook his head emphatically. "I'm not doing it, Hunt. Melissa would hate—"

"Either you call him or I'll do it myself. Melissa is not going to handle Edward's latest little stunt on her own." Not stopping to see if his old friend was in agreement, Hunt sprinted across the lawn to the garage where his car was parked.

All the way downtown Hunt kept telling himself he was making a mistake. Melissa would hate him for interfering. Nevertheless, this time he had to do what he thought was best for her. "To hell with her stupid, stubborn pride," he muttered, getting out of his car at the city jail.

He wasn't allowed to talk with Edward. He had to sit in the lobby for over an hour until Beau and his father showed up with a bail bondsman. Then it was another thirty minutes before bail was arranged. Even with Beau's father's influence, it was New Year's Eve, a busy night at most any jail.

The young man who at last walked out to the lobby with his uncle bore little resemblance to the swaggering, angry Edward whom Hunt remembered from their last encounter. He was pale, and his blue eyes, so like Melissa's, were overlarge in his drawn face. *He's scared to death,* Hunt thought.

"Where's Melissa?" Edward demanded instantly.

Hunt's eyes were steady on his. "I didn't tell her."

The young man cursed.

"Edward," Beau said quietly, "I'd suggest you keep your mouth shut."

"Yes," his father agreed. "Disorderly conduct, resisting arrest and possession of marijuana are not exactly minor offenses—"

"The guy had no right to pull me over in the first place," Edward insisted in loud, angry tones.

"Let's get him out of here before they charge him with something else," Beau said.

Together the three men hustled Edward out of the building.

"What about my car?" he asked.

Beau's father held up the keys. "I think I'll take it home, Edward. You can pick it up at my house tomorrow." Not waiting for a reply, he went back into the building.

Hunt hooked his hand over Edward's elbow. "You're coming with me."

"No!"

The younger man tried to jerk away, but Hunt's grasp tightened on his arm as he spun him around. In the dim light of the streetlamp, they faced one another, both furious, both ready for a fight.

"You're coming with me," Hunt ground out between clenched teeth, thankful that he still had some semblance of control left. "We're going to talk." His grip loosened, allowing Edward to shrug away. Evidently he'd convinced Melissa's brother he wouldn't stand for any more nonsense, for he simply stood a little to the side, not attempting to get away.

"Want me to come with you?" Beau asked Hunt in a low voice.

"No, I think this is something I have to do on my own."

"I called Melissa's father. He'll be here as soon as he can get a flight. Probably in the morning." Beau paused. "I'm afraid Melissa will have a fit."

Hunt let out a tired sigh and rubbed a hand through his hair. "Yeah, I've probably blown it all to hell."

"I hope not."

"Thanks for you help." The two men shook hands, and with a last look at Edward, Beau headed down the street to where he'd parked his car. Hunt turned back to Edward.

"My car's over here." He started walking, forcing the young man to fall in step beside him.

"Why are you doing this?" Edward demanded in a low voice, his breath forming a vapor in the cold air.

"For Melissa," Hunt said quietly, stopping beside his blue Mercedes.

"She didn't ask you to. You said you didn't even tell her where I was—"

"Did you really want her to sit and wait for you in there?" The blood roared in Hunt's ears as he struggled with his anger.

Edward gulped, his eyes flicking back to the building they'd just vacated.

"Jails aren't really her style, are they?" Hunt pressed.

"No, but I—"

"But what? Do you think Melissa would have just bailed you out—no questions, no lecture?"

Edward pushed a hand through his shaggy blond hair. "She would have been mad, but Missy always—"

"She always fights your battles for you," Hunt completed for him.

"I didn't say that—"

Hunt laughed derisively.

"You don't understand," Edward said defensively.

Hunt's fist clenched at his side as fury swept through him anew. "I wish you could hear how weak and pitiful you sound, moaning about how no one understands you. Do you think you're the only person in the world whose parents got divorced?"

"That's not—"

"Are you going to ruin your whole life because your father had an affair, because he's remarried with a new family?"

"You don't—" Edward stopped himself, his gaze swinging guiltily to Hunt's face.

"Don't tell me I don't understand," Hunt said sharply. "Melissa told me all about your father's other son. If you're so concerned that your father loves Joey more than you, why don't you do something that will make him want to love you? It seems to me that all you do is hurt the people who care about you. You certainly do enough to hurt Melissa."

"Just shut up!" Edward cried, charging at Hunt with fists flying.

Hunt sidestepped the attack neatly, managing to grab one of the younger man's arms. Twisting it around Edward's back, he shoved him against the car.

Edward swore. "Just wait till Melissa—"

"Can't stop hiding behind her, can you?"

"Damn you—"

Hunt let go of Edward's arm and stepped back, but Melissa's brother didn't move. "All right," he said, "I'm taking you home to her, but I swear, if you try playing your little games with her, I'll make you wish we'd left you in jail."

After rounding the car, Hunt got in, releasing the lock so that Edward could get in also. He turned the ignition and drove down the nearly deserted streets, the quiet purr of the engine the only sound penetrating the silence inside.

"I don't want to hurt her," Edward said softly, about midway to River Rest. "I don't want to hurt anyone."

The sadness in his voice pulled at Hunt. He glanced over at the young man. "Just stop taking advantage of her sympathy."

"I never thought of it as taking advantage. She's my sister—"

"And she's also a person with pain and problems of her own," Hunt said bluntly. "Melissa wasn't put on this earth to be your crying towel."

"I know that—"

"Then act like it."

"Listen," Edward began with spirit returning to his voice, "I've never meant to hurt Melissa. She means more to me than anyone on earth—"

"Oh, yeah?" Hunt returned, glancing at him again. "Then maybe you and I have something in common after all."

The words hung in the silence of the car for the rest of the drive.

Still wearing their silly party hats and tooting their noise-makers, the last of the New Year's Eve crowd was flowing through River Rest's front doors by one o'clock. Melissa stood to the side, trying to maintain her cheerful smile. *Where is Hunt?* she thought for perhaps the hundredth time of the evening.

Both Hunt and Beau had disappeared around eleven. Then there'd been that strange phone call from Beau's mother, asking if everything had been straightened out. Confused, Melissa had asked Aunt Martha what she was referring to, and the older woman had practically hung up. When Melissa called her back, all she got was a busy signal.

Something's happened and Hunt is involved, Melissa decided, a spark of anger replacing the worry she'd been experiencing for hours. She thought of the chilled champagne, the carefully laid fire and the assortment of fruits and cheeses waiting upstairs. When she'd planned this romantic evening with Hunt, she'd certainly never thought he'd disappear.

She locked the front door behind the last giggling group and turned back to the foyer. *Where is Hunt?* Melissa asked herself again.

Employees rushed around, clearing away the last of the mess, eager to get started on their well-deserved holiday. When only a few people remained Melissa took the evening's receipts and wearily climbed the stairs.

She met Hunt in the upstairs hall. He was coming from the back staircase with Edward in tow.

"What are you doing here?" Melissa demanded breathlessly of her brother, taking in his disheveled appearance.

"I...I was..." Edward began and then glanced at Hunt, as if asking for help. Hunt shook his head.

Melissa glanced from one to the other. "Okay, what's going on?"

"I got arrested," Edward said in a rush. "Hunt and Beau had Uncle Perry arrange bail."

"Why?" Melissa murmured, her voice sounding faint, even to her own ears. "Why did they arrest you?"

"Possession and resisting arrest," Edward supplied bluntly. "I'm sorry, Melissa."

She stared at him for a long moment and then groped blindly for a means of support. Her hand encountered the wall, and she leaned against it, fighting for breath. This was hard to believe. Edward had pulled plenty of wild stunts in desperate bids for attention, but he'd never gone this far.

"Why didn't you tell me?" she demanded of Hunt.

Here it comes, he thought, *and I can't stand here while she defends this punk.* Hunt avoided her eyes while answering. "I wanted to get him home before you had to deal with it. I knew Beau's father could probably help. I thought it was best—"

"I should have been told," Melissa insisted, her voice rising.

Edward turned to Hunt with an ill-concealed smirk. "I told you—"

"Shut up!" Melissa shouted. Both men stared at her as if in shock.

"I should have been told," she repeated in a softer voice. "If you'd talked to me about it, you wouldn't have had to call Uncle Perry. I'd have left him in jail."

"Melissa!" Edward protested. Hunt was sure it was raw terror he saw on the young man's face.

"You be quiet!" Melissa wrestled with a red, blinding fury. "Maybe in a jail full of New Year's Eve drunks you'd have realized a few things. Maybe you'd have learned a lesson. What did you think, Edward? That I'd just run down there and pat you on the head like I always do?"

Her brother bowed his head.

"Look at me!" Melissa dropped the box of receipts and money she held. They tumbled across the floor, but she paid no attention as she stepped forward to grasp Edward's shoulders. "Ever since I can remember, I've been getting you out of trouble. But I'm not going to do it anymore. This is it. You're on your own." She gave him a vicious shake.

"Melissa, I'm sorry," Edward murmured, raising tear-filled blue eyes to hers. "It all gets so jumbled up in my mind. Mother doesn't want me. Neither does Father. Nadine hates me. You're the only one—"

"I'm the only one who still listens to your self-pitying garbage," Melissa completed. "I'm the only one you can still fool. Isn't that right?"

"No," Edward insisted. "You're the only one who loves me—"

"No, I'm not," she said, for the first time resisting the misery in his voice. "Mother and Father love you, Edward. They just don't know how to show it. Unfortunately, they've never known how to show either one of us." Melissa shut her eyes to stop the threatening wash of tears.

"But why—"

"I don't know why!" She gave Edward another impatient little shake, then cupped his face with her hands, her voice fierce as she said, "You've got to stop worrying about all the things you can't change. Mother and Father are just the way they are. You can't do anything about it. You've tried. Now you've got to get yourself straightened out—not for them. Not for me. For you."

"I try, but then I think about everything they've done and I get so angry." Edward's eyes were full of pain. "It's like before I know it, I've done something stupid again."

Melissa's voice softened. "You're just like I was. You're so afraid of failing or being hurt that you don't give anyone—least of all yourself—a chance. The only difference between us is that you strike out at people, before they can hurt you. Me? I just lock all my feelings inside. If Hunt hadn't come along . . ."

Melissa's voice broke, and she had to swallow deeply before continuing. "Edward, you've got to stop running from all the pain. I got lucky and found Hunt, and he filled in the empty places. But you've got to do it yourself. Now. You may not get as lucky as I did."

A spark of understanding lit her brother's blue eyes.

Maybe he grasped part of what I said, Melissa thought. That was all she could do for her brother now. The rest was up to him, and besides, she had to talk with Hunt. If he hadn't already guessed from what she'd told Edward, she had to tell him how very much she loved him.

"Hunt," she began, turning toward where he'd been standing last. "Hunt, I have to talk . . ." The words trailed away as she saw that he wasn't there. The hall was empty.

"Hunt?" Melissa said, raising her voice. Perhaps he hadn't wanted to intrude on her talk with Edward. She'd asked him over and over again not to interfere, but of course he'd gone ahead and interfered anyway by not telling her of Edward's arrest. Now he probably thought she was really angry about it. Maybe that was why he left.

"Hunt?" she called, louder now as she hurried back down the hall. She had to find him and explain that the anger had been directed at Edward, not him. *I have to thank him for his help. I have to tell him I love him,* Melissa thought, starting down the stairs.

And just then—sounding faraway, like distant thunder—the front door slammed shut.

Chapter Eleven

With an icy persistence, the wind slapped at Hunt as he hurried from the all-night convenience store to his car. Once inside, he took a grateful sip of scalding hot coffee, but it failed to warm him. The coldness in him had nothing to do with the weather; it had started with Melissa's cool, hard anger.

He had no one but himself to blame. He'd known she would be furious at his interference with Edward, yet he'd done it anyway. Then, afraid that his actions had at last been more than Melissa's independent nature could endure, he had run away; he'd been running all night. He'd driven aimlessly until he was forced to stop for fuel and coffee here in an unfamiliar section of the city.

Trying to block out her image, he concentrated on the Christmas lights in the store window. They blinked on and off, providing a garish background for the grinning Santas and snowmen that had been painted on the glass. Just like all decorations at the end of the holiday season, to Hunt these seemed almost desperate, as if they knew their time was slipping away.

"Slipping away," he murmured, repeating his thought out loud. That was exactly what he was allowing to happen with Melissa—she was slipping quickly out of his life. He kept doing all the wrong things.

Shivering, he started the car, turned up the heater and huddled in his inadequate tuxedo jacket, trying to remember why it had seemed so important to handle Edward's problem by himself tonight. He'd wanted to spare Melissa that agonizing wait in the lobby of the police station, spare her the indignity of arranging bail, of facing her brother in front of others.

What Edward had done wasn't the end of the world; he wasn't the first mixed-up kid to land in jail. However, he was Melissa's brother, the one she loved despite his troubles or his tantrums. When he hurt, so did she. For that reason, and that reason alone, Hunt had tried to cushion tonight's trauma.

He didn't know if he'd succeeded. Melissa had merely seemed angry. Of course, he had been happy to see some of that fury turned on Edward. Hunt doubted that she would have really left her brother in jail, but planting that doubt in the young man's head had been effective shock treatment. Edward needed to realize he could no longer cruise through life, breaking all the rules and expecting Melissa or anyone else to pick up the pieces. Perhaps Melissa was going to finally force Edward to grow up.

And what about her? Hunt thought. When was Melissa going to grow up and realize that everyone who loved her was not trying to use her? Would love always be synonymous with domination in her mind?

He shook his head. He couldn't believe that. She was too smart to live with those old fears. In the few short months they'd been together, she'd already changed so much—too much for him to back off now.

Hunt was jerked out of his reverie by a tap on the window. The convenience store clerk was hunched over in the cold, peering into the car.

"Something wrong?" Hunt said after rolling down the window a bit.

The burly man frowned. "I was about to ask you the same thing. You've been sitting out here for a long time."

"I had a lot of thinking to do."

"In twenty-degree weather?" The man rolled his eyes. "It must be a woman."

Hunt gave a hollow little laugh.

"Take my advice, bud, there ain't nothin' to be gained by avoiding the trouble. Go home and fight it out. But don't sit out here and freeze. The boss wouldn't like it if you died out here in front of the store, all right?"

Nodding, Hunt watched as the clerk scampered back into the store before he rolled up the window and put his car in gear. The man was right; there was nothing to be gained by avoiding Melissa. So she was angry. It wasn't the first time. It wouldn't be the last. She'd probably always be extrasensitive about him intruding on what she perceived to be her own personal business. He'd have to show her that he was acting out of love, not some twisted desire to dominate her.

I can show her, Hunt promised himself fiercely. There'd be no more pretending that he'd never said he loved her. He was going to say it every chance he got. She was going to have to get used to it. And someday, Melissa was going to feel free enough to acknowledge that she loved him, too. That hope almost made him smile.

Dawn was brightening the clear winter sky as Hunt worked his way through the unfamiliar streets. It's New Year's Day, he thought, a time for fresh starts and resolutions. It was definitely that time for him and Melissa.

After Hunt's abrupt departure, Melissa spent a miserable night. She supposed she should have been grateful that he left her alone with Edward. After all, wasn't that what she had told him she wanted—to be allowed to deal with her problems on her own?

Yet she couldn't help wishing for Hunt's clear, controlled logic as she talked with her brother. Edward was full of confusion and contradictions. He was twenty years old, with no direction and no plans, and Melissa didn't have any answers for him. Though she repeated the offer of a job and a place to stay, she made it clear that tonight's escapade or anything like it wouldn't be tolerated. This time, at least, Edward seemed to take her seriously.

Finally, looking completely exhausted, he'd gone off to bed, while Melissa huddled on the couch in her apartment. On the coffee table her romantic New Year's Eve supper went to waste. The ice melted around the champagne; the fire burned lower and lower. Close to dawn Melissa finally dozed off, but the buzzing of the front door jerked her awake only a short while later.

"Hunt," she murmured, jumping off the couch to rush downstairs. It was only as she reached the bottom of the main staircase that she realized Hunt had no need to ring the doorbell. Nevertheless, breathless with exertion, she was still full of hope as she swung the door open.

It was her father, not Hunt, who was waiting on the porch.

Malcolm Chambers had changed little in the six months since Melissa had seen him. The blond hair was almost completely silver, and perhaps there were a few more lines beside the blue eyes and the handsome, mobile mouth. However, about him there still clung that indefinable air of vitality, of power. No matter how old he gets, Melissa thought, as long as he has that air, he'll always seem young.

"Melissa," he said, eyes crinkling into a smile. "How are you?"

"I'm fine," she answered, thinking how inane these pleasantries sounded. There was no warmth, none of the closeness that should be found between a father and daughter. Suddenly aware of the cold, she stepped back. "Come in, please."

"Thank you." Malcolm stepped into the foyer, glancing about him with interest. "The house looks just terrific," he said with what Melissa hoped was genuine approval. "I hope things are going well?"

"Very well," she murmured, taking his heavy tweed overcoat. As always, she felt messy and gauche beside his tailored elegance. Her sleep-tousled hair and rumpled blue jogging suit didn't exactly inspire confidence, and that was what she needed most around Malcolm.

Her father turned to face her, a frown creasing his forehead. "Where is Edward?"

"Edward?" How had he known about Edward?

"Yes, Beau called me last night. I got on the first available flight—"

"Beau called you?" Melissa echoed, puzzled. Calling her father was something she'd never expect from her cousin.

"That's right," Malcolm said with a trace of impatience. "Not knowing exactly what had happened, I came here first. Was bail arranged? Do I need—"

"Uncle Perry took care of that."

Melissa and her father wheeled around at the sound of Edward's voice. Looking pale but determined, he was coming down the stairs. "Hunt and Beau called Uncle Perry. He brought a bondsman down to bail me out," he continued.

"Hunt?" Malcolm asked, stepping toward his son.

"My partner," Melissa supplied, glancing from father to son, noting the almost palpable tension in the air. "Listen, why don't you two go on up to my office? I'll make us some breakfast...." Her voice trailed away as she saw that neither her brother or father were paying the slightest bit of attention to her.

"I'm surprised that you're here," Edward said, his chin lifting in challenge.

"I'd expect you to say that," Malcolm returned stoutly. "You always expect me to be the villain."

"An expectation you have often fulfilled." Edward had paused about five stairs from the bottom so that his father was forced to look up at him.

Malcolm's head bowed, and Melissa saw the muscles working in his jaw, but he didn't reply to his son's remark.

"Let's go sit in here," she insisted, leading them into the first dining area to the right. "I'll get some coffee—"

"You're acting just like Mother used to, Melissa," Edward said shortly. "By the time she'd stopped fussing over us, getting refreshments and arranging a nice little atmosphere in which to talk, everyone would have forgotten what the problem was." He flung himself into a chair at the nearest table.

Melissa paused in the doorway, realizing with a guilty start that her brother was exactly right. Malcolm took the seat opposite his son.

"I'm sorry I ruined your New Year's Eve," Edward muttered. "I'm sure *sweet* Nadine was furious."

"Nadine is worried about you—"

"Oh sure!" Edward exclaimed sarcastically, not even bothering to look up. "Tell me another one, Father."

Melissa watched the lines on her father's face settle into a sad mask. He looked suddenly older. Slowly, keeping his eyes on Edward's downcast head, he said, "I don't want to argue about Nadine, Edward. What's important now is you. Are you in serious trouble?"

Edward didn't answer, so Melissa recited the charges which had been brought against him.

"That's not the end of the world," Malcolm answered, looking a little relieved. "I'll have a word with your Uncle Perry. I'm sure that—"

"No!" The word seemed to explode from Edward. "I want you to just stay out of it."

"But Edward," Melissa protested.

"Son, I was not suggesting that we pay off the judge or anything so dramatic," Malcolm said sternly. "The charges are basically misdemeanors. Whatever else I think of your uncle, I'll admit that he's a fine attorney, and I think he can handle this."

The room was silent then. Edward stared angrily at the tabletop. Melissa still hovered by the door. Her father's gaze traveled back and forth between them.

Malcolm finally gave a heavy sigh. "You know, I keep thinking that this is the first time the three of us have been together in a long, long time."

"And whose fault is that?" Edward demanded.

"Mine, of course," his father admitted. His chair scraped across the floor as he pushed away from the table. Hands in trouser pockets, he took a few steps away and then turned back to face his children. His words came out in a rush. "I've made a lot of mistakes."

Edward gave a short, mirthless laugh, but Melissa stepped farther into the room, eyes never wavering from her father's face.

He continued, "First I forced my family to center their lives around my political ambitions, and then I threw those ambitions away. I was selfish from start to finish. I hurt you both, and I'm sorry."

Sorry. That was one word Melissa had seldom heard her father say. An apology was the last thing she'd ever expected from him.

"I'm not apologizing for loving Nadine or for beginning a new life with her," Malcolm added. "The mistake I made was in deceiving your mother. I was a coward, and I cheated all of you, as well as Nadine and Joey."

Edward made a disgusted sound.

"It's true," his father insisted. "One of these days your brother is going to ask me why I didn't marry his mother before he was born. I'm ashamed of that."

"He's not my brother," Edward said sharply.

Malcolm shook his head. "I wish you didn't feel that way, Edward. I don't love Joey more than I love you. No one could take your place in my heart. I wish I could make you understand that, and that you'd stop blaming him. He's a little boy, and he's totally innocent. He never did anything to hurt either of you."

"No," Melissa agreed, "but it always seems easier to pretend that he doesn't exist."

Malcolm nodded his head. "I suppose I can understand that. I've done a lot of pretending over the past few years, too. My favorite fantasy was the one in which the two of you forgave me, and we became a family again."

"Oh, get real," Edward declared bitterly. "We were never a family. We were an attractive political photograph."

His father's head bowed again, as if he struggled with the burden of that truth. When he looked up again, his eyes were bright with emotion. "Your mother says we'd all have been better off if she and I had ended the marriage sooner."

"Mother says?" Melissa echoed. "Do you and Mother talk?"

"Of course," Malcolm replied, looking surprised. "It took a while, but I think she's finally forgiven me for the things I put her through. Our marriage was over long before I ever met Nadine. We stayed together for the sake of my career. Your mother was as dedicated to it as I, you know. That was the real betrayal—I took away her life's work."

Melissa stared at him. She'd believed her mother's heartbreak had been over losing the man, not the political office.

"And why shouldn't your mother and I talk?" Malcolm continued. "After all, we still share something we both love dearly. You."

Neither Melissa nor Edward said a word.

"Being a parent isn't something everyone does naturally," Malcolm said softly. "Nadine is good at it. She's open and loving. Your mother and I, well, we had a harder time communicating—"

Edward sat up, muttering, "That's the understatement of the century."

His father sighed. "I know, Edward, your mother and I are lousy parents. You've spent the last few years reminding us of that at every turn, and you've been exactly right. But the point I'm trying to make is that it's harder for me to connect with you. I'd like to try and make that connection now."

Melissa cleared her throat. With the changes she'd made recently in her life and attitude, it would have been easy, too easy, to just reach out to her father. But she couldn't just forget all the pain he'd caused. "It's not as simple as saying you're sorry," she told him.

He nodded in agreement. "I know that. I'm not asking you two to forgive me. God knows, it'll take more years than I probably have left for me to earn your forgiveness. But if we can just try to understand each other. If I can just be a part of your lives. I want to." He paused, glancing from one to the other. "Can we try?"

It surprised Melissa when Edward answered. "You know," he said slowly, "I am tired of fighting with all of you. Melissa said a few things that made a lot of sense to me last night—about letting go of the past. I think *everything* that happened last night made me do some real thinking." He looked up at his father. "I don't know if I can forgive you, but I do know I can't live in that house with you and Nadine and Joey. I resent your little family unit, because it's something I never really had."

"Edward," his father interrupted. "I'm sorry—"

Edward stopped him with an upraised hand. "Don't say that. I don't want to hear your apologies. I just want to get on with my life. I want to go back to school." He grinned ruefully at Melissa. "I even want to try and stay out of trouble. How about a job, Sis?"

"You've got it," she said, coming forward to lay a hand on his shoulder.

"I'll try not to hate you anymore, Father," Edward said bluntly, looking up at Malcolm. "I can't promise anything else."

"That's a start. It's probably more than I deserve," the older man said softly, his gaze lingering on his son's face. Then he glanced at Melissa. They looked at each other for a long moment.

Hidden beneath the silver hair and the lines, Melissa could see a younger man. She was always subtracting the years from her father's face. Indeed, whenever she even thought about him, it was always as he'd looked when she was a little girl. Tall and handsome, smile flashing, every blond hair smoothly in place, he had been the sort of father many little girls might yearn for. He'd been busy all the time, of course, with little time for picnics or bedtime stories. Yet sometimes when he was at home, working in his study, she'd slip in the door and silently watch him, admiring him from a distance. More often than not, he'd see her and she'd wind up on his lap.

Then, very seriously, she'd ask him what he was doing. He never brushed aside her questions. Instead he'd tell her about some bill he was drafting or some committee he was working on. And always, he'd explain it in terms of what he was trying to do for the people who'd elected him. She'd thought him the most important man in the world, as generous as Robin Hood, as handsome as any fairy-tale prince. No wonder she'd been willing to do anything he asked of her. No wonder it had been so hard when she'd found out he was only human, after all.

But she could still love a real-life father, even with all his flaws, Melissa decided. No, she couldn't forget all the things

he'd done, but she could choose to forgive. She simply ha
to accept the love he was willing to give, love that she no
could see was without qualifications, without a price. Be
cause of Hunt she now knew that sort of love was possible

So Melissa smiled and whispered, "I love you, Father.
always have."

The tense lines around his mouth relaxed into an answer
ing smile.

Feeling like an intruder, Hunt watched from the door
way. The three people in the room had been so intent on on
another that they hadn't even heard him come into th
foyer. So he'd stood outside, listening to the little dram
unfold, feeling happy for Melissa and hoping she could f
nally set some of her bitterness aside.

Malcolm saw Hunt first, and the smile he'd been bestow
ing on his daughter dimmed a little. "Yes?" he said, an
Melissa turned around.

The look of relief and welcome on her face surprise
Hunt just a little. He'd still expected her to be furious.

"Hunt," she said, coming toward him. "Where have yo
been?"

"Lost somewhere in the far reaches of a city I don't kno
very well," he answered, trying to smile.

"Lost?" Confused, her glance dropped to his rumple
tuxedo.

"I went for a drive. A long drive." Hunt laughed. "I'
explain it to you later." He stepped forward, extending h
hand toward Malcolm. "You must be Melissa's father."

"Yes," she said as the two men shook hands. "Hunt, thi
is my father, Malcolm Chambers. And Father, this…" Sh
paused, her eyes steady on Hunt's. "Father, this is Hun
Kirkland, the man I love."

The statement momentarily robbed Hunt of speech. He simply stood, grasping her father's hand but staring open-mouthed at Melissa.

"Well," Malcolm said, breaking the awkward pause. "It seems that you two have been collaborating on more than a restaurant."

"Yes, we have," Hunt murmured, dropping the man's hand but continuing to look at Melissa. Had he heard correctly? Had she really said she loved him?

"It was Hunt who actually came and got me last night," Edward told his father.

"Then I have to thank you," Malcolm said.

"Yeah." Edward stood and put out his hand to Hunt. "I didn't mention it then, but I appreciate everything you did for me last night."

Wonders will never cease, Hunt thought, even while he accepted the younger man's handshake. "You're welcome, but it was really Beau. All I did was have him call his father and yours."

"So you're the reason Father is here," Melissa said.

Hunt faced her again, again half expecting anger.

Instead she merely whispered, "Thank you."

"I just didn't want you to have to handle all this alone," he said, struck by the tenderness in her gaze. "I thought you'd be angry."

Melissa just shook her head and smiled.

She thought her father sensed that she and Hunt needed to be alone. At any rate, he turned to Edward. "Any chance you and I could have a private talk, Son?"

Edward started to protest, then appeared to think better of it. "I guess so," he agreed. "You could buy me some breakfast." Grinning slightly, he glanced from Hunt to his sister. "I don't think River Rest's kitchen is going to be serving today."

"Fine," Malcolm said. Before leaving, he paused to shake Hunt's hand again. "I don't have to know much about you to know you're a very special person. Otherwise, she never would have chosen you." He turned to Melissa, his eyes softening. "I think I've got a pretty smart daughter."

"Yes, you do," she agreed proudly. "I've finally got it all together."

"Yes, I believe you really have." Malcolm's glance took in the whole room. "I'm very proud of what you've done here, Melissa. Several old friends have called to tell me what a wonderful job you've done with this restaurant."

"Are you sure you didn't call them—just to check up on me?" Melissa teased.

He gave a guilty smile. "Well, maybe. I hope that's okay?"

She actually laughed. When was the last time she'd done that with her father? Melissa thought. "I don't mind," she told him. "But the next time you want to know how things are going, just call me."

Watching her father and brother leave together, Melissa felt as if the burdens of the world had been lifted from her shoulders.

The front door had barely closed behind them when Hunt pulled her gently into his arms. "Tell me I'm not dreaming. Did I hear you say that I'm the man you love?"

Softly, she touched his cheek with her hand. "No dreams. Simple reality. I love you, Hunt Kirkland." Her lips lifted to his and conveyed all the reassurance he could have needed.

"I have to know," he said after several minutes had passed. "How did this miraculous discovery take place? I came in here today prepared to wait years to hear those words.''

"It was my grandmother who convinced me.''

"Your grandmother?'' Hunt repeated, eyes widening. "She spoke to you from beyond?''

Melissa relayed to him the conversation she'd had with her grandmother long ago. "So you see, I finally realized I didn't have to be afraid of loving you. Instead of stealing my heart, you simply make me whole.''

His gaze swept across her lovely, expectant features. *God, how I love this woman,* Hunt thought with a fierceness that was almost frightening in its strength. He was going to do everything in his power to make sure she was never hurt again, but there were a couple of things they still had to straighten out.

"You know that there are going to be times when I will seem to be interfering,'' he said quietly.

"I think it's just your nature to do everything you can for those you love.'' Melissa grinned and pressed a kiss to the dimple that creased his cheek.

"Just keep in mind that I'm acting out of love,'' Hunt added.

"I will,'' she promised so solemnly that he felt compelled to kiss away the serious set of her mouth.

As it always happened when Hunt kissed her, Melissa felt the rest of the world slip away. Until him, she'd never dreamed she'd be capable of so much passion. *I doubt that we're ever going to have a quiet, settled kind of love,* she thought.

"You're going to have to marry me soon,'' he murmured, lips trailing across the curve of her jaw.

"Oh, really?'' Melissa pulled away. "That wasn't a very romantic proposal, Mr. Kirkland.''

He had the grace to look a little apologetic. "I'm sorry. Do you want the full treatment—on bended knee?"

"Actually," she murmured, undoing the buttons of his shirt. "I was thinking the whole thing might go much better in bed."

Her blue eyes were full of mischief, and Hunt wondered if it was possible that she was as filled with need as he. She took his hand and pulled him toward the stairs.

"We ought to get this settled before Edward and my father come back."

"If you insist," he agreed, smiling at her eagerness.

It was some time later that Hunt actually got around to a properly romantic proposal. Naked, on bended knee in the middle of the bed, he looked so adorable while he proposed that it was longer still before Melissa got around to accepting.

"I guess this will make us partners in every way," she said, nestling close to his strong, warm body.

"Does that mean I get to help you run River Rest?"

She glanced up at his face. He looked serious. "I guess so. If you can keep in line."

Hunt grinned. "I'll try."

"Good." Melissa laid her head back on his shoulder.

"But I'll probably want to make some changes."

She sat up. "What? What changes?"

"Oh, a few menu additions, a few price changes, a couple of shifts in personnel, bar specials—"

Gently, Melissa put her hand over his mouth. "I think in some respects, I like you better as a silent partner."

He pulled her hand away, his brown eyes merry as they smiled up at her. "And how do you propose to keep me quiet?"

"Like this." Melissa covered his lips with her own again.

"Now this is the perfect partnership," Hunt murmured against her mouth.

* * * * *

Silhouette Special Edition

WHITE LIES*
by
Linda Howard

Bestselling author Linda Howard is back with a story that is exciting, enticing and—most of all—compellingly romantic.

Heroine Jay Granger's life was turned upside down when she was called to her ex-husband's side. Now, injured and unconscious, he needed her more than he ever had during their brief marriage. Finally he awoke, and Jay found him stronger and more fascinating than before. Was she asking too much, or could they have a chance to recapture the past and learn the value of love the second time around?

Find out the answer next month, only in SILHOUETTE SPECIAL EDITION.

*Previously advertised as MIRRORS.

COMING IN MAY

SSE452

ATTRACTIVE, SPACE SAVING BOOK RACK

Display your most prized novels on this handsome and sturdy book rack. The hand-rubbed walnut finish will blend into your library decor with quiet elegance, providing a practical organizer for your favorite hard-or soft-covered books.

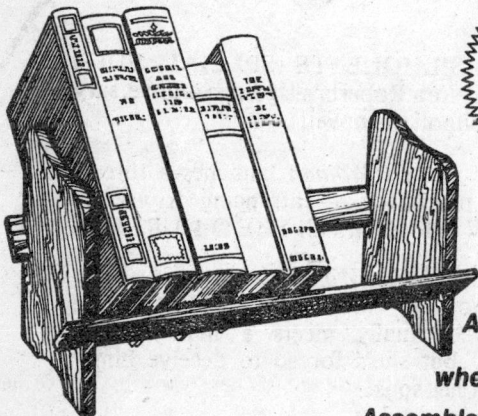

Only $9.95

Approximately 16" x 8" when assembled

Assembles in seconds!

To order, rush your name, address and zip code, along with a check or money order for $10.70* ($9.95 plus 75¢ postage and handling) payable to *Silhouette Books.*

Silhouette Books
Book Rack Offer
901 Fuhrmann Blvd.
P.O. Box 1396
Buffalo, NY 14269-1396

Offer not available in Canada.

*New York and Iowa residents add appropriate sales tax.

BKR-2A